# THE PRIVATE PARTS OF WOMEN

# THE PRIVATE PARTS OF WOMEN

## Lesley Glaister

BLOOMSBURY

First published 1996
This paperback edition 1996
Copyright © 1996 by Lesley Glaister

Bloomsbury Publishing plc, 38 Soho Square, London W1V 5DF

A CIP catalogue record for this book
is available from the British Library

10 9 8 7 6 5 4 3 2

ISBN 0 7475 2603 6

Typeset in Great Britain by Hewer Text Composition Services, Edinburgh
Printed in Great Britain by Clays Ltd, St Ives PLC

*for*
*Pat Durrant*

# INIS

I could have, should have, gone round the world. I should have taken a plane and flown to a different continent, a different climate. I should have done the job properly, changed my name, had my teeth done, a nose-job, siliconed breasts, augmented cheekbones. I should have done hard, definite, permanent things instead of this soft, temporary, half-hearted means of disguise. Only hair. I should have got them to pare my bones, stuff me with something artificial. Something that doesn't feel.

I should have gone to Madagascar or Patagonia, lost myself in New York or Rome. I could have flown round the globe. I could have soared away from my old life on eagles' wings. I could have dared the sun, jumped the equator like a skipping rope, to-and-fro, to-and-fro. But what do I do?

Go two hundred miles. Rent a dreary little house in a dreary post-industrial city. Keep on doing what I do. Photographs. Scald the edges of my mind where it tries to bleed into the past. Suffer. Play safe. Even in my flight, my grand gesture, my great escape I play it safe. I do it the English, female way, the little hen way. I am no eagle, I am a scared brown hen pecking and pecking. I am little and pathetic and hindered by edges.

February is a desperate month. Whenever I said that, Richard disagreed.

'No!' he said when I tried to explain how it depressed me. 'No, it is *not* depressing, quite the reverse.'

He pointed out how buds were fattening; how shoots were poking up through the soil; how evenings were lengthening; how sometimes the sun shone warm enough through glass to mimic the summer. So I was wrong.

But wrong or not, I still don't like it. It's cold but not proper winter any more – not deep, dark-at-four-o'clock winter when it feels all right to stay in. I hate taking children to the park when it's cold. I hate standing shivering by the swings pushing and pushing and pushing. I hate the undependability of the sunshine, the teasing snatches. I hate the papery crocuses, purple, yellow, that die softly in the frost, too, too tender. I hate the snotty noses; Richard's bleeper going off in the night; his worthy weariness; shreds of paper tissue flecking all the washing in the machine.

February is a terrible time to move into an empty house. The cold has owned the house by then. It squats possessively, despite the radiators clanking and occasionally leaking, despite the gas-fire. It hides in cupboards and curtain folds and as soon as the heating goes off it creeps out again with its sad, damp stench.

Oh God, listen to me. Self-pity or *what*?

I'm going to paint the walls, everything white. I've bought several 2½-litre tins of brilliant white emulsion and I'm painting every room on top of whatever's there which would send Richard into a fit if he was here. He's the type that likes to strip things down and do a job properly, whereas I don't care to peel off old paper. I don't care what's underneath, as long as it stays underneath.

I've had my hair cut very short and bleached it white. Roberto, the hairdresser, was unwilling. 'You'll regret it,' he warned, fingering the long brown stuff, 'such lovely natural lights.' And when it fell from my head, drifted in toffee-coloured waves on to the floor, on to my lap, I did feel a sense of loss but such a trivial loss it was almost a relief.

'White,' I said.

'Not something subtler?' he encouraged. 'Cheryl, fetch me the shade chart.' He pointed out little tufts of nylon hair, all soft and subtle blondes. 'Most of my ladies take it in stages,' he said. 'How about a warmer shade – muffin or sun-set?'

'White,' I said.

He sighed. 'Even with our advanced treatments, it strips the hair. Plays merry hell with condition.'

'Good,' I said.

'On your head be it,' he waved his hand in the air. I laughed.

The bleach was cold and sticky on my scalp. I sat under a lamp, with a mug of bitter coffee, flicking through a magazine, noticing how many of the models had long and flowing hair, feeling perversely satisfied.

Before and after.

Before: a long-haired woman with a push-chair and toddler attached. After: a peroxide blonde absolutely unattached. I will still carry a camera. But I will hardly be myself at all.

After a time, the bleach began to sting and caused my eyes to water. Not tears, only a reaction to the peroxide on my tender scalp. Eventually a piercing bleep signalled that I was done. The lamp was wheeled away, my hair was rinsed, Roberto dried the white fluff, lifting it with his fingers.

'If you rub a spot of wax in,' he demonstrated, 'give it a bit of movement.' He stood back and considered my reflection in the mirror. 'Hmm not too bad,' he said. 'I think I can see what you're after.'

My hair was white as frost and my face had changed. My skin looked dark, my eyebrows fierce, my brown eyes startling. I lifted my chin, hardened my mouth, narrowed my eyes. It was started. I did not look pretty any more and that was a relief, because I am not really pretty. Not inside.

I paid my money and stalked off, hard-faced into the February cold of my new self.

# TRIXIE

I do so hate an empty house. Not that I want company, I like to keep myself to myself. It's just that empty houses scare me, call to mind dead people, bodies without souls. All draughts and decay and what have you – but no light in the eyes, no light behind the windows.

Yesterday, the landlord showed someone round next door – a girl with long brown hair. I hope that means what I think it means. That house has been empty for a year – more. If my luck's in she'll be a gardener – that garden! It's a disgrace, a proper eyesore. Long grass and thistles tangled with all sorts: polythene rags, beer cans and a mattress thrown out by the butcher's family when they left. And a laburnum dropping its poisonous black hooks over *my* side.

Fifty years in Sheffield and what is there to show for it? Only my garden like a picture in a magazine. Half a century slipped away somehow when I wasn't looking. *Half a century*. Why Sheffield? Why indeed. When I had to flee my old life I looked at a map of England and put my finger in the middle and there was Sheffield. I knew next to nothing about it, nothing and nobody. It meant nothing to me but knives and forks.

Mercy Terrace. I thought that had a nice ring to it. It's nothing remarkable. Just a low back street that runs along behind the shops at the bottom of a steep hill. I'm at the end. Over the road is the back entrance to a greengrocer's shop where, in the morning, every day save Sunday, a lorry chugs outside at eight o'clock, men unloading sacks of spuds, greens, carrots – you name it – and on hot days there's the sweet smell of squashed strawberries in the air.

It's a quiet street. The tarmac has worn away in patches, showing up the old cobbles underneath. Under the houses a river runs. The cellar is useless, damp at best, and after heavy rains the water rises an inch or more, all black and stinking. In the old days I'd be down there with my mop, sloshing about, doing battle. But now I leave it be. It always goes down in the end.

The butcher's family were a law unto themselves. *He* had big thick hands the colour of the slabs of meat in his shop. *She* was all frosty blonde – a beautician. The children – to speak plainly – were yobs. *Huge.* All that meat I suppose. They moved away eventually to a bigger house, a posher area. There used to be such a slamming of doors, such rows, such *language*. So little shame. And the minute Mr and Mrs were out – which was frequent – hordes of teenagers would congregate outside, filling the passage between my house and theirs, actually lounging sometimes against my own front door. The music would thud so loud the windows rattled in their frames. I used to lie in bed composing complaints, very civil mind you, and fair. But . . . well, if the truth be told I was a bit wary of them; so bold and cheeky. Respect for their elders? Don't make me laugh. And I didn't want to speak to them anyway, not really, didn't want to get myself embroiled. So I'd grit my teeth and stick my head under my pillow and wait for the parents to return and the slamming shouting and slapping that followed before you could hear yourself think again. Or some nights I would sing too, at the top of my voice, and stamp and shake my tambourine.

They moved out in the summer. Never a word said, just a van drawing up one morning, a lot of palaver, as you'd expect, and they were off. At first I liked the quietness and privacy, relished it. Nobody to watch me in the garden, not a sound through the walls at night. But when the nights began to draw in, I did miss the companionship of a light next door of an evening. I hated the sight of those blank windows, the dark. Rather a row I thought; rather the sight of a butcher making love to a beautician against the kitchen sink; rather a string of teenage obscenities and so-called music, than nothing. The house had never stood empty for so long in all the time I've been here. I thought if nothing else there would be bound to be students in September or October but no. There was nothing. Only silence and dark.

# HYACINTHS

Between the curtains, Trixie sees a white-haired person in the garden. Just for a second she thinks it's an old person, then a teenage bleach-haired boy, then she recognises the figure of a young woman. She is wearing a knee-length sweater splashed with white paint and her hands are clasped round a mug. She is standing in her garden, poking at the weeds with her foot.

Trixie is relieved. Last night she saw the oblong of frosted glass in her neighbour's front door illuminated, the blur of red stair-carpet inside. It is good to have a neighbour again, and a quiet one at that. There wasn't a sound last night, though Trixie strained her ears for the chatter of the television or music. No noisy children, just a young woman alone – possibly the ideal neighbour. Although she doesn't want to get involved, although she likes to keep herself to herself, relief and curiosity drive her to put on her coat and outdoor shoes and open her own back door.

The girl doesn't look up at first. She is staring at something on the ground. The steam from her mug, which she holds at chin level, has made her face look moist and pink. The sun hasn't got on to the gardens yet and the grass is weighed down with thick feathers of frost. Trixie looks proudly at her own garden. The pink and grey crazy-paving is surrounded on three sides with neat clumped shrubs, clipped and huddled down against the cold, but still there is colour, orange berries glow on the cotoneaster, and there is *order*. She does hope her new neighbour is a gardener.

'Bitter,' she says and the girl jumps.

'Oh . . .'

'Bitterly cold,' Trixie says.

'I was just looking at these snowdrops . . .' The girl indicates them with her toe. She wears clumsy black boots, like men's work boots.

Trixie comes closer to her little hedge to look over and sure enough, there poking their heads out beneath a stiff flop of frozen grass is a frail group of snowdrops, drips of cream grown out of the frost.

'Like a miracle,' Trixie says, 'first sign of spring. Crocuses next. Look . . .' She points at the little striped spears of crocus leaves. The girl is silent, gazing at them.

'I'm Trixie,' Trixie tries. 'Thought I'd best make myself known.' It is so hard to talk, she has almost forgotten how – and this girl is no help.

'Inis,' she mumbles.

'Sorry?'

'My name is Inis.'

'Unusual.'

'Mmmm.'

'English?'

Inis shrugs. Like squeezing blood from a stone, Trixie thinks, but then the girl does look troubled. Reminds her of someone, somehow. Something about those heavy-lidded eyes.

'How about a cup of tea?' Trixie suggests. 'I've got the kettle on.'

Inis holds up her mug.

'Go on, keep me company. You needn't worry,' Trixie adds, 'I'm not the sociable type. You won't know I'm here as a rule – only I thought I'd make myself known.'

Inis looks at her properly for the first time. 'All right then, thanks.' She pushes open the rickety wooden gate between them.

Inside it is dim. There is a sweet rank stench Inis can't

8

immediately identify. The electric-fire is burning, an orange slash in the dullness. The television flickers, a cookery programme, a Chinese chef. Trixie turns down the sound.

'Sit yourself down,' she says. The imitation sheepskin by the fire makes Inis sad. No reason except that she is prone to sadness. A quick hand shreds chicken on the screen.

'Do you like cooking?' Trixie asks. 'If you like Chinese food there's one of those takeaway affairs down the road, I've never tried it myself, not something I particularly fancy.'

Trixie goes into the little offshot kitchen to make the tea and Inis follows her with her eyes. The house is a mirror image of Inis's in design: the sink, the window on the opposite wall so that they can gaze out of their kitchen windows at each other. Trixie sighs and breathes stertorously in the kitchen in the unselfconscious way live-alone people do.

Trixie arranges a tray and carries it precariously through. Two elderly best cups and saucers full of pale, slopping tea, a plate of biscuits, an embroidered tray-cloth.

'How nice,' Inis says. The cups are white with green leaves on them and a worn gold rim. The handles are gold too, they look delicate and snappable.

'You'll find I'm not much of a one for company,' Trixie says. They sit and sip their tea watching the silent sizzling on the screen. 'Television's company though,' she says. 'Don't know what I'd do without my telly.'

'I haven't got one,' Inis offers.

'Oh dear . . .'

'By choice,' Inis says.

'Busy I expect.' Trixie grates the bottom of her cup across the saucer, pours the slops back into the cup and drinks them.

They lapse into silence again. Trixie looks captivated by the chef spinning a nest of golden hairs out of melted sugar. Her eyes are very bright with the television light in them and little puckered purses stand out under each one. Inis eats a soft petticoat-tail and looks round the room. On the window-sill is a row of yoghurt pots full of spindly seedlings, craning towards the light. There's a piano against the opposite wall, covered in a chenille cloth and on top of it a glass fruit bowl full of pink breakfast grapefruit and pale green apples. There are sepia photographs in dark frames, she can't see the detail, posed figures. There are three hyacinths in a white china bowl. That's what the smell is, hyacinth breath stifled and baked in the electric heat. One of the blooms is strong and fat, fully open, glimmering white; one slimmer, a little behind in its development; the third has lost the fight for root space, it is only a puny thing, loose in its green sheath. They are as competitive as people, Inis thinks, those hyacinths in the bowl.

# BOY

It is time to come out

I have been asleep but now I am awake

I want to come out now and . . . I don't know what

I don't know how

I am shouting to Trixie and moving my arm

She will not hear me

I am stuck in Trixie

And she will not know

# LIAR

I make a speciality of not remembering. I have done for years but now . . . It's like my will power is unravelling. What is it about that girl? Inis, bizarre name. Nothing sort of a name. In. Is. She has stirred me up. Ever since she went home the memories have been flocking. It's something about the look in her eyes, something familiar and lost. She does remind me of someone – it's a proper tease, that's what it is, a conundrum.

I should never have asked her in. Not grateful. Not friendly, not particularly. Not that I want friends, but a smile wouldn't go amiss. I've noticed how mean they are with smiles, these days, the young. I want to shake them by the shoulders sometimes, the sulky louts, and say, *What's the matter with you? A smile costs nothing.* Although I never will.

Not that *Inis* is all that young.

The television is on loud to try and drown my thoughts and it's my quiz, 'Countdown'. You make the longest possible word from nine random letters against a hectic ticking clock and I can do it well, usually I can, sometimes I beat the contestants. I've even thought of sending up my name and taking part but I would never really do such a thing, never in a month of Sundays. Then you have to do a sum, I'm not so good at that. Sometimes Blowski comes to join me at this time, for a cup of tea and 'Countdown', but I always beat him, well he is a Pole and never has caught on properly to English words.

Memories are rarely good, Trixie Bell. Best to steer clear, live in the present, by far the best way.

But coming to in the pantry my mouth stuffed full of raisins; stinking stuff smeared on the walls and my fingers dirty; a torn skirt; suddenly being in a strange street alone with no hand to hold; a stinging leg; a huge face pushed into mine, shouting, shouting. Flecks of spittle.

Because always there were absences.

Sometimes I dream about dark and soft stuff in my face, everything cool and thick and dusty so I think I will choke, beating my hands against fur and cloth. No light or air.

I did not know it is not like this for everyone.

Now I am one. I am healed.

But there *were* the gaps. Somehow I would part from myself and come to somewhere I shouldn't have been. Sometimes I'd come to and find myself in the corner; sometimes a stain on my clean dress; a foul taste in my mouth, a scrape on my knee.

Gaps then but not clean. I try not to remember. When I would come back it was like trying to remember a dream. Only the *feeling* is left, a trace of sensation, dim memories. No. I don't mean memories exactly, something more like a finger prodding inside my soft brain, something physical.

I was a bad girl. Somehow I was and there was guilt. Bad things happened: marzipan went missing, the cherries from the trifle. Someone scribbled on the wall. Father's letters got thrown away. A bite was taken from every apple in the bowl.

No, it was not like dreaming. You don't get in trouble for dreaming. You don't get accused of lying. They always called me a liar, before I even knew what the word meant. 'You *did* it, Trixie,' Mother's face too close to mine. 'Useless to lie, we *know*. You are a liar.' Useless to protest. The unfairness battered about inside me like something wild in a box. But I kept my mouth shut, I did learn that, for whatever I said would only make things worse.

I was a still and silent child. Indeed I was afraid to move. I tried so hard to be good and sweet and silent. Usually, I wore white. I sat with my feet together and my hands in my lap. I tried to be seen and not heard. I only ever wanted to be good.

When I was five my father went to France to fight. My mother thought he would never come back. She took me to be photographed on my sixth birthday, a photograph to send to him. In it, my eyes are huge and frightened, my mouth so small it is only a dot. The thing was battering inside me. The dress, the special dress that Mother had knitted me for the occasion, all thin and lacy gossamer wool was stretched and baggy as if I had stretched it over my knees which Mother had warned me not to do. I did not do it and yet the dress was stretched. My leg was stinging where she'd slapped me. She was glaring at me from behind the photographer and whatever he said, that man, I could not smile or watch the birdie: there was no birdie to watch. There I stood in my sagging, ruined dress and my mother's eyes burned at me, promising punishment. *Your poor father out there risking his life for King and Country and you can't even keep yourself decent* . . . And there I am still, caught in a frame and terrified, my hands screwed into fists at my sides. The photograph has darkened after all those years, is stained, as if the badness has seeped out. And Father came home anyway, before it could be sent. Discharged for his bad nerves.

All my childhood, I was frightened to move. I hardly did a thing. And yet the evidence of my badness was forever there. I would try so hard to be still and silent but suddenly there I'd be with a trailing hem and bits of twig caught in my hair. 'I didn't do it,' I used to say before I learned better. 'I didn't, I haven't . . . *I* didn't do it.' And they would get so terribly angry and their breath would be hot in my face. 'The evidence is *here*,' they might shout. 'As if it's not bad enough that you do these things . . . but then against all the evidence to deny them! It defies reason.'

It hurt me so much that they wouldn't believe me. But then, who on God's earth would?

'The girl's an imbecile,' Father might say.

'The Devil's in her,' Mother might add.

And then there were the punishments.

# WHITE

Now all the walls are white. The bedroom looks all right, the bathroom too because it is mostly grey tiles mottled with white anyway. The white painted over a crust of mould makes it bright. It might come through again, the black mould, but I don't care. It's temporary this, little boxy, two-up, two-down, attic, offshot. Like a doll's house, pretend.

I love the smell of emulsion paint. It is almost delicious and just for the odd moment when I was painting, I was almost absorbed, almost, when I could just *do* it, let my hand roll the oozing foam roller to and fro, listening to the licky sticky sound of paint. I would not even begin to approach the word happy, but I was almost content.

In the sitting-room though, the wallpaper flowers loom through the whiteness no matter how many coats I do. The old paper that looked so well stuck on I couldn't face stripping it, has bubbled away from the wall. It looks awful, blisters and bruisy flowers. How Richard would scoff. The Indian bedspread I've used as a curtain, tacked to the frame so you can't draw it back, but who wants to look out? Looks OK. In the evening, with the gas-fire lit and a brass-based lamp I found in a skip, it looks all right. It looks possible. It's only in the daytime when light forces itself through the rusty cotton weave that it appears amateurish – no, what do I mean? It does look pretend.

I look in the bathroom mirror, it's still a shock to see my new white-haired self. I've had long chestnut brown hair ever since I was about two. *Lovely hair* all my lovers and friends have always said, and my parents' friends, stroking, *so glossy, such a colour with the sun on it.* And now it is short and no colour at all. When I got home from the hairdresser's and looked in the mirror I saw I had little flecks of dark hair stuck to my face, gathered in little drifts under my eyes. My eyebrows looked heavy and too dark for the first time so I began to pluck them, but it made me sneeze, made my eyes water again. All the stinging, all the little trivial physical tears. I wanted to pluck my eyebrows because I thought fine brows would look better with my short white hair. You see? There I go again, wanting to look better which is a step towards prettier, which is a lie.

I am a terrible woman. I have done a terrible thing. I have left my children. A month ago I was a mother now I am not. Though that is not absolutely true. Once you have been a mother you can never stop being one, not entirely, whatever happens, because becoming a mother does something . . . does something to your soul. But in *practice* I am not a mother any more.

I have brought with me some clothes, some photographs, my cameras, some rolls of film I shot in the last weeks. I have left behind two precious children and a man I cannot blame. He is a terrible man, terribly good, patient, understanding. I left the children in front of 'Fantasia' on the video recorder; I left a note which tried to explain; I left my door-key and my sad reflection in the hall mirror. I left the house tidy, bleach in the toilets, the freezer stuffed, milk in the fridge. I left friends who will be hurt and angry that I never confided the despair I felt. But then I did not know I felt despair. It was just that it reared up one day without warning. Oh yes I had been miserable, depressed, Richard thought, but I was also safe, appreciated, loved.

Somehow I couldn't stand it.

And now I am here in this white painted dump. The only room that is not white is the attic. I have curtained off a section for a darkroom – fortunately there is a basin up there. It is a perfect space. I've invested in new equipment, delivered yesterday. So

I am set up. I will not waste time. I want to work. Looking at whatshername – Trixie – today I thought I might ask her if I could take some pictures. Her face is beautifully old and she has a sort of dignity. All the same there's something not quite right about her, the way she drifts off. But thank Christ I've not landed up next door to a family, other people's kids. That I could *not* stand.

'You are greedy,' Richard said to me once, long ago, before the children.

'Greedy?' I didn't understand. We were in Greece, on a ferry travelling between islands. He was basking in the sunny slop of light, I was squinting through my camera lens at plush green feathers of cyprus against the intense blue sky.

'Why don't you just enjoy it?'

'I *am* enjoying it.'

'Why don't you put your camera down? Just look and let it go. You never just *look*. You always have to try and *keep* it.'

I laughed at him and went on clicking. The wind got up as we moved out into the open sea and I photographed Richard leaning over the ship's rail, his hair blowing, a spray of rainbow prisms behind him. We were in love and he was always teasing me. I took no notice. But now I see what he meant and partly agree. I do have this habit, that infuriates him, of lifting up my hands, angling my two forefingers and thumbs into a rectangle through which to frame a scene. Even without my camera, to impose edges. Now my memory is composed of rectangles.

My head aches. Perhaps I regret the rectangles. I don't know. I strain to see round the edges of the things I remember, to remember the things outside the frame that I wilfully did not see. Or wilfully did not feel.

I used to photograph sunrises and sunsets. One year, when Robin was a baby, we rented a house on the Isle of Skye. And because I was feeding at funny times I would be awake to see the sky lighten and I'd photograph the rosy or greenish or pearl grey dawn. And late at night – it must have been midsummer to have made it so late – I'd try and capture the sunset, the fantastic rose, gold, lilac, lime, all the incredible colours. I don't develop colour film, so I took them to the studio but when I got them back I was disappointed. I didn't say. Richard liked them. A pile of shiny colours, skies, clouds, vanishing sun, but still, lying on the kitchen table they seemed dead things. Of course they did, because the magic was in the sky itself, in the transience of the light. Impossible to shrink it through a camera lens. Audacity to think you can keep it. You might as well spear a butterfly with a pin.

I'd forgotten until now, but last night, just as I was drifting off to sleep, which I make myself do by drinking hot milk, honey and a good shot of Scotch, I heard singing – hymns. A loud, strong, woman's voice and the thump of a beat, maybe her foot on the floor. It could only have been Trixie, though I would not have thought such a voice could come from her she looks so done in, sort of defeated. 'Onward Christian Soldiers' she sang, and 'He Who Would Valiant Be' and I went to sleep trying to remember the words. I used to love singing hymns at school. I wonder if children still sing hymns like that in assembly. I wonder if my children will?

# THE DEVIL

If I screw up my eyes and try to picture my mother as she appeared to me as a child, I see fine wriggly scribbles that were the strands of escaped hair. Before she was ill her hair was black and though she pulled it back, coiled it at the nape of her neck and stuck it with long, pearl-headed pins, little fizzes always sprang up around her hairline. I see her hair first, then hear the swish of her skirt, the invisible legs moving inside. When she was well and clean she always smelled of lily-of-the-valley. She had ivory skin and brown eyes. Her eyebrows were clear, straight and black. Her head was neat and oval as a wooden doll's.

Before she was ill she sometimes used to stand on the dining-room table with a tablecloth wrapped round her and recite, 'The Wreck of the Hesperus'. She would put one hand to her brow, and the other to her heart and sob her way through the last lines:

> At daybreak, on the bleak sea-beach a fisherman stood aghast,
> To see the form of a maiden fair lashed close to a drifting
>   mast.
> The salt sea was frozen on her breast, the salt tears in
>   her eyes;
> And he saw her hair, like the brown sea-weed, on the billows
>   fall and rise.

But only when Father was out.

Father's skin was always closely shaved and he smelled of his pipe tobacco and Silvikrin hair tonic. I remember the feel of his newly shaved cheek, silk smooth if you stroked one way, cat's tongue rough the other. I must have been very young to have been allowed to, to have wished to, touch his face like that. Although his skin was so well shaved there were bundles of bristles coming out of his nostrils and ears as if he was really stuffed with straw. His eyes were the colour of cloudy ice, frozen with flecks.

I had no brothers or sisters to help bear the burden of my parents.

I don't want to go remembering all that, but somehow I can't seem to help it. The memories are like itches you must try not to scratch but then you forget and you are scratching again and I am remembering and it feels dangerous. I feel like a bad child on a railway track, running through a tunnel just for the risk, haring back down into the darkness of my own past. Back into that big house on a tree-lined road in Holloway, hating that house, sometimes almost blaming it.

I can't blame next door. Inis. But she has set me off. What is it about her? I don't know. What is it about her eyes?

I don't know if the punishment came first. I mean, if the punishments were for the absences or the absences were a result of the punishments.

This was one thing and it doesn't *sound* too bad. I had to stare into a mirror, at my own face. Mother said it was for three hours – it was Mother's punishment. I do not know if it was really three hours. To begin with I had no idea how long an hour was. The end of three hours was as hopelessly distant then as the thought of Christmas in July. I had no control, and no clock. Only the oval mirror in a wooden frame. The mirror was big enough to reflect my face and most of the room behind me, including the locked door. Sometimes Mother would be reflected behind me, standing at my shoulder. In the mirror her face was slightly twisted as if someone had pulled her jaw to one side, narrowed one of her eyes. In the mirror the curly hairs round her forehead looked like stiff wires, though I knew that really they were soft. My own face, too, looked odd. Now I think the glass was warped; then, I was afraid of the odd twist the mirror gave, that made what was familiar so frightening.

'Look Trixie,' Mother would say, leaning forward so that her face loomed beside my own. 'Look deep into your eyes. Search your eyes for the truth.' The edge of the glass was bevelled. If I moved my head a little and squinted through my lashes, sometimes I could see rainbows.

'Don't shut your eyes,' she'd say. 'Don't blink. I want you to stand there and look inside yourself until you recognise the badness in you. I want you to look until you recognise the Devil, all your badness and lies.'

Then she would leave the room for a long time. There was a window overlooking the street where people passed by, sometimes I heard children shouting. I never shouted. I did not go to the window. I did not leave the mirror. I hardly dared to let my eyes wander from the mirror eyes. I did look at the frame. I think it was mahogany, a deeply polished, warm wood. There were little scratches on the frame and one on the glass made, Father told me, by a diamond; the hardest thing in the physical world.

In the room for oceans of time, there would be only me. I would stand in front of the mirror with my arms folded and stare at the mirror eyes and the longer I stared the less they were my eyes. I cannot explain the dread. It does not *sound* too bad, I think, as a punishment. Not cruel. The mirror eyes were pale. They looked not at me but through me and my face melted away, became a white cloud on the glass, like breath that would condense and run away.

Sometimes I fainted. My face would dissolve around the two dark spots, like frogspawn spots that were the pupils of my eyes. A sick hunger would well up from my bowels and my breath would turn to stone in my lungs and I would swallow as if seized by a dreadful thirst that turned to a thirst for air and I would open my mouth that would turn to a dark gasp in the glass before I fell, seeing through the fizzing sparkle in my head the sinking of my eyes from the glass, their vanishing.

If I did not faint, if my face did not dissolve, I would learn that it was not mine. It lost its meaning as my face or any face. The lips were like two pink worms, fat pink edges of a trap. The cheeks were lumps of meat, the nostrils damp holes. I could stretch it and if I opened the trap I could see teeth and a moving tongue like a snake that the mirror creature had swallowed, that flickered up from inside.

But sometimes even while I was being punished for my absences I would have one. It was all right in the end if I could just be there in the cold room. If I could just remain there for three hours until Mother came back. If I told the lie, 'Yes Mother, I saw the Devil and I told him to go away.' Then that would be an end of it. We could go and sit by the fire and eat our tea although I did not want it. I was never hungry and had to force the buttered bread and the little cakes down my throat, past the thick snake in my throat. I only wanted to get into my own bed and be alone. I had a rabbit my Auntie Ba had knitted for me when I was a baby, a grey floppy thing, and I liked to curl under the covers in the safe dark and suck his ears.

But sometimes I would not stay. That is why the door was locked, why there were bars on the window, because otherwise, in an absence, my body would not stay in the room. When I came to from an absence in that room I might be bruised where my head had been smashed on the wall, I might have tooth marks on my arm, my clothes might be ripped. I might have nothing on at all. So frightening to find yourself, suddenly, naked and alone in a cold room with a locked door and a prison window and eyes sad and accusing in the mirror, when you looked.

Once I woke in bed with my arms strapped to my sides with soft bandages and dry lint stuffed in my mouth. The doctor was there, solemn with his grey, whiskery face. 'A fit,' he pronounced. 'A most hysterical child.' He put his fingers in my mouth and pulled out the lint and it was as if my tongue went with it and I was dumb for a week, afraid to speak, afraid of whose voice was living in my throat.

That was one thing. Mother's punishment. Father's was quite another. And until I knew about the boy, it made no sense.

# ADA

Trixie and me and that boy. Why Trixie is the main one I will never understand, not that *he* could ever be. But I saw the opportunities for fun that she did not take. Trixie was a lump and I was her spirit but then I was dumb. I was her good spirit and the boy, oh *he* was her bad.

I watched but then you see I had no strength. I could not move. I was in Trixie moving slow like underwater. I could not move out till we were a woman.
Being good, being punished when it was not her that did the bad things.
Oh that boy!
Poor Trixie.

But me, being suddenly a young woman.
I could not move till I was a woman in love.

> *Call me romantic,*
> *but still I maintain,*
> *I was born to lo – ove.*

If you could see Trixie's little hands clenched in her lap while my arms wanted to fly in dance, my hair fly, my feet spin . . .
I was not born to be a child.
But *he* oh some *people* they never grow up.

# PARTY

I'm tempted to get a television or a radio at least. I miss noise, chatter. God, how I used to wish it could be quiet. Just for a moment, to coast on a clear smooth wave of silence but there was always something. If it wasn't the children squealing, or the television, Richard's music – lovely music, Handel, Bach, but too persistent – or the radio, and that was my fault, I had the radio on most of the time just to hear a sane, adult, BBC voice, if it wasn't any of those it would be the washing-machine churning, or the kettle rushing up to a boil, taps running, the microwave pinging, Robin's battery robot, Billie's squeaky toys, Richard's bleeper, the alarm-clock, the door-bell, the telephone. Even if it was quiet in the house there was the sound of cars starting up on the road outside, the maddening sound of a car alarm, or sometimes our neighbour's faulty burglar alarm that would go on and on and drive me round the bend, or a siren – somebody else's emergency – and always as a background the grey roar of distant mingled traffic.

If I could just have silence, I used to think or say or sometimes shout, then I would be all right. Now I have silence more or less. I have no TV, radio, no washing-machine. The telephone, like myself, is unconnected and I will leave it that way. No one ever comes to the door. I can hear Trixie's television sometimes, or her singing at night. Cars rarely pass because it's a dead end, and although the main road isn't far away, by some acoustic freak you cannot hear it from here. When I am up in my attic I can hear nothing at all. Funny. We lived in a *nice* suburb, gardens, trees, what you might think of as a quiet place. Now I live in the inner city and it is quieter. What I always wanted. But my mind scrambles quite desperately for distraction.

I want to buy a radio, at least, but I won't. I wonder if I did I'd hear Richard's voice appealing for my return. No, because then he'd be breaking his promise and Richard would never do that. *I* promised, when I phoned that if he leaves me alone, doesn't try to find me, I'll send a postcard every week so they'll know I'm all right. So I do that, cheerful words, pictures that the children will like because of their colours. A red Matisse; a Bonnard with a red checked tablecloth, a woman and a black dog like the dog I used to have. Bonny, that's funny, Bonny, Bonnard. No it's not. I loved that dog. I used to take her to walk along the beach by the golf course in Felixstowe where I grew up, and sometimes right along the beach and across to Bawdsey in a little ferry rowed by an old man. We'd walk on the steep curves of brown shingle, by the sudden plunges of grey water where it was dangerous to swim and then miles across the estuary mud, Bonny's paw prints looping and tangling round the neat twinned line of my footprints that would slowly fill with shining water. Sometimes, she'd roll in a dead fish or sea-gull and have to be bathed when I got home and the whole house would stink of wet dog. She'd follow my dad around, shaking all over him. My mum would grumble about the black hairs that made a wavy ring round the bath and the dog smell. Because I had no brothers or sisters, Bonny was like my sister.

My dad was a doctor. It's funny that I married Richard without even thinking about that. You wouldn't think it was possible to have so little insight. My parents were killed in an aeroplane crash when I was eighteen. I should have been with them. They'd been on holiday in Tuscany. I'd met a boy, my first lover, a fortnight before the holiday and decided I could not go. I could not be parted from him for three weeks – and besides the house would be empty. I pretended I wanted to stay to look after Bonny who had been ill, who would have been miserable in kennels. They were very dubious.

'You will be sensible, won't you?'

'At least you can water the tomatoes.'

I waved them off and as the car rounded the corner of the road a surge of excitement rushed through me. The sun was hot and quivery on the road and the next three weeks were mine. I went and watered the tomatoes straight away, picked a few red ones. The greenhouse was humid, thick with the rank cattish stink of the plants. The fruit was developing at the bottom, growing like fat little green pearls halfway up and at the top the plants still bore little spiky yellow flowers beaded with wetness where I'd sprayed them. I thought, what must it be like to be grown-up, so grown-up that you grow tomatoes, have a nearly adult daughter you can leave at home and trust.

I cooked proper meals for the first time, meals for Mark, meals for other friends. We gave a dinner party with candles and wine. I did gazpacho and spent an entire day making ravioli, rolling the pasta thin as paper and parcelling up minced mushrooms. I made a lemon soufflé that rose like a cloud. And I slept for twenty-one nights in my parents' bed with Mark and had my first orgasm on the twentieth night. On the twenty-first night we had a party.

All day, Mark, my friend Louise and her boyfriend moved furniture and rolled up rugs and compiled tapes of dance music. I made giant pizzas and gallons of pink fruity punch. It was exciting and frightening. It was a good party at first but too many people came. Older people I didn't know who wouldn't take no for an answer. One even brought a baby in a carry-cot. I tried to get Mark to help me throw them out but he was very drunk and said to leave it. I was wearing tight jeans and only a silk scarf tied round my breasts since it was a hot night. And people kept looking at me and I knew how beautiful I was, seemed to be. So I got drunk too. People were smoking dope and I tried some and forgot for a while where I was, that this was my parents' house. Mark made love to me in the garden, where there were other people who might have seen but I didn't care, I even wanted them to see how happy I was.

Bonny followed me around anxiously all night, like a fretful aunt, her brown eyes reproachful, but I ignored her. I think someone must have given her something, some sort of drug or drink because she started yelping and running round in crazy circles, chasing her tail like she did as a puppy, then rolling about on the carpet, then falling asleep sprawled on the sofa where she was not allowed to be.

The silk scarf came off and I walked about topless after that. I can't believe I did that now but I wasn't the only one and people caressed me as I passed them, not my friends who had started leaving by then, but strange men and even a woman who kissed me in the hall. I saw Mark kissing someone else too, one of the older women who was holding a joint out with one hand and running the other over his bum but I didn't mind. I felt generous and proud. This was my home and my party and it was the greatest thing ever.

I went upstairs to the loo and saw two people screwing on my parents' bed and suddenly I felt sick. In the bathroom mirror I looked shameless, my little breasts bare, my face flushed, my eyes blazing horribly. I went into my room, which seemed a very childish safe room with its shelf of dolls in national dress, the posters and books, and put a T-shirt on. I went downstairs and made coffee. I felt wobbly and frightened of the drugs and sex and drunkenness. The woman still had hold of Mark and she had taken off her shirt and her breasts were very big and floppy and adult looking and Mark's childish hand with its chewed fingernails was on one. It wasn't all right any more and I know it was my own fault, I started it, I know.

I thought what would my parents say if they walked in now, their lovely house with its polished parquet floors full of – mostly – strangers because it was late and everyone I knew – apart from Mark – had gone home. There were all these grown-up strangers who didn't even know it was *my* house, who looked down their drunken noses at me as if I was only a child.

I didn't know how to stop it. I tried to get Mark away from the woman but he was too drunk to listen.

'Come on Mark,' I said. 'I think we should be kicking people out.'

'The night is young,' the woman said, although the hall clock right in front of her nose showed that it was half-past two. 'This your place?'

'Yes, and *my* boyfriend,' I said stiffly.

'Cool,' she said. The music was too loud and the place so smoky it was as if there was fog in the house. I had an idea. I went into the cellar and switched off the electricity. My dad had shown me how to do this before they left in case of emergency. 'Like what?' I'd teased, but he was not thinking about this, I'm sure. The cellar smelt comfortingly of creosote and bicycle tyres. I stayed in the dark, lights flashing in my eyes, feeling sick, feeling as if the top of my head was coming off. I stayed underneath the feet and the grumbling and the door slamming. And then, when it was quiet, I turned the power back on and went to switch off the tape-player that had screamed back to life.

Everyone had gone except Mark who sat on the bottom stair as if he'd been shipwrecked, 'Christ, Inis,' he said.

'We've got to clear up,' I said.

'Inna morning,' he said and crawled upstairs.

I wandered around looking at the chaos and imagining how horrified my parents would be, how my mum would shriek at the cigarette burns on the hall carpet, how my dad would react to the ruined parquet. But I was too tired to do more than empty an ashtray into the overflowing kitchen bin. I went upstairs and slept beside Mark on my mum's side of the bed.

In the morning we drank coffee and cleaned. I was outside picking up cans when the man next door stuck his head over the hedge. 'Doug and Betty back?' 'No,' I said. 'Only I want to complain about that racket last night. Beverley never got a wink.' 'Complain to me.' 'Don't you worry, young lady, soon as that car draws in I'll be round to tell them your carryings on. We're not blind you know, nor deaf.' 'Fine,' I said, quailing inside. 'Do.' My head was throbbing and I felt sick every time I bent over to retrieve something. From inside I heard the roar of the vacuum cleaner.

They were due home in the early evening. Mark went home in the late afternoon. I took the washed sheets off the line, ironed them and put them back on the double bed. I shut some of the windows which had been open to let out the smell of smoke. I picked tomatoes and made a salad ready for them. I gathered some roses and only then did I notice that my mother's favourite cut-glass vase was missing – Venetian glass, a wedding present from her grandfather. I found it smashed behind the sofa. I'd put it there to be safe. I don't know how it got smashed. It lay on a whitened patch where the water had soaked into the parquet and dried, a mess of glittering crystal and broken lupins.

I was standing looking at it, filled with dread, thinking that it was the one thing, the *one* thing, Mum would really mind, that could not properly be replaced when the door-bell rang. When I saw the dark blue uniforms through the glass door I thought it was about last night, about the drugs or the noise. But it was not that.

I hope they had a good holiday. I hope they got drunk and made love every hot afternoon. I hope they walked along hand in hand like young lovers again, not the stiff English people they had grown into. I hope it was so quick they never knew what was happening.

My first thought, this is terrible to admit, but my first thought when the policewoman went to put on the kettle, to ring my aunt and ask her to come and be with me, was that I would never have to tell Mum about the vase. I felt relief.

After that grief.

And after that guilt. Somehow I felt that if I hadn't so thoroughly and joyously lost my virginity in their bed it wouldn't have happened, the engines failing, the plane falling, tons of it, dropping like a mountain from the sky and breaking into tiny pieces. I saw a tangle of warped metal and soft limbs, like the glass and the petals. If I hadn't had the party . . . if I hadn't let those people defile their house . . . I felt sick of myself, sick with guilt. And I should have been with them on that plane. I should have been dead too.

Bonny had known. Earlier in the afternoon I'd tried to take her to the baker's with me, she wouldn't come. Usually when anyone went near her lead that hung on a hook by the kitchen door, she'd whimper and frisk her stiff old body about, but this time she shrunk away. She went and lay on the hall floor outside my parents' bedroom door, her nose hidden under her paws, crying, trembling. I was too busy cleaning to take much notice. But of course, she knew.

# PIGEON PAIR

Sometimes when I looked in the mirror I saw a boy. I believe this was before I even knew there was a boy. I cannot be quite sure about that, of course. At eighty-four, I find, the memory will play such tricks. I hate it. But I am swept along. I remember things I could never have done . . . I say I could never have done but . . . oh how I ramble. One thing at a time. About the boy.

As a child I felt unwanted. That is a hard thing to say, but true. They were cruel to me. Mother with her punishment. Father with his.

Sometimes when Mother gave me the Reflective Punishment, which is what she called it, even when I was so small I had to stand on a chair to see myself in the mirror, my eyes would play tricks. They would tire with staring at the surface of the glass and sink through, focus back far inside the mirror as if it was a deep pool of light, focus past the reflection of door, wallpaper, ceiling rose and pale girl's face to discover a swimmy picture of a familiar boy. Familiar because he looked like family. He looked like me, or like I might have looked if I'd been a boy. I saw him for years. I liked seeing him. On those occasions I didn't faint. If I saw him the punishment wasn't so bad. It was as if I got a sort of comfort from his presence, as if something inside me relaxed, a sense of completion. I didn't think that then, of course, it was only that I felt happy, as if a little bubble had expanded in my chest.

Anyway, I never asked Mother or Father about the boy in the mirror. We hardly talked about the punishment at all. It was quite

33

by chance that I learned about the boy. I often used to sit on the window-sill in the sitting-room, a wooden space, wide enough for me to sit with my knees drawn up to my chin if I moved the china vase. In winter I would sit behind the brown velvet curtain. I won't say I was hiding, though I was hidden. I didn't think they liked me to sit with them and I didn't like to anyway. When the fire was lit the room got stuffy, I didn't like the heat, it made me breathless. Behind the curtain was a slice of cold air. I leant my cheek against the cold window-glass and watched the condensation trickle down. Sometimes in the winter there were frosty ferns and feather faces peeping through.

Once I was there – I think Mother had forgotten me – and Father came in for his tea. They were talking. I was barely listening, my mind elsewhere, watching the black hole my breath melted in the frost, squinting through it into the silver and dark fuzz of the garden, when I heard Father say '. . . if the boy had lived.'

'There's no use harking on at that again,' Mother said. I tried to rush my memory back to what else Father had said, but it was not there in my mind and anyway now I prickled with questions. Boy? What boy? I knew if I came out then I would be in trouble, they would say I was a sneaking eavesdropper but I did not care. I wanted to know so badly.

I must have been very young not to have been more afraid. I know I was young because I remember my feet didn't touch the floor, my heels banged against the skirting-board and then the vase smashed. I don't know how, maybe the hem of my dress caught it. I don't know, but I'm sure it was an accident. It seemed to hang in the air for a moment, opening a flap in the curtains through which my fire-lit parents' faces burned. My mouth opened in a balloon of panic, and then the vase smashed. It smashed in sharp, curved pieces and there was the stench of rotten flower water and broken chrysanthemums, petals scattered, slimy stalks. The curtain was whipped back and my cheek was stung by the hard flat of a hand. I was wrenched into the hot light of the room, I was slapped again, I was pushed and I fell. My head hit the hearth.

I remember nothing more until I woke up in my own bed. The first thing I saw was a vase of flowers on the window-sill, a different vase of course, and different flowers but still they hurled the memory back into my aching head.

Mother came into the room then and stood against the light so that she was as dark and flat as a shadow except for the frizz of escaped hairs round her brow.

'Woken up then,' she said. She leant over and became pink and round. She kissed me. I breathed her cool, lily-of-the-valley scent. She held my hand. 'You had us worried,' she said, 'falling like that. You must be more careful.' I tried to lift my head off the pillow but it was heavy and my neck hurt as well as the place on my temple where I had bashed it. Mother sat on the edge of the bed. 'You clumsy darling,' she said and stroked my hand. I liked it when she was like that, like a mother who loved me.

'Sorry,' I said.

'Least said: soonest mended.' She looked down at me and her eyes shone like wet pebbles in the sun. I wanted to ask her about what Father had said but I was scared it would make her angry, make her eyes go dry and hard, make her leave the room. But I had to know about the boy. You could never tell with Mother whether she might not be soft and open because sometimes she was. Sometimes she really was a good kind mother.

I held my breath and dared. 'I heard Father say,' I began, 'I heard him say about a boy.' Her eyes stayed bright. She stroked the palm of my hand with her thumb over and over. I saw that she was not angry but sad. She sighed, opened her mouth and closed it again.

'What, Mother?'

She breathed in and her nostrils fluttered like little dark moth's wings. 'You were born a twin,' she said finally. 'Two of you, two babies, first a boy – the boy your father wanted, and then you, the girl. A pigeon pair.'

35

'So, so I had a brother . . .' I struggled to sit up but my head was as heavy as if it had been nailed to the bed.

'Benjamin Charles,' she said. 'Benjamin Charles came first but Benjamin Charles was born dead. And then you. They took him away, tried to revive him. Alone I gave birth to you. And how you yelled!' I could not tell what her smile meant. 'How *you* yelled and flailed. Nothing wrong with *you*. But all the time, Benjamin Charles was dead.' She gazed out of the window and I looked too but there was nothing to see, only grubby clouds. Only the wobbly black M of a bird.

'"It's a mercy she's got the one," they said,' she said bitterly. She continued stroking my palm with her thumb but now I could feel the edge of her nail and the thinness of my bones between her fingers. 'How little they knew! How little insight . . . Charles wanted a boy, do you understand that?' She looked at me fiercely. 'Do you, can you understand the . . . disappointment is too slight a word. He wanted a son. And there was this son, a fine boy, handsome, perfect in every respect . . . but dead. It killed something in him. Do you understand that?' I winced at the pain of her hard fingers.

She sat still for a moment and I listened to her breathing calm. She loosened my hand quite suddenly and stood up. 'A dull day,' she said and twitched the curtain. 'I'll send Louise up with some soup.' And then she left the room.

If it had been the other way round I wouldn't have existed. That is what they would have preferred. Benjamin Charles and not Trixie. I lifted my hand and studied it. It seemed a horrible guilty thing that hand – a hand that had no right to be.

After that, when I saw the boy, I knew him for what he was. The brother I had killed. It was not for a long time because there were no punishments from Mother for a while. After she told me about Benjamin Charles, she was ill. I do not know the name of her illness but it meant that she sat still for hours at a time, her eyes open but unseeing, her fists clenched on the arms of her chair. Sometimes a string of dribble would dangle from her chin, sometimes a tear trickled down her cheek. And sometimes when Father – or Auntie Ba, who always came to help when Mother was ill – sometimes when they moved her there was a terrible dark wet patch on her chair cushion that made me hot and crawly with shame.

I think Mother was ill for weeks or months that time. I don't know. I think spring turned to summer because I remember the curtains drawn against the light when I went to bed. Auntie Ba used to sing to me about the gypsies and I liked it so much when she sang:

> What care I for my goose-feather bed,
> With the sheets turned down so bravely, oh?
> Tonight I will sleep in a cold open field,
> Along with the Raggle Taggle Gypsies, oh!

It gave me a feeling of lightness inside as if a little bit of gypsy freedom had got into me from the song. I used to try and sing but my voice had gone very small after my accident, like a little shivery thing huddled under my tongue so Auntie Ba had to put her ear against my mouth to hear me.

'What's got into you?' she'd say, but kindly, and she cuddled me when I shook my head. She was lovely my Aunt Barbaria – that's what I called her when I was learning to talk, trying to pronounce Barbara and it was one of the only times that I can remember when Father was pleased with me. 'What's that? Barbaria?' he shouted, thumping the table so the knives and forks jumped. 'Barbaria! That's a good one.'

She was really my mother's aunt though not much older than her and looked very much the same only her hair was cut short in a way that made Father hoot with scorn behind her back. And she was kinder with soft hands and little gifts of time in her lap, up her sleeves, in her pockets, time to give to me. She had had four children, though her first son, Tom, the oldest by several years, had just been killed in the trenches. She bore it well, Mother said. I never saw her cry, though if his name was ever mentioned, her hand flew softly to her heart as if to hold it still.

I did not dare ask Auntie Ba about the boy, not at first. But one night when she sat on the edge of my bed after her song she said something that made me sad and afraid. 'Trixie love,' she began. 'I'm going home in a day or two. Jack and the others need me . . . and your mummy's nearly better now. Why, today she ate a bit of Welsh rarebit and asked about the laundry. What's that long face for now?'

'Can I come with you?' I asked. 'Can I be your little girl?'

She sighed and kissed me. 'Silly. You're your mummy's little girl . . . What would she say if I took you away?'

'She wouldn't mind. You see, they really wanted the boy.'

Auntie Ba sat up very straight and her pink smiling mouth went straight. I could see she was older than Mother then with deep lines printed on her forehead.

'Now that is nonsense,' she said. 'Nonsense good and proper. Whatever in the world?'

'She said . . .'

'Forget about it,' she said, smiling again, though not with her eyes.

'Father blamed Mother, and Mother blames me.'

'Blame! These things happen. How could you even think it! You've misunderstood, my love. Put it out of your mind.' She sat me up and held me against her, the edge of her brooch digging into my cheek, but I didn't mind. I started to cry which was a horrible, dirty, leaky, weak thing to do. Crying was nearly as bad as wetting yourself Mother said, and I never ever did it. I kept my eyes dry. *Tears smell*, she said, though there were her tears when she was ill, water came from every part of her that I could not bear to see, could not bear to breathe in the smell.

'That poor baby died, but *you* lived, that was the important thing. Oh she always was a tragedy queen that mother of yours. Why she didn't get straight down to it and have another one,

38

I don't know. Oh my poor lamb, I almost think I *should* take you home.'

'It's all right,' I said suddenly, pulling back, dashing the tears from my eyes. I thought Auntie Ba might go and tell Father what I'd said and he might come and see me. He'd hardly noticed me since Mother was ill and that was the best thing.

'She didn't exactly say I was to blame,' I said. 'I just thought . . .'

'Well you can just unthink . . .' She wiped my eyes with an embroidered hanky. Then she ran her finger along the scar on my forehead. It was healed but still a bright shiny pink like an upside-down smile above my eyebrow. '*How* did you say you did this?' she asked. She had asked before but I had only said I'd fallen. 'By being clumsy,' I said and she smiled, comforted I think, and kissed me goodnight.

When I was older I learned how babies grow in their mothers' wombs. That a womb is like an upside-down draw-string bag inside the mother and when the baby is ready the string loosens and it comes out. The bag is full of water in which the baby swims like a fish. After that, I had dreams about the boy and me. I saw us swimming in a tank in our coats and shoes, tiny children in Sunday hats with bubbles streaming from our mouths. That was a happy dream but another was terrible. It was a dark, cramped, slippery dream of slithering limbs and a struggle in which I killed Benjamin Charles who was not separate at all but was another part of me. I knew, even when I was a little girl, that I could never ever have a baby. That I could not be trusted with a baby.

Father's punishment. He stripped me of my clothes. Hard and rough, his face a blank, his fingers cold as metal fingers. He stared at me as if he hated me, looking at my shivery body. Then he made me dress in boy's clothes: underwear, buttoned shirt, trousers, jacket, woollen socks. My fingers fumbled with the buttons. He stood over me watching every move. And when

I was dressed he would look at me with tears standing in his eyes, and a white tremble in a muscle by his mouth.

'Boy,' he would say. And then he would open the wardrobe door and push me in and lock it behind me. The lock had a tickly curved sound like a silver S. Then I would hear the bedroom door slam, then silence. Almost silence. I'd have my face pressed into the folds of Mother's dresses and coats, silk, velvet, fur. Sometimes my mouth filled up with fur. She had a beaded dress that rattled softly when I moved. There was a choking smell of camphor and stale perfume. There was no light, not the merest chink round the door.

I thought I would choke to death in the folds of the clothes, the stiff, scratchy and soft fabrics against my face, the beads so smoothly cold they felt wet. My legs would tire and I'd sink down among the lumps of shoes and other things on the bottom of the wardrobe. Once I put my hand by accident into the pocket of a fur coat and I pulled out something hairy, sticky, an old peppermint sweet that I sucked.

I did not fight or scream because I thought I would suffocate. There was no air only cloth and fur. Perhaps I slept because I never remember coming out of the wardrobe, only going in.

# BOY

Couldn't Father see me?

When I stood in front of him

Me

He only saw Trixie

I was out and I did bad things for him

To show him

But he looked at me and saw Trixie

He wanted not her but me

I made Trixie let me do things

Steal things, eat things, spoil things

Run and climb and hurt

I was strong then

I am strong now and I am awake

Why can't I get out?

I am getting stronger

I am moving in her and shouting

# BONNY

Our kitchen windows face each other over the fence so we could smile at each other, Trixie and I, as we stand at our sinks, but we don't. We preserve the pretence of privacy. There is a Venetian blind pulled up above the sink with a greasy black knotted string but it is too disgusting to use. I let it down once and bits of God-knows-what fell out from between its slats so I pulled it quickly back up and left it. I considered getting a new one but it would seem rude to stop pretending not to see and put a real one up.

It might be nice to have a pet. Maybe I should get myself a dog, a puppy. For what? To clutter up and complicate my life. Why can't I just *be*. Anyway it would seem disloyal to Bonny, my dog-sister I used to call her as a child.

Before my parents went away, Bonny had been ill. I thought she'd seemed better during the holiday but when they didn't return she got worse. My parents' house was sold very quickly and I went to live with my aunt in Colchester. I was rich for a young girl, but useless. I was a few weeks off starting my teaching degree. I should have been looking for somewhere of my own but I couldn't do it. My aunt, Daphne, said I could stay with her until I felt better, me and Bonny. Bonny hated it there. It was a cats' house. There were three of them, sneaky looking creatures with long, liquid eyes and lashing tails. They perched high up on shelves and window-sills and regarded Bonny scornfully.

Daphne was like a cat herself, graceful and self-sufficient.

She moved about her little house on silent feet and was always startling me by suddenly being there, behind or beside me. Not that she had much to do with me. She was a painter, a vague woman who lived outside the normal rules of time. I remembered my mother describing her as scatty, but she was not at all. She was quite methodical, it's just that because she was used to living alone she didn't subscribe to things like mealtimes or bedtimes. She tended to sleep more in the day and rise at night. For days there would be nothing but fruit to eat in the house and then I'd be woken up at 3 a.m. by the smell of frying mackerel.

We didn't like each other very much. She was my mother's much younger half-sister. We had nothing in common. She smelled of linseed oil and wore long, paint-splashed skirts with fishermen's smocks over the top. I don't know if she'd ever had a lover. I don't think she could have stood one. She couldn't bear touching. She gave me one stiff, sympathetic hug at the funeral but I could tell she was flinching inside. After that, no more touching, though she lavished love and kisses on her ginger cats and cooked them little messes of chicken and fish which they'd eat fastidiously with their paws.

About a month after we'd moved in, five weeks after my parents' death, Bonny died. She wouldn't eat, she whined and moped and shrank. One day I realised with a shock that her coat slid loosely over her rib-cage, there was no flesh in between the skin and the bone. A few days later she refused to go for walks any more. I took her to the vet who called her a poor old lady and offered to put her to sleep. I refused. I would have felt like a murderer. I took her back to Daphne's and there, after two days, she died. I knew it was the end by the odd smell that came from her and the noisy way she was breathing. Her nose was hot and dry but her eyes were bright, and between naps, she kept her eyes on me, looking deep into my eyes as if she was trying to communicate something. Right to the very end, when I stroked her head and spoke to her she wagged the tip of her feathery black tail. And then it stopped wagging and she gave a rattly sigh, closed her eyes and was gone.

I cried more for Bonny than for my parents. Or was it myself I was crying for? Daphne kindly took Bonny's body to the vet's to be hygienically disposed of since there wasn't anywhere in her tiny garden to bury her. I manoeuvred the heavy, blanket-wrapped body into the back of her 2CV but stayed at home. I didn't want to think about what they'd do with her. If we'd been at home, my dad and I would have buried her behind the greenhouse and we all would have mourned.

Daphne was kind in her cool vague way. She made me a little meal, like a cat's meal, of lightly-cooked chicken breast and poured me a tiny glass of thin, pale sherry.

'Fino,' she said. 'I know how I'd feel if it was one of my sweethearts . . .'

The next week I went to college and hardly ever returned to Daphne's house after that. I doubt if she noticed. Less than a year into my degree, I met Richard. Dr Goodie. He was a junior houseman, worn down with all the hours and the strain of the job. I fell in love with his exhaustion which was so impressively greater than my own. I quickly moved out of my stuffy hall-of-residence and in with him. I was in love with his need for me. I made coffee and took his clothes to the launderette and was always ready to make love at any odd time that he had the energy. I never decided to give up my degree, it just slipped away, became irrelevant. I loved him partly because he understood death, or so I thought, because he had seen it. I wonder if people fall in love with murderers for the same reason? I suppose I thought he was wise.

When I remember that time, I can hardly believe I am remembering myself. It is all so dim and far away, like the memory of an old film. After Bonny's death I don't think I felt anything else strongly, not even love. I felt nothing much except guilt and loneliness and then immense relief at being needed by Richard, wanted and loved. I felt nothing strongly until the birth of Robin, and then I felt too much.

# A FUNNY TURN

Mother and Father kept me a child for longer, far longer, than it was true. I was bad, 'a problem child' though I don't think such a handy phrase was in currency then. I was lonely, cruelly sheltered even into my early twenties. I don't blame them. I was not safe to be left alone, that's how they saw it. They were afraid of my growing up, quite sensibly frightened of how I would cope with the world. I was no better. Still the blank spells came, though sometimes I was able to cover up the absences, for I was left very much alone.

The house was quiet. Father was out a good deal of the time. He was having trouble with labour relations in his rubber goods' factories. Demands for better conditions, shorter hours, more pay. Father was incensed by the ingratitude of his workers. At breakfast each morning, the newspaper would tremble in his hands. 'Two million unemployed!' he might say, waving the headlines in my face. 'And still they threaten action.' Then he'd subside behind his paper, muttering, *Commie traitors*, and *Bolsheviks*. He always drank his tea too hot, slurping it. The noise made me wince. There was no conversation. Father didn't like to talk at breakfast-time. Louise, the cook, served our food and slunk away, repelled I'm sure by the atmosphere. Father would have preferred to be alone, but he pretended, quite successfully mostly, that we weren't there. And sometimes, I think, I wasn't. And neither was Mother.

One day we were eating sausages, I remember, slightly

blackened, and I suddenly saw us as we were: Father muttering over his newspaper, chewing and slurping; Mother silent, staring wild-eyed at the tea pot; myself, a woman dressed as a child, eating neatly, cutting my sausages into tiny pieces and chewing each one twelve times, and it made me laugh. Laughter was a rare sound. Mother did not seem to notice. Father whipped his paper down and gave me a look. Louise who had come in with fresh toast, pulled a droll face at me and backed out of the room closing the door behind her.

'I fail to see the joke,' Father said. He had a smear of fat on his immaculately shaved chin. I thought it funny, him so dignified, a scarecrow dressed for the office. Oh I knew he was a scarecrow, I could still see the straw sticking in bunches from his nostrils and ears. 'Pray enlighten me,' he said. Red spots were growing on his cheeks though his lips were white.

Mother reached out for the tea pot. 'Another cup, Charles?' she asked, though her eyes were not with us. He banged on the table with his fist and my tea slopped on the tablecloth.

My laughter stopped. I don't know how I had dared. It's just . . . it's as if sometimes the light changes and makes quite ordinary things seem absurd. Looking at a bus, I sometimes want to laugh even now. All those people, two tiers of them, sitting still and travelling forward; sometimes the bus disappears, that is all that makes sense of it, the bus and then all that's left are the absurd people plunging seriously forward through the air.

Apart from breakfast I never saw Father. He was always at work or out elsewhere. Mother had settled into a sort of trance. She wouldn't move for hours, sometimes days. She emerged briefly sometimes, like a dreamer, wild-eyed with dreams, fighting the descending blanket of sleep. I sat with her, tried to bring her back. '*It was the schooner Hesperus that sailed the wintry sea* . . .' I kept starting to try and rouse her, but her eyes were empty. It drove me half mad. Louise clattered in the kitchen and moved about the house, making pleasant remarks, even singing sometimes, and it was as if a real bright person moved among ghosts.

I read the newspaper and the Bible. I was Mother's nurse. Auntie Ba didn't come any more now that I was grown-up, she said that, *grown-up*, though it made Father snort. He was glad to see the back of her though, he'd always despised her. So I was left alone for much of the time – except for Mother. I sat with her, sometimes reading aloud; when she was at her worst, wiping her dribble, holding a spoonful of broth to her mouth.

Louise, who lived in, extended her duties and helped me get Mother up and washed, and later, put her to bed. I don't know what made Louise stay as long as she did. Father paid her very little and it must have been like living in an asylum. She was what you might call 'strapping', very matter-of-fact. Her face was pale and pitted as a crumpet. 'She'll never marry,' Father used to say with satisfaction, 'not with all the young men of her class shot to smithereens in France. Not with a face like that.'

I wish I had been more friendly to her. Though she didn't encourage it. She was pleasant enough but . . . well because of Father probably . . . she knew her place. She would never criticise them, never side with me. She did her job, cooked piles of plain food, was polite and helpful. I can't complain.

One day, I found myself outside. There was the familiar and sickening lurch back into consciousness like the moment of falling in a dream. Another absence, another frantic looking round to find myself. I don't think I'd done anything bad except walk out alone with no coat or hat, quite normal as far as the world was concerned. There was nothing strange in my pockets, no dirt or damage to my clothes. I asked directions back to Holloway – and found I'd walked miles. I was in Stratford, an area I didn't know. I was full of the sick, startled sensation that always followed a significant absence.

I hurried along, troubled and tired, anxious that I might have been missed, when I came to an ugly square red-brick building. Something made me stop and look instead of hurrying past.

47

Inside, someone was playing a trombone. Above the door it said: CURRY STREET CITADEL. I hesitated. I felt unwell, faint and weak and torn. What I should do was hurry home. I didn't know what state Mother would be in, what trouble I'd get into from Father. But the trombone sounded like a message, reaching out especially to me. Years before I had heard a Sally Army band and believed that it beckoned me. I had almost forgotten, but the rich brass slither brought it back to me. I looked around but there was no one on the street to see. I went through the front door into a lobby, and looked through another door into the main hall.

A young man in shirt-sleeves was standing with one foot on a chair, a beam of sunshine from a high window shone down and lit up his trombone like gold. He was laughing down at a young woman in Salvation Army uniform. She held her bonnet in her hand and was looking up at him, smiling and scolding. She looked utterly happy and herself. I wanted quite suddenly and badly to be her. To laugh. To scold flirtatiously. I wanted that young man with his trombone and his floppy black hair to be smiling down at *me*.

They noticed me at the same instant. The woman smoothed down her wavy hair and with it her expression. She replaced her bonnet. The man took his foot off the chair.

'Can we help you?' the woman asked.

'I was just walking past,' I said. 'I didn't feel well . . . I heard the trombone . . . Oh I don't know . . .'

'Sit down a minute,' the man said brushing the chair with his hand. The woman took my arm and sat me down.

'You're very pale. Water,' she offered, 'or tea?'

'Just water,' I said. I could hardly look at them, they were so kind.

'What's your name?' the man drew up a chair and sat close beside me.

'Trixie . . . Trixie Bell.'

'I'm Harold Brown, Lieutenant,' he added with a grin, 'and

48

this,' he indicated the woman who returned with my drink, 'is Lieutenant Mary Bright.'

'I heard a Salvation Army band once, at Harrogate,' I said. I sipped the water. I could feel the blood returning to my head. The hall was lofty, full of echoes and splinters, the windows so high you could see nothing out of them but sky. There were posters on the walls advertising meetings, Battles for Souls. There were texts in great black letters, some I recognised from my own reading, that almost made me feel at home.

Harold had a narrow face, a long nose, shadowy, speckled cheeks. He was a big heavy man and he smelled slightly of sweat.

'I thought they were wonderful,' I continued. 'But my father doesn't approve . . .'

'We thrive on disapproval,' Harold said, grinning.

'Have you been to a meeting?' Mary asked.

'No, I was only a child then and I . . . well it would be impossible, I care for my mother, you see, I don't get much time.'

'Could you not make a little time?' Harold leant towards me.

'I don't know . . . perhaps . . . one day.'

'Do you feel better?' Mary asked. 'You looked like a ghost when you came in, I thought you were going to pass out.'

I nodded. 'Yes, thank you . . . I came over tired . . . just a funny turn.'

'Where do you live?'

'Holloway.'

'You've walked all that way?'

'I like to walk,' I said.

'Evidently.' She looked down at my dusty shoes and smiled.

'We'll go a little way with you,' Harold said standing up. 'We could walk in that direction.'

'No,' I said. I handed Mary the cup. 'Thank you. I must go. Mother might miss me. Thank you again. I will *try* and come to a meeting.'

I fled. I was not used to people or to making conversation. I could not believe my nerve. The idea that I might attend one of their meetings seemed preposterous, seemed a lie. I hurried through the streets towards home, head down, terrified that I would be seen, or that Father would have returned home unexpectedly and discovered Mother alone.

But as I hurried I knew that that is what I wanted. That it was not really preposterous, not a lie. One day I could be one of them. I could be a Salvationist. I could wear a uniform like Mary's. Maybe I could even be called Lieutenant. Lieutenant Bell. It was a glorious thought.

I opened the door cautiously and crept inside, terrified that I had been missed. But it was all right. It was as if I had never left. The grandfather-clock ticked sluggishly in the hall. Mother still sat in her chair: that her chest was dark with dribble was the only sign of neglect. The dreary smell of braising liver floated from the kitchen. I went to fetch a cup of tea. Louise, chopping carrots, only looked up and smiled.

# BINDWEED

I have got myself involved. Christ knows I didn't mean to but what can you do when someone needs help and you are there?

First thing, I was coming back from a walk yesterday. I'd walked through the parks taking pictures of the wintery trees, the mill-dam, branches, leaves frozen into the ice and the ducks waddling and sliding. Now it was getting dusky, I was tired and wanted only to get inside and drink coffee. But when I got back, there was a man standing in the passage between my front door and Trixie's. He was standing facing her door as if he'd knocked and was waiting for an answer, a small man in an overcoat and trilby.

'Hello?' I said.

'Ah!' He raised his hand and shook mine. 'You are Inis, yes? The new neighbour.'

'Yes.'

'Honoured to meet you.' He took off his trilby and executed a little bow. 'I am Blowski, Stefan.' He looked as if he expected that I knew of him.

'Yes?'

'A friend of Trixie Bell.'

'Pleased to meet you,' I said. I moved towards my door and he moved reluctantly aside.

'I want you to know it is relief to me that Trixie have neighbour, nice neighbour. I worry about her, alone.'

'She's OK,' I said, fumbling in my bag for my key. 'She knows

I'm here.' I just wanted to get inside, switch on the gas-fire and drink coffee. I found my key and put it in the lock.

'She keep herself to herself,' he said, 'but she need . . .'

'Me too,' I said opening the door. 'I keep myself to myself too.' I stepped inside and was enveloped by the cold smell of new paint. I flicked on the light and it shone out on Mr Blowski, a quite charming old man, I saw, with a wizened monkey face, wild wiry white eyebrows and a most glamorous puff of silvery hair. 'Goodbye,' I said.

'She no ordinary woman,' Mr Blowski was saying as I shut the door.

I made a jug of coffee and crouched beside the gas-fire drinking mug after mug, scorching my face, feeling guilty that I had been so rude. The flowers loomed through the white paint like faces through fog. It was too quiet. I wondered if Mr Bloswski was still standing in the passage, waiting for Trixie to open her door. *No ordinary woman.* Funny, I had thought she was just that, an ordinary old woman, wandering a bit perhaps, but that's normal surely at her age. Though there were the hymns she bellowed out at night. I shook myself, irritated to feel that she had got her hooks into me, only soft ones, more like the tendrils of a creeper – bindweed – tendrils that seem so slight and tender but will never let go once they have a grip, unless you break them.

When I'd drained the last drop of coffee, I went up to my dark-room and switched on the red light. Some other photographers I know hate this part of the job, find it tedious, the processing, but I love it almost more than taking the photographs, the small space, the red light making rosy shadows, even the vinegary whiff of the chemicals.

I had several reels of film taken in Sheffield – roadworks, street scenes, shopping-complexes, trees – Sheffield is full of trees, I'm surprised to find. I've been wandering around shooting this and that, groping towards a theme. None of this is my usual style. I am a portrait photographer by trade and inclination. I work best with a long lens, a dense point of focus. Character in close up is my forte. I also had some rolls of undeveloped film I'd brought with me, some of the last I shot before I left. It was one of those I picked up first, rather numbly, scarcely thinking why. Wondering instead, as I tested the exposure, what Mr Blowski meant. *No ordinary woman*. Well nor am I. Who is?

I filled the baths with stop and fix, rolled on my rubber-gloves and watched my family bloom up through the wet like Chinese water-flowers.

Christmas day:

A bulging stocking hanging at the bed-head of a sleeping boy.

A tousled man sitting up in bed eating a chocolate snowman.

A boy in a bear mask, his pyjama-trousers falling down.

A baby half-buried in crumpled wrapping-paper.

A boy building with new bricks. Expression of fierce concentration.

A baby girl regarding a Christmas cracker with wonder.

A man holding up a glass of wine, eyes shining love at the photographer.

And more and more and more. I hardly even cried. I pegged the prints up to dry, like so much washing, and went to bed.

I woke thinking I *will not* get involved, feeling cross with the little man who had presumed so much. Just because I live next door to Trixie doesn't make her my responsibility. I don't want responsibility, that is the point, that is why I am here. Just because I'm a woman he thinks I must care. How wrong about someone can you be?

And then this morning I saw Trixie in her garden. I was about to go out to hang some knickers and T-shirts on the line, but when I saw she was out there, I waited. I didn't want to talk to her or anyone. I wanted only to work, though I was losing heart with all the wandering and searching. I needed a subject.

Trixie was wearing a pale green raincoat. As I watched from the back window, she knelt slowly and stiffly down on a cushion and began to weed her garden. There's not a weed to be seen but she was pulling something like invisible hairs from the soil. And then she leant forward and stooped right down low with her face only inches from a clump of golden crocuses, glowing as if they had electric light-bulbs inside, grown so quickly from the little green spears she'd pointed out. She was quite still. I couldn't see whether her eyes were shut or not but she looked as if she was engaged in an act of worship or devotion. Embarrassed to be spying on her in this attitude, I turned away from the window, wishing I could capture her like that, on film.

Next thing, I heard a cry. I looked out again and saw that Trixie had fallen forward, her face in the flowers, her legs unfolding awkwardly behind her. I went out, through the gate. Her face had broken the crocuses.

'Trixie . . .' I was thinking about strokes, heart attacks, all the things that lie in wait for old people, the things that have punctuated so many of Richard's (and my own) nights. 'Are you all right?'

She turned her head to the side. There was yellow pollen on her cheek and soil between her lips. 'Perfectly, thank you,' she said with such aplomb I almost laughed.

'I heard you shout. Did you fall?'

'Just trying to get up, dear. Always clumsy, always was.'

I struggled to help her to her feet. I hadn't realised how big she was, not tall, but solid and sturdy under her layers of clothes. When she was up I helped her inside, she was limping badly, when she was sitting down on a kitchen chair, I saw that she had scraped her shin and knee.

'I'll make some tea, shall I?' I said. 'But we'd better wash that.' Her stocking was ruined and dark gritty blood was slowly oozing. I could feel my morning oozing away too and felt guilty for minding. She wouldn't let me lift her skirt to unfasten her stocking so I cut it open with scissors. A child's graze is different; tight, healthy skin skimmed off and bright healthy blood speckling underneath. Robin used to wriggle and scream while I bathed his grazed knees in warm water with TCP but as soon as he had a plaster on he'd be proud and happy.

'Look,' he'd say to anyone at all, 'I've graved myself.'

But old skin is loose. It tears and hangs in flimsy rags. The blood is thick and dark, it wells up sluggish and stubborn.

'Perhaps you should go to A and E,' I suggested.

'What's that when it's at home?'

'Accident and Emergency. You know, Casualty. I'll go out and phone for a taxi ...'

'No, no.'

I started dabbing at her knee with Dettol, since that's all she had, and tissues. She made a strange quiet groan and I looked up to see that her face had turned the colour of putty and her eyelids were fluttering. I stuck a couple of pieces of lint over the grazes with some scraps of plaster. 'I'd better make your tea,' I said, frightened she was going to collapse on the floor, finding myself wishing that Richard was here, capable and confident, so I could slope off.

'Want to lie down,' she mumbled. There was no way I was going to get her up the steep stairs, heavy and faint as she was, so we went into the cold front room and she lay down on a sofa that was covered in crackly plastic. I tried to take it off before she lay down but she resisted. The curtains were drawn. 'Shall I let a bit of light in?' I suggested, but she shook her head and closed her eyes. I switched on the electric-fire that stood on the hearth and the dust on it fizzed.

Waiting for the kettle to boil, I found myself blaming Mr Blowski for this; as if him asking me to keep an eye on her had caused it. I wandered round, looking at this and that, all the old-ladyish things. One of the photographs on the piano showed a little girl in a floppy white dress, a look almost of terror on her face. Another one was of a plump woman with unsuitably shingled hair with some older children and the same little girl. Trixie presumably, though not recognisably. Stuck into the edge of the frame was a photo-booth shot of Mr Blowski, baring his NHS teeth in a fierce smile.

The kettle boiled and I made leaf tea in a pot, something I never bother with any more myself, a tea-bag in a cup does me, besides it's hotter. I couldn't find the china cups but there was a Bovril mug hanging on a hook so I poured it out in that with a couple of spoonfuls of sugar for shock. Trixie struggled to a sitting position when I went in, she looked much better.

'I'm quite recovered now, thank you dear. Oh that's Blowski's mug – never mind. You get back to your . . .'

'I *have* got some work on the go,' I said. 'I'm a photographer.'

'Is that a job?'

'Of course.'

'For the newspapers?'

'Not generally no . . . I do portraits commercially and . . .' I don't know what got into me then, I hadn't meant to talk about it, but I found myself rambling on about portraits of children and old people, making a kaleidoscope of images to make some sort of sense of life and death, oh I don't know, talking rubbish.

'Well I'm here, you could do me,' she said, 'that is if I'm the type . . .'

'Yes,' I said, surprised and almost touched. I thought that it was all right, this morning, this involvement, if it led me to a subject. 'I might take you up on that.'

'You get off then,' Trixie said.

'Sure you don't want anything – maybe something from the shop?'

'Oh yes,' she said, 'save me going out in this state.'

'Put a list through my door,' I said, 'I'll do it later. I'll get some stuff for your leg.'

When I got into my own house again my enthusiasm had diminished. I went and hung my washing on the line, though the sun has gone in. Trixie's crocuses are smashed like a yellow sunburst on the soil. I feel cross that I've got myself involved. I feel the clinging tendrils of her need. Like bindweed, yes. Or babies' fingers.

# SALVATION

Trixie sits on the crackling plastic watching the dark blood soak through the lint on her leg. She almost never sits in this room. Television reception is best at the back and, anyway, people gawp right in here if the curtains are open, straight through the nets. That's the worst of this house, that it has no front garden, so people pass within inches of the window and if they're talking their voices even vibrate the glass. Sometimes things are left on the outside window-sill – a sill just begging for a window-box of trailing geraniums in another setting – fizzy-drinks cans, or curry-sauce-stained polystyrene dishes, or nuggets of spat-out chewing-gum. There's no sense of privacy so she keeps this door shut and the best sofa that Blowski got her to buy how many years ago, twenty? is still pristine under its plastic cover.

'So much money!' he'd exclaimed when he'd seen her bank books. 'My God, Trixie Bell you are a woman of fortune. Why you not spend?' She'd bought the sofa to humour him but there was nothing she really wanted, not that money could buy. She sends money to charity. She likes appeals on television, for the blind and lifeboats and children struggling about with plastic limbs, she sits with her pen and pad ready, her cheque-book by her side. If she's not sure about a particular cause, God helps her, via the Bible. She opens at random, circles her finger in the air and wherever it rests she takes advice. For instance she was doubtful about the worth of the Royal Society for the Protection of Birds until her fingertip, guided by God's own, picked out: *I am become like a pelican in the wilderness and like an owl that is in the desert*, and then she wrote a most generous cheque, for what could be clearer than that? But an appeal for Relate turned up *Ye blind guides, which strain at a gnat, and swallow a camel*, and caused her to shut her cheque-book very firmly.

She heaves herself up, her knee stinging badly, and takes Blowski's mug into the kitchen to rinse. Fancy asking Inis to get her shopping! She feels cross, tetchy, having someone else knowing her business, knowing even what she eats, doing things in her own kitchen as if she's quite at home. The cheek of the young. Although she can't go out, not feeling so shaky, all at sixes and sevens. She will have to allow herself to be helped. Not that it won't be a relief to stay put, away from strangers' eyes. As long as she doesn't let Inis any further in. Something niggles her, something else, oh the photographs, yes, whatever possessed her to offer herself up like that! Must have fallen more heavily than she thought, got a knock on the head.

She tips the tea-leaves into her kitchen compost tidy and goes upstairs, feeling restless, the stairs need a brush, there are dust balls at the corners, a brush and a wipe, only a five-minute job, but not now. From her back-bedroom window she looks down at her garden. Her kneeling cushion is still where she left it on the concrete – lucky she didn't crack her head on that edge. Inis's smalls are dripping on the line – though it looks like rain. From above you can properly appreciate how organised Trixie's garden is but not how rich. It is like a mouth pursed on secrets at this time of year, all the buds and bulbs are invisible shoots of promise.

The room is small and square. Her bed is single, there is a chest of drawers, a ladderback chair and a clothes rail swathed in plastic. There is no mirror, but one painting, which she'd kept near her since childhood, of girls gathering wild flowers. Trixie pulls the plastic off the rail. She unbuttons her cardigan and unzips the front of her dress. She stands in her slip and ruined stockings for a moment, then takes some different things from the rail: a navy-blue serge skirt which will nowhere near do up and has a long mend all down the side; a crimson blouse, a navy jacket, also several sizes too small, and last of all, and almost reverently, a black bonnet with a fraying red band. Despite her grazed knee, Trixie kneels on the floor to pray, the pain of the rough carpet pressed by her weight against the sore place brings tears to her eyes but almost pleasurable tears. It is a pleasure to suffer pain in prayer. When she wears these clothes now, now that she is whole and normal she feels that any evil use they have been put to is, if not forgotten, forgiven. She nearly burnt them once, thought it best to rid the world of a Salvation Army uniform defiled, but now she is grateful that she didn't. She sends her mind back to before and, hauling herself up, picks up her tambourine and begins to sing. When her voice comes out strong and clear she knows she is forgiven, that she is healed and whole, that God is hearing her, she sings:

> Jesus, save me through and through,
> Save me from self-mending:
> Self-salvation will not do,
> Pass me through the cleansing,

which makes her think of washing-machines, and a soul as pure and blameless as a Persil-white tea-towel pegged out in the sun.

She sings for an hour until her strength gives out and when she finishes, the silence is dreadful. She strains her ears for the sound of Inis next door but she is so quiet, ideal of course to have a quiet neighbour but there seems something almost sneaky about such complete silence all the same. What sort of person goes without a television in this day and age? Just for a moment she catches herself missing the sound of the butcher shouting at his wife or the dreadful so-called music of their children.

But, as she divests herself of her Salvation Army uniform and struggles back into her crimplene dress and buttons her cardigan she banishes the ungrateful thought. Inis is good, kind and helpful. Beggars can't be choosers when all's said and done. Blowski's forever blethering on about the Social Services, home-helps, guardian angels (ha), but Trixie is not having that sort of carry on, not in her house, not nosing strangers. She could afford the most luxurious nursing-home there is, satin sheets no doubt and whirlpools and black-pudding and champagne for breakfast every day (that is, if she drank) but no. None of that razzmatazz is for her. Here she'll stay until she goes out feet first, her money secure in the bank and in stocks and bonds and goodness knows what else, all safely bequeathed to the Salvation Army, because there was nothing in her father's will to stipulate the recipient of the money *after* her death. He never thought of that.

# ROOKS

I fetched Trixie's shopping – eggs, yoghurt, plasters, Germolene – but I did not stay and talk. She was all right, recovered, she'd been singing, I'd heard her. I'd worked in the darkroom most of the rest of that day, exposing trees and holes in the road. When I'd finished I was dazzled and despondent. They didn't add up to anything. Every print shouted, *so what*?

And there were the blown-up faces of Robin and Billie, and Richard's dark eyes shining innocence of what was about to happen. I thought, what if I go back, now, I *could*, I could just go back. There is nothing here I would not leave like that, a snap of the fingers, without a backward glance. Standing among the glossy familiar faces, I allowed myself a day-dream. I could be back in a few hours. I imagined walking in. The gasps of surprise, the children's delight. Robin running to me, jumping up, his legs round me, hard shoes, wet kisses on my cheek. An open baby smile from Billie who might say 'Mama' for the first time, seeing me, remembering me. My face buried in her velvet fragrant skin. Richard's more measured relief, his firm lips against mine, his dark eyes promising, *later* . . . Precious infant bodies in the bath, clean pyjamas, kisses, stories. Then Richard would cook something, no, no, we'd get a takeaway, he'd fetch a bottle of my favourite Cabernet Sauvignon from the off-licence, and pick up flowers from the garage on the way home. He would understand. He would not be angry. After dinner we'd . . . But there it all dissolved because I cannot open up. I do not want to make love. That is gone. I can't remember how it feels to want it, that ramming, sticky closeness, that ridiculous expenditure of energy. Richard panting in my ear, thrusting over and over. Him taking my groans of discomfort, or simply the air being banged audibly from my lungs as sounds of pleasure. And anyway it might not be like that. What if I got back and the children looked at me without recognition? What if Richard was out with another woman? What if they didn't want me back?

I could not sleep last night, and today, to occupy myself, to keep myself away from Trixie, away from the temptation to flee again, I went to Blackpool. The train was almost empty, February isn't a Blackpool sort of month. The tall buildings along the front sulked. It had snowed in Lancashire and heaps of it slumped against the fronts of the gift shops. OPEN AT EASTER or CLOSED TILL EASTER said curled signs in the windows. The red and white-striped canopy outside a café where I stopped for coffee had torn with the weight of the snow that melted through in long, sloppy drips. I found one gift shop that was open. A man in an anorak sat by a fan-heater, eating Jaffa Cakes and watching snooker on a black-and-white television. He jumped when I entered.

All the bright things looked sad: faded plastic buckets and spades, a net of swirly plastic balls, foam-rubber flip-flops, a half-inflated porpoise. I stood looking at a rack of dirty postcards – man with bulging swimming trunks holding fish, busty woman in bikini saying, *Oooh what a whoppa*! man pulsating with pride – gulping back the tears that tried to come. Robin would have loved this shop. He would have wanted to buy something, anything, it didn't matter what. He always wanted a bit of wherever he went to keep, my Robin.

I bought two sticks of rock, gaudy pink with white inside and the word BLACKPOOL running through it in red letters. The man took my money morosely, hardly taking his eyes from the grey balls rolling on the grey table. He said nothing and neither did I.

For a minute I felt a sort of complicitous misery that was nearly cheering.

I went out of the fusty, almost-warmth of the shop into the blade of the wind. I crossed the road to the beach. I wore a thick sweater, a long wool coat, a woollen hat that the wind wanted, sheepskin mittens and a long scarf, but still I could feel the wind on my skin that tightened and goose-pimpled. My nipples were screwed up so tight they hurt, my ears ached and the gold of my earrings burnt cold through the perforations in my ears. Tears ran from my eyes, not of true sorrow, but only of sorry-for-myselfness. The tide was out and the beach vast and flat and empty but for a minute figure in the distance with a prancing dog.

The brown sand was powdered with white snow which scrunched more softly under my boots than the sand. Sometimes the wind snatched up a handful of the snow and flung it in a gritty flurry in the air. I walked towards the sea where the sand was wet and brown. As I walked, each footstep blanched the sand and then, when I turned to look the footprint had filled with water. The sea moaned. Despite the wind it was not very rough, the waves were small and messy. It was no colour but grey and the foam was yellow. Gulls flew and blew like so much litter in the sky.

I took shots of the pattern of my footprints in the sand, the snow footprints on the drier sand, the closed-up shops, the juxtapositions of lilos and snow, the torn canopy outside the café, I unwrapped a stick of rock as I walked back to the station. There was a small grey picture of Blackpool. The pink was sticky on the Cellophane. I sucked hard at the sweet mintiness as I walked until I'd sucked it into a long sharp point. It made my tongue sore. The word BLACKPOOL slid back in tiny red distorted letters where it was uncovered by my sucking.

And now I'm back. Now what?

Sometimes this house feels like a cage. It is night again. I've eaten fish and chips and drunk a pot of coffee. Stupid, now I won't sleep again. I went to Blackpool this morning because I couldn't sleep *last* night. I only went to sleep as morning came and then something woke me, suddenly, and I didn't know where I was. It was as if something had come loose and I couldn't catch it. Like trying to catch a dream but I was trying to catch what was real. And then I remembered. It was so quiet. I held my breath and listened – I could hear nothing. And the sound of nothing was terrible in my ears because it should have been a treat. For Christ's sake, that is what I wanted, that is what this is all about, or part of it, me being here. And then when I was awake I found I was heartbroken, really as if there were deep fissures in my heart that ached and welled blood in all the wrong directions. And the morning I left home came pressing in on me and that is why I went to the station and went anywhere that was further away from home, and the train to Blackpool was the first one going north that came.

Now I won't sleep and that morning *will* come back. You can only stall memory, not staunch it.

Billie woke us up as usual. Richard fetched her from her cot, took off her wet nappy, put on a dry one, gave her a bottle and brought her back to bed with us. She snuggled between us, sucking noisily on her rubber teat. She felt like a live toy in her zip-up fluffy-yellow sleep-suit with its cold plastic footsoles. I kept my eyes closed when I felt her face close to mine. She kept saying 'Dadababa,' and blowing splashy raspberries, her new favourite noise and then laughing. I turned away from her and hid my face under the quilt.

'Shhhh,' Richard said. 'Let Mummy sleep.' He pulled Billie away on to his side of the bed but she wanted to play, so eventually he got up with her and went out, closing the door behind him leaving me in peace. I opened my eyes a crack and looked at the clock. Five past six. I had another hour, I was just drifting off when Robin opened the door and came in.

'Mummy?'

'Go away.'

64

'But Mummy, I need a carrot for my snowman. He do need a nose don't he?'

'Has it snowed then?' I asked from under the quilt, my interest snagged.

'No, but it is winter, isn't it?'

'Go away,' I said. I had hardly ever said that to him before. I did not shout it. I lay with my head covered. I heard him sigh, a terribly adult sigh and the door closed behind him with a disappointed click. And then I could not get back to sleep. I was wide awake and filled with guilt. He is only four. He is a lovely boy, my first child, my truest love. And I told him to go away and suddenly it was terrible that he had obeyed me, with that resigned sigh. Why had he not refused to go, climbed into bed with me, plagued me with his icy sharp toes and his questions?

I could hear them in the kitchen if I strained my ears. The low grumble of the radio spilling news, Richard's calm deep voice, the sounds of spoons in bowls, Billie's occasional shriek, the upward swing of Robin's questions. At seven o'clock, I knew, Richard would bring me a cup of tea. He would put it down quietly beside the bed, bend over, find my face amongst the quilt and my tangled hair, kiss me and say, 'Tea, darling.' Knowing this made me start to cry and then I found I could not stop.

My dad used to bring me tea every morning. His dressing-gown cord would be tied as neatly round his stout middle as string round a parcel. He'd put it down quietly but he wouldn't say a word. He brought my mum and me tea in bed every morning and even poured Bonny a bowl of tea to lap with her morning Bonio. Remembering that increased my tears and as I lay sobbing I floated above myself amazed. I could not imagine where all the tears were coming from. It was as if there was a reservoir that I should have drawn on in the past. If I'd known, if I'd shed the tears gradually over the years, perhaps it wouldn't have burst like that. Perhaps I wouldn't be here. How can I know?

Richard came in with my tea.

'Oh darling,' he said when he saw that I was crying, for there was no hiding it. The tears leapt from my eyes and my throat was hollowed with sobs. 'Whatever is it? Oh sweetheart.' He tried to hold me but I couldn't let him. He stood awkwardly by the bed. From downstairs Robin shouted and Billie screeched. I could see him torn, see him sway towards the door, his eyes fixed on me.

'Go and see,' I sobbed. I didn't want this bloody patient man staring at me.

'I've got to shave,' he said. 'I'll sort them out . . . we'll have to talk . . . I can't leave you like . . .'

I put my head under the pillow where it was cool. My mouth was full of tears and hair. A dream came floating back to me, a dream so sad and terrible it made me moan aloud. I pushed it out of my head, thought, instead, about later.

I could just imagine it. Another day achieved. The children in bed. Bathed and put there by Richard who came in like the Lone Ranger every teatime just in time to save the day. If I hadn't cooked the meal by the time he'd finished, he'd start slicing onions and tipping rice or pasta into a pan. We would eat and drink a glass of wine. Then he'd wash up while I threw a few toys in a box. Then he'd put on a CD, Mozart perhaps, and we'd sit together on the futon. He'd put his arm round me and his armpit would smell of sweat reminding me that he'd worked hard all day and not had a moment to himself, not time for a shower. And he'd ask me what's up.

'Is it the . . . ?' he'd say. Fitting, that. The dot dot dot, the nothing. The baby that never was.

I lay under the pillow until it got too hot. The radiator was creaking out its warmth now, the pillow was sodden. When I pulled my face out I could hear cartoons in the distance. That showed that this was an emergency – there is a rule in our house, no TV in the mornings. I could hear the buzz of Richard's razor in the bathroom. I got out of bed. The tears had ceased but my chest and shoulders shook spasmodically. I went into the bathroom to pee. Richard looked round, he pulled his mouth to one side the better to shave his cheek. He switched off the razor and tapped it on the edge of the wash basin. The fine black dust of his bristles fell out with a scorched smell.

'Oh, you're up,' he said. 'Good.'

He bent to kiss me but I turned my face aside. I didn't want to be kissed, certainly not while sitting on the lavatory.

'So you're all right?' he asked. 'I don't like to leave you all upset but . . .' He indicated his watch.

'I'm fine.' I flushed the toilet and went to the basin to wash. He hovered in the bathroom doorway. I wondered who he was and what he was doing here and why he was so fucking kind. 'Absolutely fantastic,' I said. 'Just go.' I turned to look at him. I hated his skin when it was just shaved, it reminded me of fish skin with the scales scraped off. I didn't like his droopy shoulders or his look of concern.

'Sure?'

'I think I can just about manage.'

'I don't want you just about managing, I want you to . . .'

'Just fuck off,' I said. His face stiffened.

'Fine,' he said. 'Right, I'll just fuck off then and leave you to just fucking manage. Fine.' He went out of the bathroom looking as if he might cry. We did not do this. We did not swear at each other. Particularly, he did not swear.

'He's wonderful,' people said, all my friends, his patients, his family. 'Aren't *you* the lucky one to have a man like that.'

And oh yes, yes, I was lucky. I can't fault him. He looks good. He works hard. He is faithful, I'm pretty sure. He's a GP, forever climbing out of bed in the night to go to someone's aid, sorting out the children, doing most of the housework, never reproaching me. I stopped working hard. I tried to but after the children, particularly after Billie, it all drizzled away, all my energy, enthusiasm. I couldn't manage the house or the children. Dirt and mess grew and flourished like jungle plants faster than I could clean. And I lost my patience with the children.

He went downstairs. I took off my nightdress. He said

something to the children. Robin followed him out into the hall asking something. I rubbed a little nub of strawberry soap that smelled of jam on to my flannel. Robin's Christmas-stocking soap. I washed under my arms. The front door banged. I washed between my legs. My stomach was skinny and hollow. I dried myself. I heard the car starting. I put deodorant under my arms, two sharp jets of it, man's deodorant. His. I heard him drive away.

'Mummy,' Robin shouted up the stairs. Billie began to cry. I looked with surprise at my body in the mirror. It was like a stranger's. I live in that, I thought, it's mine, freehold till the day I die. And then, but what am I that lives in that? That is my last clear memory of that morning although I know I did certain things. I dressed and threw some clothes in a case, packed up my cameras. I wrote a note that asked Richard to let me go for now, promising I would keep in touch if he would not try and find me. *Try and I will disappear*, I wrote, melodramatic but sincere. I went downstairs and took my building society book from the dresser drawer. I put 'Fantasia' on for the children. I gave Billie a bottle and a rusk and Robin an apple and a biscuit. I secured the fireguard. I phoned for a taxi and stood behind the children watching the film, watching the shadowy orchestra playing Bach's solemn and portentous 'Toccata and Fugue in D minor' turn to dancing lights in the sky until the taxi came. Then I slipped out, they didn't even look round, Billie was falling asleep. She would stay asleep for an hour or so, while Robin went into a trance in front of the screen and they would come to no harm. I propped my note up on the stairs where Richard would see it as soon as he walked in. I closed the door very quietly and locked it. From a call-box at the station I rang Richard's surgery. 'Tell Dr Goodie he must go home at once. It's an emergency. The children are alone,' I said to the receptionist and put the phone down before she could ask any questions. I knew she would tell him and I knew he would try and phone and no one would answer, or Robin would, and

Richard would drive straight home. They were quite safe. I had an empty swooping feeling inside, excitement and terror and yet I was not quite there. I was not quite doing this, leaving my children. I could not quite do that, what mother could?

The train brought me to Sheffield which is a city I didn't know. I know no one here, except, now, Trixie. I telephoned Richard from the station, to make sure he was home, and put the phone down before he could say anything. I stayed in a guest-house while I found a house to rent. It was two weeks I think. I sent postcards to the children. I spoke to no one in the guest-house unless it was necessary although I was perfectly civil. The guest-house overlooked a park. My room was at the back, a small room the window rectangle crammed with bare black branches clotted with the nests of rooks. They sound so sad, rooks. They are the black-feathered spirits of sorrow when they cry out the way they do, when they slow hand-clap themselves through the sky like old black gloves.

I watched no television, I read no papers, I was enclosed in a slab of dullness the shape and size of the telephone-box from which I had made my call. Once again during that fortnight I rang the house to hear Richard's voice. I did not speak but I listened for a few seconds, long enough to gather that they were all right, nothing had happened to the children, they were safe and well, and then I cut myself off.

# SONGBIRD

When I joined the Salvation Army, I left my family. I had no choice. You cannot secretly be a Soldier. As soon as I was Saved, I told my father. He did not shout or rage. I had a choice, he said, to give up the monstrous charade or to leave home. I did not have to think long. As soon as I was accepted as a Recruit, I took my new uniform home and changed into it in my room, gladly stripping off my childish dress. It felt freeing and wonderful to wear the sober clothes, the shirt was crisp and mannish. I tied my bonnet-string under my chin and went downstairs.

I walked into the room and stood before them, brave for Jesus. The Salvationist must gladly endure persecution. My father folded his arms and looked at my mother but there was no use looking at her – she was sitting rigidly in her chair, staring at the carpet as she did for hours on end. If you touched her when she was like that she was as cold as a statue, and almost as stiff.

I clasped my trembling hands behind my back, told myself I did not care what he said. The Salvation Army was my family now. In the month between becoming a Convert and then a Recruit, I had managed to leave the house for several Meetings. Now I was ready to sign the Articles of War, to be publicly sworn in, to have my name entered on the Soldiers' Roll of the Corps.

'You are leaving this house?' Father asked mildly.

'Only if you wish me to,' I said.

I looked past him. The rain was rolling down the window. The garden looked like underwater, green things swaying through the grey.

'It is your choice,' he said. 'And I must be certain that you understand the consequences.'

'Yes,' I said. I did not care what the consequences were. I was strengthened by Jesus and my friends to this extent: that I would give up, throw off anything, without regret. I guessed he meant my inheritance. I would forfeit his wealth. I thought nothing of that . . . houses, factories, investments . . . all wordly stuff that had brought not a shaft of happiness into my childhood. I didn't want Father's wealth, though I knew that the Salvation Army would have welcomed it. I thought if I didn't join the Salvation Army, but waited till he was dead which might not have been for another twenty years, the fortune would have been mine to spend as I wished. While if I joined them, it wouldn't. Surely they would rather have had me than money, I thought.

'If you walk out of that door in order to join that common, stinking, hysterical bunch of cranks,' he said, in the most reasonable of voices, 'then you are no longer my daughter. You never, ever dare to set foot in this house again. Do you hear? We wash our hands of you. I speak for your mother – see what you've already done to her with your . . . proclivities – and myself.'

I looked at my mother. She gave no sign of having heard.

'I need you to help with your mother,' he continued. 'She needs you. If you go, you are wicked, you neglect your duty as a daughter. What kind of religion encourages people to turn their back on their duty?'

'Goodbye Father,' I said. 'Goodbye Mother.'

I turned away and as I opened the door and stepped out into the warm lashing rain, the sense of sudden freedom was dizzying. I felt purified. My childhood was a dirty thing. Sinful. I was grateful to my father for cutting me off. I did not want him saved, or my mother. That is wrong and I know it now and I knew it then. Their Salvation should have been my first preoccupation. But I wanted them left behind. How can I bear to say this? Standing there so pious, in my uniform, I wanted them damned. I didn't think it then, not so clearly. But my distrust of them, my fear and loathing was so complete that if, by some miracle, he had made a different response, had said:

'Well Trixie, if you're so wholehearted then I'm pleased for you. Maybe there's something in it . . . you have our support.' If he'd attended a Meeting, if he'd repented and become a Salvationist which *should* have been my deepest desire, if so, it would have been ruined for me. If that had been his response I might not have done it. I needed to oppose him. I wanted him to cut me off. That is my thought now. I felt pain as the heavy front door slammed behind me as if it chopped off a limb and I gasped with shock and my mouth filled with rain. Then there was the dizzying freedom. I walked down the front path and had to steady myself on the gatepost for fear that I would faint. White lilac flowers shook scented raindrops into my face. Through my wet eyelashes I saw the outline of my father's figure behind the lace curtains. I turned and walked away.

For a time I forgot them. If that is possible. Anyway, they did not live in my waking mind. I had some independent money, enough to donate my 10 per cent Cartridge and live comfortably enough. I had no other employment, I dedicated myself to the Army, selling the *War Cry* in public houses, working in the Bothwell Street Shelter for down-and-outs, attending meetings, processions. I was not disturbed by the rift with my parents, rather strengthened.

I would have been happy if I could just have shaken off the shadow and terror of the absences. There was a brief time, though long enough to fool me, when I seemed to be whole. I seemed to be one single solid human being with my name through the middle. A simple human being with one simple faithful soul. I grew more confident, I made friends. And I discovered I had a voice – that was the most glorious thing, the greatest gift.

My speaking voice had always been small and I had hardly

ever sung. There must have been nursery rhymes, surely? But there was no music in our house. It was Mother's nerves that stopped us getting a piano, and Father would not entertain the thought of a wireless. So there was no music – except when Auntie Ba was there. *She* always sang to me.

Whenever she sang, I could hear my own voice in my head. *Away with the Raggle Taggle Gypsies, oh*. 'Come on Trixie Bell, you sing it,' she'd urge but my voice was dull and flat, a fearful voice with no music in it. Auntie Ba would shake her head. 'Ah well Trixie Bell, we can't all be songbirds.'

But once I'd left home and dedicated my life to Jesus I found I *did* have a voice. I had always been ashamed when I joined in the hymns and choruses. I would have avoided it, but in the Salvation Army you *have* to sing, you *have* to join in, voices in unison provide volume. And with the casting off of my childhood, a voice came to live in my throat and what else could that have been but a gift from God? A sign that I was truly Saved, truly Forgiven – even for the fault at the outset of my Army career, my own failure to forgive and to pray for the Salvation of my parents.

I can remember the very hymn. My heart was still full and fat and sore from the split with my parents and with the huge love I had embraced. I was tender and trembling and open. My voice was its usual low inhibited growl. We were standing, a little group of us on a corner. It was a week or two after I'd left home. I had signed the Articles, made public my testimony. I was a Soldier. It was a warm Sunday, the air full of the scent of flowers. There were six of us, no band, just six voices and tambourines. Children had gathered to listen – and one or two men on their way to the pub. 'Can you do "Let Us With A Gladsome Mind"?' a little child asked. And that is what we sang and as we sang my voice climbed. Like a butterfly breaking free of its chrysalis, my voice emerged and sprouted wings. By the fourth verse, *He the golden tressed sun, Caused all day his course to run*, it was a noticeable voice and by the end it was rising above the voices

73

of my fellows, strong and clear and strange in my throat. Mary, holding my elbow on the way back to the lodgings we shared said: 'You enjoyed the singing today, Trixie,' and her eyes were full of warmth and shine.

'Everyone has a voice, you just have to learn to use it,' she had said to me more than once, when I'd complained of my lack. I had hoped but not believed that she was right but now I knew and could hardly stop myself singing, I was like an excited child with a new toy. All the time there was a new song in my heart and rising through my lips.

# ADA

I have talent. I can dance and sing. My lips are the most kissable you have ever seen and my eyes! How they flash, big and black, seductive. How the men fall like nine-pins. It is a waste to have been stuck in Trixie all and for ever.

But not a waste entirely, because when she was a woman I got out.

Suddenly I was in front. I was the one with the arms in her flesh and I was the mover. My feet at once able to dance through her feet. My body, through her body, to love. For I was born to love.

It was my destiny to fall in love. Sitting behind the face of someone but being someone else. Can you imagine it? O la la! A pale Anglo-Saxon and me with the fiery Mediterranean blood racing in my veins.

Was it perversity that made me choose Frank out of all the men there were? A reaction to Trixie and her Salvation Army? Bad, handsome Frank.

Poor Trixie. You cannot help to feel sorry for someone with no spark. I am the spark! If only she would see!

# EGG

One night, in the guest-house, I dreamed that there were babies crying in the trees, high up, tangled in the cold wire branches, babies I couldn't reach.

I wish he had reproached me. More. I wish he had been angry. I wish he had slapped me, punched me, punished me – because then I could have hit back. I wish he had been frail. I could not stand his understanding. He was so patient with me as if I *was* one of his patients. He was patient and sensitive when what I needed was a smack.

Can you believe I'm saying this?

I woke up with the babies' cries in my ears and my hands all slithery wet clutching nothing.

At breakfast the egg was gelatinous and raw on top. Why do they never cook the tops of eggs in these places? I thought *egg*. I thought of what it is, genetic material. I couldn't stomach that genetic slime.

The only other guests were men who smoked through breakfast and kept their newspapers propped up in front of them like screens.

'Everything all right?' said the girl who served. She was very young with bitten nails and bare legs marbled with the cold. She wore a brown-and-white-checked overall stretched across her chest and love-bites on her neck.

'Yes,' I said. 'Not hungry, that's all.'

'More tea?'

'Thank you, yes.' I drank the tea. I did not feel nauseous, I had not, I realised, for days. It does not go instantly when you stop a child. It hangs on, the hormones are confused. That was what I'd wanted an end to most desperately, that nausea, but it hung on for a week or more.

The tea was hot, it was good. 'Good water for tea, Sheffield water,' the landlady had said when I'd remarked on it, 'better than London water. That where you're from?' I nodded and then shook my head. 'Not really, no.' Just in case, just in case she'd guessed I was a woman on the run.

It took me a couple of weeks to find this house. This narrow road behind the shops. Strange that it is so quiet. Last night I heard a rushing noise, I thought it was in my ears, this morning I realised what it is, it is the river running under the road and under the houses. The cellar is wet, the landlord warned me not to keep things down there, but I made no connection with the rough brown river that emerges here and there from its channels under the roads. It is high now, full of winter rain and melted snow from the hills. Beside the church on the main road, it is quite a thrilling thing to see, a full, peat-brown rush, carrying leaves and sticks with it, gorging its banks and then vanishing again, under the road. But it is still there, of course, and I can hear it rushing.

I stood in my little garden at first light. 'Are you going to see to it?' Trixie asked me. I don't think so. That is not what I am about, tending a garden, tending anything except myself. It is a mess though, long grass and weeds, a rotting mattress, slugs everywhere and snails. The laburnum tree has no shoots yet, just warped old seed cases, dropping occasionally into the grass. The snowdrops have finished.

I do love Billie. I do. It's just that after the birth I couldn't pull myself together. That is a dead as a doornail (ha) metaphor, but it is so apt. I could not pull together the unravelling strands. I could not get the will, the sense, my centre back, it hung just out of reach, a loose end. I should have said, Richard would have understood if I had said, would have understood more of my . . . I don't know, of my unravelling. Is there anything he wouldn't understand?

A little girl. It's what I wanted. She was born last May. I expected an easy birth. Robin's was easy. I read books, did exercises, Richard came to classes with me and we practised breathing together. Labour was manageable agony. I remained in control. And when I held the squirming hot wet boy in my arms there was never a second when I did not love him more than my own self. My heart opened like a rose, all the fat petals of love unfurling at the sight of his crumpled red face, his downy cheeks, the dark liquid of his new eyes, the greedy lips that clamped on to my nipple and sucked so fervently, so expertly as if he'd been practising for a hundred years. It was love like no other love I have ever known or would ever want to know.

It was a terror-filled love. I used to wake at night, suddenly sit up sweating and gasping my way out of dreams of fire or flood or falling where I could not reach my baby, could not save him. I used to stop frozen at the top of the stairs, with him in my arms, afraid that I would fall or drop him. I could not drive for weeks after Robin was born, I couldn't trust myself or other drivers. War in the Gulf broke out soon after his birth and sometimes, as I fed him, I watched the war on the television and tears would stand in my eyes. It petrified me to realise how little control I had, that I could not make the world safe for him.

I took ridiculous numbers of photographs as if in that way I could keep moments. At least that moment was safe, at least that moment was happy, I would think, hoarding the past as if it is of some use when it is the future that is the danger. There are albums and albums of pictures of Robin, the walls at home are covered, every expression, every movement he made practically in the first few months. Richard thought I was obsessed. He wanted us to have another, get on with it, 'get the babies had' was his curious expression, 'and then get on with our lives'.

I kept putting it off. I didn't want to have another. I didn't want anyone else. I didn't even want Richard half the time, but he insisted that I made time for him. Sometimes he arranged a baby-sitter and took me out to dinner or to a concert or film. Sometimes I quite enjoyed it, sometimes I relaxed, but I could never wait to get home. I was always relieved that it was over so that I could stand in Robin's room and watch him sleep. Secretly I used to lick his sleeping cheek, just for the soapy taste.

Not until Robin was two did I want sex again, and hardly then. I let Richard do it to me once a week or so but I breast-fed Robin until he was nearly two and my body felt like *his*. I did not want any hot and hairy man on it or in it. It wasn't Richard's fault; no matter how kind he was, no matter how much he touched or kissed me, I felt nothing. He was so patient, so insistent that I enjoy myself that I used to pretend, to gasp and shudder and sigh, with my eyes on the clock calculating hours of sleep. Only when he believed that I was satisfied would he come. I wanted to tell him not to bother – but how could I? He was so wonderful, as always, such a diligent lover. I should have been grateful.

When Robin was two and a bit, Richard arranged a surprise for me. It was the middle of August, a Saturday, my birthday. Hot sunlight glowed through the red curtains on to our bed. Richard brought me coffee and the room was filled with its scent and that of a sheaf of red carnations. Robin gave me a card with a picture of a tractor on it that he'd drawn himself and a box of chocolates. Richard gave me a long, expensive-looking box. Inside was the most fantastic watch: a silver bracelet, each section set with a fleck of glittering stone, two glittering claws holding the oval face, as tiny as my little fingernail.

'I love you,' Richard said. 'Old woman, thirty-two eh?' he kissed me. Robin bounced on the edge of the bed, his pyjamas wet, his nappy all skew-whiff. Two faces pressed against mine, one stiff and scratchy, the other cool and soft.

'Granny coming,' Robin announced.

'Is that the surprise?' I asked, for a surprise had been promised. I had been told to keep the weekend free.

'An essential part of it,' Richard said. He was sitting on the bed beside me, wearing only a crumpled pair of pale blue boxer-shorts.' I looked at the line of hair on his belly like the tail of a butterfly, its wings of hair on his chest. He had a smile on his face as if a secret was pressing against his lips and I was afraid. I was afraid that I would not want the surprise, and I did not want to hurt him. I pulled Robin on to my lap. 'Happy birfday to you,' he sang. He smelled of small boy and sleep and pee.

'Robin needs a bath,' I said.

'Put it on,' Robin said, picking up the watch.

'Yes,' said Richard, 'put it on and I'll tell you.'

I fiddled with the clasp and he had to do it up for me. It was a beautiful watch and I hated it. The claws that held the watch-face were sinister, pointed, greedy. Little hairs on the back of my wrist caught between the silver segments. I held it up to my ear to hear its tick, a tiny tutting tongue.

'I thought it would be nice for evenings,' Richard said.

'It's lovely.'

'Thirty-two,' Richard said again, looking at me with his head on one side. 'You look . . . eighteen, twenty-one at most.' He touched my cheek. I was glad Robin was there, I could see the stirring in Richard's shorts, knew the look he was giving me.

'Let me drink my coffee,' I said.

Robin climbed off the bed and began to fiddle with my earrings which were hooked through a long scarf hanging on the wall. He liked to unhook them and put them back.

'So,' Richard said, sliding his hand under the quilt and up my thigh, 'don't you want to know?' He settled his hand between my legs but kept it still. It felt nice, felt friendly though it was proprietorial of course. He was saying with his hand that I was his and later on he'd have me. But that was all right because it was safely later on.

'Go on then,' I said. 'I'm all ears.'

'And a face and a tummy,' Robin corrected.

'And a bottom,' Richard added giving me a squeeze.

Robin giggled. 'Bottom!' I sipped my coffee. 'Two parrots,' Robin said to the earrings, 'two paceshits.'

'Not spaceships, silly,' I said, but when Robin held up the two long silver earrings, I saw that he was right, they *were* spaceships.

'Mum should arrive around twelve,' Richard said. 'We'll have a bit of lunch with her – I've got chicken and salad-stuff. And then, darling, I'm spiriting you away for the night. To pastures new.'

'Oh,' I said. 'Where?'

'Derbyshire, the Peaks. I've booked a night in a great hotel, recommended by Lucy. She and Dick keep going back.'

The sun was very hot in the bedroom. We'd bought thick red curtains to keep it out but still it got in, thick and oily and choking.

'That's a nice thought,' I said, 'thanks Richard . . . so Pauline's coming all this way . . . just for lunch? She's not coming with us?'

'No, dope, she's staying here.'

'But why . . . ?' I began. But I knew why. Robin wasn't included. Richard had been threatening to 'get me away from it all' as he said, as if all I wanted wasn't here at home. 'Just the two of us,' he was always saying, 'an affirmation. Romantic.'

So Robin would be staying with Pauline, with his very nice granny who'd been plotting a way to get him to herself ever since she'd first clapped eyes on him. 'The image of Richard,' she'd said and I'd seen the greedy look in her eyes. Sometimes when she'd visited, she'd called him Richard by mistake as if she was the mother and he her son, and me? I was nobody. She got out photographs of Richard as a baby to show how uncanny the likeness was and yes . . . to some extent . . . both dark-haired, round-faced with wide dark eyes. But there was me in him too, no one could see it but me, there is a lot of me in him, but I have no parents left to point it out. Pauline is the only grandparent Robin's got.

Whenever I went quiet when Pauline was there, or whenever I criticised her, Richard sprang to her defence. Of course she loves Robin,' he'd say. 'He's her only grandchild. It's quite normal, you should be glad, relax. Don't begrudge her this pleasure. She's lonely.'

But he couldn't see what I could see, the criticism in her eyes when she watched me fumble with him. I only fumbled when she watched. And traitorous Robin lapped up her adoration, he took his first solo steps when she was there, toddling towards her with open arms and a big dribble-bright grin on his face.

'I don't want to leave Robin with Pauline.'

Richard sighed. He removed his hand. 'I know,' he said, 'I knew you'd say that, but you'll be fine. Soon as we're off . . .'

'Can you open the curtains?' I said.

He got up and did so and the bright sunshine stung my eyes.

'I don't want to leave Robin,' I said.

'Not much of a romantic weekend then,' Richard said.

'Two moons, two wiggly worms,' said Robin, oblivious.

'I'm sorry,' Richard said. He has this way of lowering his voice when he's angry instead of raising it. 'But it's all arranged. Mum's on her way. The hotel's booked. Robin's looking forward to Granny minding him, aren't you Robbie?'

'Granny coming!' Robin said and the scarf fell down scattering earrings on the floorboards and the rug. 'Oops,' he said, looking at me with a flinch in his eyes as if he thought I'd slap him which I never ever would.

'It's all right,' I said, 'never mind.'

'Let's pick them up again,' Richard said, kneeling down. 'The hotel is booked,' he repeated to me.

'A hotel can be unbooked,' I muttered.

'I'll see to lunch,' he said in rather a martyred voice. 'I'll tidy up. I'll see to Robin. All you have to do is pack a nice dress for tonight.'

I watched the two of them picking up the earrings, two dark curly napes bent at the same angle. I did not see how he could do this to me in the name of kindness, separate me from my son. Although, at Richard's insistence. I had recently stopped breast-feeding Robin, my breasts smarted.

Richard stood up and pinned the scarf back to the wall.

'Dere,' said Robin, rubbing his hands together.

'Let's do your bum then,' Richard opened the door and Robin trotted out to the bathroom. Richard followed him then came and put his head back round the door. 'Robin isn't the only one who needs you,' he said.

# COBBLER

I wonder how old Inis is? Early thirties? I was settled here before I was her age. I had already fled. And here I've been ever since. Over fifty years, and haven't I seen some changes? Changing faces behind shop counters, changing names, changing façades. What used to be the pork-butcher's is a second-hand book shop now; the wet-fish shop is an insurance agent's; the post-office is an Indian restaurant. Some nights the smell of curry seeps under my door, infecting my own food. I still eat like a Salvationist, simple wholesome food taken in moderation. Better to feel slightly empty than overstuffed. I have never eaten curry. Next-door does – some nights she nips out for a carton of something hot enough to burn her mouth and she drinks it with beer out of a tin. Must play havoc with her digestion. Still, modern times.

She went to Blackpool! Yes, Blackpool, in February. I ask you! She came back glum and frozen and gave me a stick of rock. It's on the mantelpiece in front of the clock. What a shocking pink. What a sticky present. I don't get presents as a rule. I'm quite out of the way of it. Blowski and I manage each other a little token now and again but otherwise . . . There's a card from 'Gregory, Gayle and the Gang', as they style themselves – Auntie Ba's grandson and his family – at Christmas. And one from me to them. I bought a box of twenty Nostalgic Christmas Scenes, years ago now and there's still ten left. But no presents. So the silly stick of rock is something a bit special. My eyes kept straying to it all last evening. I won't eat it. I'll keep it as a memento.

The cobbler's is still there, the Blowski's still live over it but it is staffed by strangers. As well as mending shoes, they cut keys and sell bags, purses, key-rings and even slippers at Christmas. The mechanical man in the window is still there, hammering, hammering, the paint on his face all chipped.

That is where I met Stefan Blowski. I didn't go there often, one doesn't have one's shoes mended every day of the week. He had what I would call a nice cheek. I don't chat. I'm not someone who hangs around the shops discussing the weather, making small talk. But Blowski used to tease me. He hardly spoke English at all, at first, but still he managed the cheek, the teasing. He'd been a lawyer in Poland, just qualified when Germany invaded, so he'd never actually practised law. He fought in the Middle East, then came to England at the end of the war. He didn't fancy returning to Poland under Soviet control. 'I'm political exile, me, not immigrant,' he was always saying. He married Brenda and together they opened a cobbler's shop – his Polish grandfather's trade. He could not practise law in England, did not want to. 'I had it with books,' he said. 'Now with my hands I work.'

I came to Sheffield a couple of years before the war, Blowski just after it. I remember his shop opening, on the corner, the opposite end of the terrace to mine. It had been empty, windows boarded-up, since I'd been in Sheffield. HIGH CLASS BOOT AND SHOE REPAIRS, said the sign, with old fashioned, buttoned boots in shiny black painted on either side. *Proprietors. S. & B. Blowski.* In the middle of the window was a mechanical wooden cobbler, who jerked his hammer up above his head then down on the sole of a boot, paused and wobbled and did it again, all day, every day. Children loved to watch him. In those days before they'd seen and done everything like children today, he seemed something miraculous. They'd press their noses flat against the glass to watch him – and every Christmas, Blowski dressed him in red felt and tied tinsel to the head of his hammer.

I met Blowski first, then Brenda. I did not take to her. A

perfectly nice woman, I'm sure, bonny, all belly and bosom and unsuitable clothes – see-through places, under-arm dampness, drooping straps, that sort of parcel, lots of doings on her face. Harsh voice unlike Blowski's which is soft. *He* was always slight. He wore a white apron in the shop scuffed at the front by dirty shoes. He had a fine face, dark eyes with long lashes. His teeth were bad though his smile was lovely. He *was* a wicked tease, still is. I suppose he teased all his customers the same.

'What you been doing?' he'd say, frowning at the heels of my shoes in disbelief, 'tripping the light fantastic?' And when I smiled he would go on about me dancing all night until the sun came up and call me young lady, and sometimes, a beautiful young lady, even when I was knocking forty. I ask you! I know it was a lark. I know he teased all his female customers like that, but still it gave me a sort of thrill. To be looked at, spoken to, like *that*, flirted with, you might say. Even as a joke. Funny that it didn't offend me. It didn't because Blowski was, and is, good.

If she heard him, Brenda would come slopping forward from the back of the shop saying, 'Take no notice, love. He's all trousers, our Stefan, all talk and trousers aren't you my cherub?' and she'd pinch his cheek between her fingers and kiss him on the forehead – she was inches taller – as if he was some sort of pet when to me he seemed such a man.

Yes, I don't mind admitting I had a thing about Blowski for a while, I used to walk miles to wear my heels out so that I could get them mended. Not only for that, for exercise too. I had no real intentions. Him a Married Man, and me . . . well. I walked miles between the trees, following the river out through the parks, right out into the countryside sometimes. When I took my shoes to be mended, I'd walk past the shop once first, glance in, past the mechanical cobbler, just to be sure it was Blowski behind the counter. If he wasn't there, I'd try again next day. Oh I did love the smell of that shop, pungent glue and rubber, the sort of smell you could get drunk on.

One day, an icy day, years after we'd known each other

slightly, maybe fifteen years, he knocked at my door. When I opened the door and found him there I was so surprised I was struck dumb. He held out my mended shoes. 'Special delivery for special lady,' he said. 'We have no bloody boiler today so shop shut. So today, you understand Blowski have different hat. Delivery boy, today, me.'

I asked him in and made tea. It was odd to have a man in the house, to have anyone in for that matter. I saw his eyes travelling round. Funny to see your house through someone else's eyes. I was almost embarrassed although it was quite respectable, just dull and poky. Plenty good enough for me alone. But it was like a private bit of me all on show.

'Aah,' he breathed. 'Piano. You play?'

'Barely,' I said. 'It was my aunt's, she left it to me in her will. She wanted me to learn but . . . I can pick out tunes, but not what you might call *play*.'

'Me,' said Blowski, taking off his gloves with a flourish. '*I* play. I may?' I nodded. He lifted the cloth I keep draped over and folded it back. Then he sat down and stiffly at first, then more easily began to play. They were not tunes I'd heard before. It was dance music, waltzes, mazurkas. I went into the kitchen and poured the tea, smiling all over my face at the sound, the fact of him in my house. When I came back into the room he stopped playing, and I saw that his cheeks were wet. He didn't mind me seeing, he wiped the tears away with the back of his hand.

'I big baby, I know. I not play since . . .' He sat on the stool with his back to the piano and accepted his cup of tea.

'You don't have a piano?' I asked.

'Brenda, she not to hear of piano in our house. "Ugly thing," she say, "taking up so much space." But I, "What we want more space for," I say, "more bloody china dog?"'

'You must come and play whenever you like,' I said.

'Maybe we get it tune?' he suggested and I felt a softness inside my chest, a warmth at his use of the word 'we'. I had not been part of a 'we' for so, so long. 'Miss Bell, you funny,' he said. 'You mind me saying?' I shook my head. 'You are beautiful sometime, but you all alone. No children shoes, no man's, only your little shoes with heels worn away.'

'I prefer my own company,' I said.

He smiled at me in a quizzical way that made me uncomfortable, as he finished his tea and got up to go. 'More shoes to take,' he said. 'Thank you for tea.'

'You'll come again and play for me?'

'Ah . . . you not like so much always your own company?' he said as he left. I sat down at the piano and picked out the tune of a hymn, feeling a bit put out as well as pleased. I was in two minds about him at first, just like I am about that Inis now. But I don't know what I'd have done without Blowski, all these years, I really don't.

I can't go out, not in the street. That fall in the garden has done for me. What if I was to go down like that out the front? Strangers helping me up and I don't know what. Coming in, nosing into my business, *invading*. So I needed help – and help has come. Like the answer to a prayer, God has sent me Inis. Or has He? Was it God or was it the other one? I am not such a fool as to take anyone at face value. Not after my life. Is she real, this good neighbour of mine, or does she masquerade? Swap two letters of her name and what do you get: I sin. That floated into my head the other night. A devilish joke. Don't think *that's* escaped me.

'Met your friend Mr Blowski,' she said yesterday when she called with my vegetables, all sweetness and light. 'Nice old fellow.'

*And what did he tell you about me*? I wanted to say, poking her in the chest with my sharp finger because she has a nose on her. I see it when I let her in, like a bloodhound, snooping and sniffing, her eyes swivelling everywhere. But I didn't say that, or poke her, of course. I was noncommittal. 'Yes,' I agreed, 'very nice.' I must be fair. Perhaps it *is* only neighbourly interest, concern. The second commandment incarnate – ha, I don't think so. Well, whatever, I'm not having her camera in here.

There, that's a decision made. I'm not having her lens pointing, snapping, snipping moments away from me. I know what I said and I don't go back on my word as a rule but I can't be . . . compromised, that's the word.

What has happened to my Christian charity?

I said nothing more to Inis on the subject of Blowski. I don't want to encourage interest. I don't want them putting their heads together behind my back, that's the last thing I want. I want them separate. She can help me with the practical side of things. He can give me friendship. Blowski, arthritic old Pole.

We have a history, Blowski and me and I don't want her in it. He used to come to play the piano. Sometimes I opened the door to him, sometimes not. Brenda gave me suspicious looks from the back of the shop when I went in. I really couldn't imagine what he saw in her. I'm not a snob I don't think, the things I've seen, the people I've known, but she was . . . not common, I have no argument with common. She was coarse. That's it: she was coarse and he was fine. It didn't seem right somehow, they weren't a fit pair. I don't think I was jealous. I didn't *want* him. Even if Brenda had gone up in a puff of smoke. I have to be alone.

I think there was talk on Mercy Terrace. I'm certain there was: the married Polish cobbler visiting the standoffish spinster from number 101.

The night before last I didn't open the door to him. I don't know why. I so look forward to his visits but somehow I wasn't up to it, talk, closeness. I heard him knock and there was a sinking in my stomach like a sponge when you open the oven door too soon. And then I heard him talking to Inis, not the words, just their voices and her door shutting. For a minute I thought he'd gone in and I went cold all over, but then I heard him sigh and saw his shadow flit past the front-room curtains.

I am sorry now. I would like to see him now. I hope he comes tomorrow. He has grown thinner than ever lately and his knuckles are all askew. His patience is not what it was either, he's quite cantankerous at times. But still, I like him.

If he knows some of my secrets, then I certainly know his. He is a bigamist.

'There is something Brenda do not know,' he said one afternoon. He had been playing a waltz and I had been watching his quick fingers on the keys, pretending just for the duration of the waltz that he was mine. That he would finish playing and we would lock the door, go upstairs together, draw the curtains. That I was the sort of woman who could do that. His nose was rather long and sharp in profile and his chin all rough with stubble. He sighed in a shuddery way, quite theatrical.

'Yes?'

He turned to face me. 'I can trust you?' he asked. 'It is secret but it hurt always to keep it secret.' He put his hand over his heart and clenched it.

'Who would I tell?'

'I háve two wife, me,' he said. 'One, I left at home. And never return.'

'But why?' Everything he'd said had led me to believe he had nothing to go home for when his country had become communist.

'Hypocrites. Liars. Me, I hate law that betray a whole bloody people. I turn my back. Now I have no home. But Marika . . .' he said, his dark eyes glittering.

'Why didn't you go back to her . . . or couldn't she have come here? Why marry *Brenda*?'

'Oh God,' he said. 'Let me ask you, Trixie Bell. You have ever been in love . . . I mean *real*?' I started to consider but he shook his head before I could speak. 'No, I see you have not. I *love* Marika. She so . . . beautiful. I never see woman, not single woman in this whole bloody world who hold candle to Marika.' He clenched both fists against his heart now. I did not know what to say. The kettle whistled and I went to make the tea.

'So why?' I said when I'd returned.

'She not love me.'

'Oh I'm sure . . .'

'No, no, no.' He waved his hands. 'She absolutely not. "You nice man," she say. "You so kind." When we marry I think maybe she love me, but, oh she not find me *sexy*, you understand?'

I nodded. I thought he was sexy. I supposed I would have done, if I was that sort.

'So why did she marry you?'

'Ha! I was good, what you say, catch, me. Like fish, eh?' He smiled bitterly. 'Good profession, good family, good look. But someone else she like better. *Love*.' I thought for a horrible moment he was going to spit on the carpet, he said this word so fiercely. 'He strong, he loud, he big. What man! Before me, she go with him. Then we marry, I think it finish, Marika and he. Then I find out, all the time, before marry, after marry, all time she still see him. I tell you, if I went home after war Marika be with him. I know it, me. I could not bear it. So I think, Blowski, you must start again. New profession, new woman, new country, new start. And I meet Brenda, she think me sexy, think I'm bloody *miracle*. So I feel good, I feel sod Marika. I live happy with Brenda, business all right. But sometime I remember . . . the music remind and sometime you, Trixie, you remind me of Marika.'

'Oh!'

'Oh you not so beautiful . . . well you older, you not so *alive* but something in your eyes . . .'

I felt like slopping my cup of tea right in his stupid sentimental face. He was so wrapped up in himself, his eyes so far away and dreamy, he didn't even realise what he'd said. Although I don't know why I was hurt. I knew I wasn't beautiful. I even knew . . . even felt sometimes that I was only half alive, so he spoke the truth.

It was several weeks later, I don't know exactly when, that he learned *my* secret. He is the only person I still know, who knows.

I got a letter from him out of the blue and it was a letter I couldn't understand. A letter I have still.

*Dear Trixie,*
*Thank you for last night. I so surprise by you. I think you friend only. I keep think of the rose. I not think you that way. I did not mean. I only come to play piano. Of course, I don't tell Brenda. I see you soon.*
    *Best wishes, do i say love?*
                    *Stefan Blowski.*

That was the start of a bad spell for me. I didn't know what he meant. I remembered nothing, not even a blank space. I did not reply to his letter or open the door to him again for months, nearly a year. I ached inside. If there was music on the television or the radio that sounded like his music, I switched it off. I stayed put mostly. When I did go out I made detours so I did not have to pass his shop.

Often he knocked at the door. I knew his knock, always the same, ratata*ta*ta, always twice, then a wait, then once more, then he'd swivel on one heel and walk away. Then I'd sit on the floor and hug myself and moan until the misery had washed over me and left me high and dry.

But one day I met him in the street, there was no avoiding it. I'd been in the butcher's buying a lamb chop. He caught me as I came out of the shop.

'Trixie Bell!' He looked delighted. He clapped me on the upper arms with both hands, not quite a hug. The contact almost hurt. I caught a whiff of his rubbery cobbler smell. I'd forgotten how dark and wiry his eyebrows were or quite how bright his eyes. 'Stranger, eh, Trixie?' He smiled. I could not look away from him. His teeth were as bad as ever but did not spoil the warmth of his smile. He let me go. 'I miss piano,' he said, wiggling his fingers in front of him. There was no suggestiveness in his face or in his voice. 'And I miss my friend,' he said.

'You can come again.'

And we returned to the old routine, the old friendship. It was different for me, of course, because he knew a part of me I didn't know myself. Only once did he refer to what had happened.

'Blowski understand,' he said. 'You not you, and I, I take advantage. I apologise, I stupid, me. I get carried away. Not again.'

And now we are just old people who meet now and then, he plays the piano hardly at all, his hands are so warped and stiff. We drink tea together and grumble about the changing times as if we are quite normal.

# ADA

*I feel pretty, I feel pretty,*
*I feel pretty and witty and gay*

Poor Trixie. If only she would let go then she could rest. We could wear the lovely dresses. If we could reach our toenails we could paint them. Without Trixie I think *I* could, supple as I am you cannot have failed to notice. And with our scarlet toenails we could dance. If Blowski would come now and it was me. *It's alarming how charming I feel . . .*

Oh Blowski, the only one since the other one, since Frank.
Blowski, a *good* man. It is not wrong to love him.
The only one to see right through Trixie to *me*.
It used to be more. Whole evenings and nights.
Shows we went to . . .
West Side Story, Oklahoma, The King and I and what was the other . . . ?
Music and dancing. Romance. *I'm in love with a wonderful guy.*
June nights, the sky blue glass, swallows drawing loops in the air.
Walking till our feet ached.
If I'd known that was our heyday . . .
Bugs and lamps and lanterns.

94

The smell of elderflowers down by the river and the moon wobbling in the water.
The ecstasy of close warm flesh pressed the whole length of you.
The flesh of another. Separate. Being.
Without Blowski to love, Trixie and I, we could not have lived for all these years. We could not have lived.

# SWEET PICCALILLI

When Pauline arrived, Robin was ecstatic. He climbed on her lap, played with her glasses and hair, stuck his fingers in her ears, would not leave her alone. She was delighted with Robin, excited to have him to herself. She'd brought him a toy fire-engine with a diabolical siren and, for my birthday, *Delia Smith's Complete Cookery Course*. It looked overwhelming – 632 pages of things you can do with food, things which by implication *I* should do with food.

'Thank you,' I said.

'Well, it might inspire you.' I saw her eyes meet Richard's in a conspiratorial way. 'There's a lovely recipe for sweet piccalilli in there,' she added. 'Richard's always loved his pickles. Matter of fact I've brought a jar of chutney. Last year's green tomato.' She fished it from her bag.

'We can have it with lunch,' Richard said. 'Sherry? Martini?'

I tried not to behave like a sullen child. I even pretended pleasure at the thought of my break. I packed a cotton dress that Richard admired, walking boots and shorts, several rolls of film and my favourite old Pentax. I even remembered sun-tan lotion.

We set off in the early afternoon. The car seats were hot against the backs of my legs. Richard drove. Pauline stood by the gate holding Robin, encouraging him to wave. I waved my hand at them, but did not properly look. When we had rounded the corner, Richard put on a tape. Bach's

*Magnificat*. The voices filled the car and flowed out of the open windows.

'There,' Richard said. As if he had proved a point. He put his hand on my bare knee.

'There what?' Every bloody person in sight was holding the hand of a child, or pushing a push-chair or wearing a tiny baby in a sling. I could not even bear to look at the empty child-seat in the back.

Richard gave me a look and joined in with the tape. I watched his Adam's apple slide in his throat. I did love him then. Despite his confident demeanour I could see he was apprehensive about what I might do, or accuse him of. Cruelty.

'Aren't you the lucky one,' Pauline had said to me over lunch. 'I never had one single day away from Richard and Lucy. Not a single day. It never would have entered Fred's head. But then you didn't then, think of it. You didn't expect any respite, then.'

I knew I must pretend. For Richard, for Robin, for Pauline, perhaps even for myself I must pretend that I was capable of this, of letting go for thirty hours. That's what I calculated. I'd insisted that I had to be back on Sunday for Robin's bedtime and Richard had reluctantly agreed.

Richard looked across at me in the car and smiled. 'Happy?'

'Happy,' I lied. The miles pulled threads of love from the pit of my stomach all along the road behind us, catching on lamp-posts, tangling at corners. I saw that my hands were clenched into fists. I made myself open them and wiped away the little snakes of sweat on my skirt.

I knew I was pathetic, how friends of mine would leap at the chance of a break from their children but . . . I just did not.

It was a golden day. Once we'd got clear of London I noticed that the trees were a million fat greens, that the sky was stupidly, childishly blue. I shut my eyes as the miles passed, and the hours. I listened to the music and Richard's voice joining in, and dozed. When I opened my eyes again, the Derbyshire hills, like the rounded flanks of animals were sleeping in the sun, grey walls and bushes threading their creases.

'Awake now? You're not much company.'

'Sorry, where are we?'

'Nearly there.'

'Really?'

'You've been asleep for *hours*.'

'Tired.'

'Well I put my foot down. No sense wasting time.' Richard stopped the car in a lay-by and we got out.

'Smell,' Richard said and I drew in a lungful of the polleny air.

'It is beautiful,' I admitted. We stood at the roadside gazing at the complex view, hills, trees, more hills, the spire of a church emerging from amongst a dark huddle of distant trees. It was the first time I'd been outside myself since Robin had been born. For a moment I became flickers of birdsong and nodding of grasses and the deep cold creep of the river in the valley. A lightness grew around my heart. The pretence had worked.

I had almost forgotten the magic I'd learned as a child, that if you pretend very hard to feel something, then sometimes it will work and become real. Like a wish coming true. I could make myself cry by pretending to be sad. I could become truly grateful for the most hideous thing. And now the pretence of happiness, romantic happiness even, that had stuck like a seed in my throat had grown shoots and leaves. It wasn't for long after all and the countryside was so glorious – and all Richard wanted was my happiness.

We stopped in Bakewell and toured the souvenir-shops. We bought a book of walks, some plastic dinosaurs for Robin and a box of fudge for Pauline. In a café we shared a pot of tea and ate slices of Bakewell pudding, all thick and eggy. We managed to chat about something or other neutral, friends, memories, laughed at the conversation going on at the adjacent table. 'He gave me every excuse under the book,' a powdery middle-aged woman was saying. 'But I wouldn't have none of it. "I'm not having it," I says. And him with only the one leg!'

I'd forgotten how eavesdropping used to be such fun, such sneaky pleasure. Now if I was in a café or restaurant I was too completely taken up with Robin.

'God it's good to see you smile,' Richard said and touched my lips with his finger. 'Aren't you going to finish your pudding?'

'Too rich. We could take one back for Pauline.' He leaned over and finished it for me, then we walked arm in arm through the little town imagining living somewhere like this, looking in estate agents' windows and rhapsodising about rural schools.

We drove to our hotel in time to change and have a drink before dinner. The view from the hotel bar was outrageously beautiful, a steep hill plunging down to a shallow silvery river far below and hills rising in the distance that looked as if they'd been blessed by the powdery evening light. I couldn't resist that light and went out to take some photographs.

Everything conspired to be perfect: the weather, the wine, the food. My dress looked good, clung and dipped in all the right places. For the first time in years I wore lipstick and, to please Richard, I put on my new, glamorous, prickly watch. I behaved very well. Richard glanced at me anxiously from time to time and I responded with a smile. He was wearing a white shirt with a stupid collar but I pretended not to mind. As the weekend successfully progressed, his expression grew increasingly smug. He had been right after all. Doctor Goodie. All I'd needed was a break. He was partly right. I was surprised I hadn't died from the forcible separation from Robin. Whole minutes passed when he didn't even cross my mind.

After our green-lipped oysters, duck and syllabub we walked for a little in the dark. The sky was full of stars like bright press-studs and the moon was almost full, low and buttery. On the hills were the lights from scattered houses and sometimes the moving brightness of headlights on a far-off road. Richard held my hand.

'Bats,' he said. Deeper scraps of darkness swooped around us as we passed a looming barn. We heard the deep hoo-hooing of an owl.

'It is so silent,' I said. There were no traffic sounds, no voices, no wind to moan in the trees. The silence was like black velvet, thick and soft in my ears.

'When I was little,' Richard said, 'I used to think I could hear the stars.'

'What did they say?'

'Nothing. They squeaked.'

I laughed. 'Let's get back.'

'Wait.' Richard pulled me close to him and kissed me on the mouth. 'Pity we have to go back,' he murmured, 'we could do it here . . .'

'Do what?'

He kissed me again and put his hand on my breast.

'Come on.' I pulled away and walked back towards the hotel.

'No sense of adventure, that's your trouble,' he said, following.

'I'm only thinking about thistles,' I said, 'and midges and cow-pats. Just being realistic. Anyway, I'm chilly.'

He caught up with me and put his arm round my waist. 'But are you feeling randy? That's the main thing, we can do it anywhere you like, long as we do it.'

'Mmmmm,' I said. I was feeling sleepy. All I wanted to do was sleep – preferably alone – for a very long time and then drive straight home to Robin. But sex, of course, was part of the deal. That's what we'd been leading up to. And it should be what I wanted to do. I just didn't. I felt suddenly deflated, disappointed in myself.

Richard massaged me first. I tried to relax, but I was worried that the oil would get in my hair. The way he did my shoulders was lovely, but then he moved down to my buttocks and slid his slippery fingers up the insides of my thighs. How could I say I didn't want it?

We ate slices of black-pudding as big as saucers with our bacon and egg breakfast. The hills were shadowy. I was relieved to have got the night over. I had even slept and not woken until the luxurious hour of eight o'clock. We planned to walk, lunch in a pub and drive back. My heart skittered at the thought of being home again, holding Robin in my arms to kiss him goodnight.

Richard's head was bowed over the book of walks. I noticed for the first time a few grey hairs in his black curls. His chin was stubbly – he never shaved on holiday. He was wearing a black T-shirt and a little wisp of black hair curled in the hollow between his collar-bones. When we weren't in bed and there was no danger of having to make love, I sometimes still desired him.

I shot rolls and rolls of film that day: leaves against the sky; tissue-paper layers of hills; smooth dry boulders on the moors; ewes, their too-big lambs almost nudging them off their feet in a late effort to suckle; a revoltingly pretty cottage by a mill-stream. Richard smiling, frowning, pointing, concentrating on the map. We discovered a dead tree, long dead, carved by the weather into an upward spiralling shape, and what was most curious, its trunk was divided into two, so that it seemed to be standing on two legs. It looked like a fury; a woman, her arms, bones, hair all streaming upwards, swirling in a silent cry. Of course, I didn't say this to Richard.

We stopped to look round a village church and eating ice-lollies wandered round the graveyard. Every stone I saw seemed to be for a child.

'Listen to this,' Richard said:

> '*Dear is the spot to evry parent's eye,*
> *where mouldering in the dust their children lie.*
> *Thither remembrance sends their frequent moan,*
> *and fond affection marks it with a stone.*

Christ! talk about maudlin!'

Tears rose to my eyes and when Richard saw them, he stalked away, irritated. 'Come on,' he called over his shoulder, 'or we'll never get any lunch.'

I followed, wiping my eyes on the back of my hand. And then I had a sudden awful realisation.

'Richard! Last night . . . I didn't have my cap in!'

He paused. 'What? I assumed when you got up to go to the loo . . .'

'No. I don't know what . . . I just forgot. Can you believe it?' We walked in silence down the steep sunny street. Peonies, lobelia, nasturtiums tumbled from boxes on the cottage window-sills. *I* could not believe that I'd forgotten. I could never have another child, that is what I believed, what I had decided. I hadn't told Richard yet. I didn't think he'd understand my reasoning: that I loved Robin too much; that it would be a betrayal. I didn't have any more love to give and I couldn't think of giving less to Robin. I knew this would cause trouble between us. Richard wanted another child, he wanted two, close together, like himself and his sister. We went into a low dark pub full of the smell of beer and roast meat. Richard bought two halves of bitter and we sat down to look at the menu.

'Cheer up.' Richard leant over and kissed me. 'It's unlikely you've conceived – look how many tries it took for Robin. And if you have . . . well . . . it's not the worst thing that could happen. Actually, I'd be quite pleased.'

'I know *you* would.'

'Beef or lamb? And so would you once you got used to the idea. Look how much you love Robin.'

It was useless trying to explain so I shut up. He seemed to know what was best for me better than I did myself. And after all, it was me who'd forgotten my cap.

# OPENING FIRE

I am not in love with Blowski, not in a romantic way. I go back over the faces in my mind and can find nobody that I have been really *in* love with. Only Jesus, though that love is different of course. But it's only in His love that I feel at home. Though, truth be told, I have never felt really at home anywhere, not even in my self. I've always had the feeling that there is someone there, hiding behind doors in my mind, smirking through windows, rustling about under the bed of my sleep.

I remember when I first fell for Jesus. We were having a week in York, visiting Father's relatives, and Mother had insisted that we spend an afternoon in Harrogate visiting Auntie Ba and her family – though Father couldn't stick them. It was March 1926. I was sixteen. It was a bright cold day. On the Stray, crocuses like yellow and purple gas-flames flared up through the wet earth. Dogs yapped and birds fluttered about in the trees. Puddles reflected the moving sky.

I was feeling sick. I had had an absence. Father held me by the wrist, almost dragging me along. In my absence someone had smoked his pipe. I had a taste in my mouth like spewed tobacco, a bitter juice that gnawed at my tongue.

'I did not, I would not,' I had said but even as I cried I could taste the dirt, remember the hard pipe stem between my lips, the gurgle and choke of spit and smoke. But it was not my memory, it was someone else's like a cuckoo's egg hatching in my mind.

Mother was walking slightly ahead, lifting her feet high like a pony, distancing herself. Of course she was angry. I was a wicked coward. Look what I had done. Over and over I did things. 'You, Trixie, you do things and you lie. There is no sense in it. Look there is tobacco caught in your collar.' She brushed it off, her fingernail catching in the crocheted lace. Of course she was angry. I felt sick. In the trees the birds sang, a sound sweet as the milk I longed to drink to take the horrible taste out of my mouth.

And then we heard the sound of a drum, and brass – a brass-band striking up. My heart flew like one of the little birds to meet the thrilling sound. It was a hymn, 'Onward Christian Soldiers', played with gusto, not solemn but full of joy. The blue-coated band had gathered in a little square opposite the Stray where we had to cross over to reach Auntie Ba's. The banner was a sight to see, blue, gold and red: *Blood and Fire* it said. The brass sound was like fire in my blood – the boom of the bass drum, the richness of the trombone – and the cornet. Oh the cornet . . . it was high and bright, blaring out like brass petals opening. It sounded like hope, but hope with a fighting spirit, not girlish, hands-in-lap, patient hope. My feet stopped and my father yanked me on.

'Utter vulgarity,' he muttered, 'posing as religion. I ask you.'

'Don't you like the music?' I dared to ask but he did not answer and my mother did not even look round, it was as if the band did not exist. I was ashamed to walk past like that when the music called out to me so loud and important. I smiled at one of the soldiers. Her face was lit up like an angel's face under the brim of her bonnet. She returned my smile as Father dragged me away.

I liked Auntie Ba and her big, nearly grown children, but I did not like that afternoon behind thick chenille curtains in a fire-lit parlour that shut out the spring. In a cage by the window was Bertie, a pale lemon canary, huddled at one end of his perch, his feathers ruffling through the narrow metal bars. He took no notice of us at all.

'Does he sing?' I asked.

'Once or twice a year, of an evening, if the late sun strikes his cage, love, it seems to set him off, then he sings his little heart out, sings something glorious,' Auntie Ba said and her words made me want to cry for the trapped scrap of yellow in the cage.

Faint in the distance through the clinking sounds of tea, the polite conversation, I thought I could still hear the beat behind the music. My jaws chewed in time as I ate sandwiches and cake. My spoon chinked like a triangle on the rim of my cup when I sugared my tea.

It was love at first sight, it was *in love* love, though I'm not sure with what. Maybe not God exactly, not Jesus, not the band or the woman's smile. I don't know. I can't explain it. It was simply love. Well it is the nearest *I* ever got. And when I thought that I felt something squirm inside me like a damp curl, a worm in the folds of my brain. That is the Devil, I thought – the bitter taste of tobacco and smoke in my mouth, the bitter taste of guilt – the Devil squirming in fear.

They left me alone in the parlour while they all went outside to look at some storm damage to the back of the house. I wandered round the room. It was a cosy room, books and knitting, a photograph of poor Tom in his uniform in pride of place on the mantelpiece – which was a little dusty. Maybe that's why the curtains were half-drawn. That was a nice thing about Auntie Ba, her unfussiness. There would never be dust on our mantelpiece at home. I sat down at the piano and tried to pick out a tune. Then I clucked my tongue at the canary. He opened one bright eye and shivered. The bottom of his cage was spattered with seed, white droppings and minute yellow feathers; a pecked cuttle-fish bone hung from the bars. It was a little cage, too little for him to fly. Seeing him in there, unable to stretch his wings, with no other birds for company, made me almost hurt. I knew I should not but I opened the door of his cage. I knew it was wrong but I was doing wrong to do right – freeing the bird. At first he didn't move. Then he hopped along his perch towards the door, cocking his head from side to side. I clucked my tongue again, 'Come on Bertie, fly,' I whispered. And all of a sudden, startling me, he did. He hopped off his perch and darted madly round the room. I was afraid he would fly straight into the fire so I stood in front of the hearth, my arms stretched out. I thought he would tangle in my hair. I was afraid he would do that and I might have to beat him out of it, I might kill him in my fright. He perched for a moment on a chair-back, then flew up to the curtain-rail. He sang a little song, dipped his tail and did a long white dropping on the curtain.

'Go back,' I begged. The fire spat behind me, I couldn't move in case he swooped over my head and into the flames. And then they came back, first the voices in the hall, Auntie Ba saying, 'Another cup before you go,' Father saying, 'Oh no, we really must be off,' followed by the opening of the door. Auntie Ba saw at once what I'd done, looking from me to the bird. Father saw too. 'What the devil . . . Trixie . . .'

'Sonny, coax him down,' Auntie Ba said to her second son. 'Sonny's got a way with him,' she explained as the tall whiskery boy rubbed his fingers together at the bird.

Father grabbed me by the wrist, squeezing very tight so that tears came into my eyes.

'Now Charles,' Auntie Ba said, 'don't go jumping to conclusions, he's a regular Houdini that bird, always getting out.'

'Did you free the bird?' Father said. I could feel my hand swelling with trapped blood.

'No,' I lied.

'Come away from the fire Trixie, love, you'll scorch your hem,' Auntie Ba said. Father let me go and I moved away just as the bird flew down. He perched on Sonny's shoulder for a moment but as he put up a cupped hand to catch him, Bertie darted off again, flapping wildly round the room, battering his wings on the curtains.

I was scared he would land in my hair and I sat down with my hands over my head.

'What's got into the creature?' Auntie Ba said. 'Sonny stand still with your arm out . . . keep calm.' Mother backed against the door but Father stood like a statue, his eyes on me. And then the bird swooped low, flew past my face and straight into the fire. He started to rise, as if he would fly straight up the chimney, his wings all in flames. Auntie Ba screamed and Sonny threw a pot of tea into the hearth, and there was a hissing and steaming and fluttering in the heart of the coals. Then it stopped and was still. There was a terrible smell of scorched feathers. And silence.

When we left, the band had gone. The place where they had stood was empty. It was getting dark, there had been a fresh shower of rain and everything glistened. The band had gone, but pasted on a wall was a row of bright posters lit by the street-lamps. Even with the speed that we walked I could read the bold black letters

BLOOD AND FIRE
LOOK OUT! LOOK OUT!
CAPTAIN MALCOLM
AND REGULAR SOLDIERS
CHALLENGE THE DEVIL TO WAR!
HALLELUJAH BRASS
WILL OPEN FIRE AT 8 am
MARCH 8th
ALL WELCOME

and I knew it was a message to me. There was nothing I could do then, but I knew what I would do when, one day, I was free.

On the coach back to York, I sat alone in the seat in front of Mother and Father. They hardly said a word to each other and nothing at all to me. I watched the dark country pass by through the pale reflection of my face. All the way I thought about the Salvation Army Band, I could still feel the beat of the music in my bones. It was the cornet that made me free the bird. I was sorry of course, sorry that Bertie had died, ashamed that it was my fault. But . . . I felt something else too. The trumpet was like liquid fire. BLOOD AND FIRE the flyer said. I thought there was something glorious about a trapped bird flying right into the heart of the flames.

# BOY

It was good when Trixie did that

I would have done that

I smoked Father's pipe to make me smell of man

Trixie got the blame

And she was very angry

I know she was but she didn't know it

Trixie doesn't know anything

But she let the bird out

I was laughing at the stupid thing

Horrible little feathers everywhere

Burning feathers stink

But I was laughing my head off

It was good when she did that

# BULL'S EYE

Two weeks after our weekend away, I discovered that I was pregnant. Richard took a urine sample to the surgery and rang me back.

'Bull's eye,' he said.

I said nothing.

'Go on,' he said. 'Aren't you pleased – just a bit?'

'Oh . . . maybe,' I said.

'It'll work out fine. *I'm* pleased.'

'Good.'

'Look, get a sitter and we'll go out for a curry. I'm not on call.'

My mouth filled with acid. 'Not curry, no.'

'Something else then. Or a film.'

'All right.'

Robin was playing with his fire-engine on the kitchen floor. I walked round the house collecting dirty washing. I worked out that the baby would be due in May. I saw myself in the hall mirror, my hair tangled, my face fish-belly pale.

May is a good time to have a baby, I told myself, a warm, opening-up time. It'll be Taurean, a little bull. Robin was a winter baby, a child of dark skies, snowfalls and freezing night-time cries. I gave Robin some juice. I got the vacuum cleaner out to do the stairs but I felt too tired. All through the pregnancy I was ill, so tired I could hardly think, constantly nauseous yet ravenous for doughnuts and ice-cream. I put on too much weight and my own Dr Goodie nagged at me to eat salad. I grew snappy and hateful even to myself. Sex was out of the question. Dr Goodie was patient but I grew to hate his long-suffering expression. He insisted on having Pauline to stay to give me a break and I wanted to break her face and his too.

The birth was hell. I lost control. With Robin, I had stayed in control and *I* did it, *gave* birth. It was something I could do. It was almost as if Robin co-operated, that's what I think now. And when I held him in my arms for the first time and experienced that electric shock of love I was changed. Everything was changed, the colours of my world, everything.

Billie was two weeks' late. I was a belly on legs, a child's cartoon, a laugh, too grotesque in the end to leave the house. Richard wanted me to have a home birth but I didn't care where I had it. I just wanted the thing out of me. I tried to tell him how I felt. 'I don't love it,' I said, my hand on its struggling bulk. 'I can't help it. I don't know why.'

'Of course you don't,' he said. 'How can you till you've seen it? It'll be all right, you wait.'

But I knew I hadn't felt like this about Robin. I'd started to love him even as an abstract thing. Even before I'd felt him move inside me, I'd felt the beginnings of love. But I couldn't say any more, my words sounded wicked even to myself.

Billie felt it. I know she did. She knew that I did not want her. That's why she was late, she didn't want to be born at all. The labour started slowly, a couple of days of grudging contractions, the odd strong squeeze, a reminder of what pain was. I knew it had really started when I woke early one Saturday morning but I did not say. I crept downstairs and sat in the kitchen drinking tea. The sun was bright on the quarry-tiled floor, the ferns on the window-sill, Robin's cars on the floor, a sticky splash of yesterday's Ribena that I hadn't wiped up. It was not yet six o'clock and Robin was still asleep. Richard had murmured a question-mark as I got out of bed.

'Loo,' I'd whispered. 'Go back to sleep.'

It was rare to be alone in the quiet of early morning. The pains were spaced out but strong. I tried to remember how to breathe. I had been so clued up with Robin, now I could hardly remember. *By tonight you will have a new baby*, I told myself and I think I did feel a filament of excitement. It was started. It was inevitable now. It was as if I had got on to a train, slow and speeding-up that would not stop. I could not get off until the end of the line. Half-an-hour's peace first, before I woke Richard. I almost resented the thought of letting him into it, not just that, letting him take control. He would be all efficiency and phone-calls, all heartiness and professionalism. It was my body, not his. I ate a bowl of Robin's Rice Krispies. The sun was warm on my bare feet. I felt balanced, momentarily, a sensation I had forgotten. For a few quiet moments I *was* in control.

I heard Robin waking, talking to himself in his room, singing. *The wheels on the bus go round and round, round and round, round and round.* I heard him getting louder, fidgeting, then the creak of his bed, the pad of his feet on the floor. I stood up thinking I'd intercept him before he woke Richard but as I got up there was a gush of hot water between my legs and then a pain that is not describable. It was too big to be mine. It was another presence in the room. The bright kitchen swirled around me, inside rocks ground and churned. I must have cried out I think, I don't know.

'Mummy,' Robin called and his voice was high and clear like a bird's. I heard him padding down the stairs, both feet on each stair, counting. He came into the kitchen.

'Whatsamatter?' he asked. I was half-standing holding on to the table. 'Whatsat?' He looked at the spreading pool on the tiles. I could not move or stand properly, the contraction held me like a vice. I couldn't breathe.

'Go and get Daddy, darling,' I managed to say.

The day was like that. Waves of stupendous, bone-mashing pain, existing beside me, filling the rooms, my body frozen. I could not breathe through it. I was helpless. I could not even think. Richard soon stopped telling me to pull myself together. I think even he was scared. He got a friend to pick up Robin and phoned Pauline who had been waiting, bags packed, poised by her front door probably, for the past month. The midwife came but there was no question of a home delivery. 'Just put me to sleep,' I begged whenever I could get a breath. I vaguely remember the ambulance jolting, the pain squeezed in there with me. Time distorted. I was injected with something.

'Darling, you're hysterical.' Richard loomed over the bed. 'It'll be all right. Try and get a grip.'

'Fuck off Dr Goodie,' I said. I think I might have laughed, anyway I heard laughter. I remember monitors and a sudden panic about foetal distress and thinking that I was dying. I didn't think about Robin at all. I was beyond that. I would have been glad, would have been grateful to die just to stop it. Then I remember nothing.

Billie was born by emergency Caesarean section. She was badly distressed and very tiny. 'Looks prem,' I heard someone say. 'Placental insufficiency,' I heard and felt criticised. I didn't much want to see her. I was glad she wasn't a boy – I thought Robin would have been more jealous of a baby brother. All I wanted to do when I woke, groggy and sore the next morning was to go home, back to Robin, and forget the whole episode.

But we stayed in hospital for a week, Billie and me. Richard came twice a day with flowers, newspapers, good sandwiches – the hospital food was impossible – fruit, chocolate and his best bedside manner. Pauline and Robin came every afternoon. Robin got in bed with me and I sniffed his silky hair and marvelled at how huge he was, how huge his face and hands compared with the skinny baby they were bringing me every day to try and feed.

She was a difficult baby. She didn't feed well. I don't think she liked my breasts, she struggled and wailed and hurt my wound with her kicking legs. She had very pointed toes, the second one longer than the first like no one in my family's – like Richard's. She was like an alien baby. I kept thinking I'd got the wrong one that soon they would bring me mine and I would like it. But she *was* mine, Richard's. Pauline was full of how like Richard's sister Lucy as a baby she was, the dead spit. I wanted my mum to be there. I wanted to ask her what you do when you don't like your baby. I couldn't tell Richard or Pauline or any of my friends who came with books and Baby-Gros.

I dreamt one night they did come, Mum and Dad and Bonny. Mum was holding Billie wrapped up in a clear sheet of polythene like a doll. Her eyes were shut. 'Won't she suffocate?' I asked. 'Yes, but that's quite normal,' my mum said. Bonny licked my hand and my dad said, 'I can see you in her, as a baby, the dead spit.'

I woke up and looked at Billie, but she was nothing like me, nothing.

'Robin's bought a present for his sister,' Pauline said. They'd brought a hideous pink teddy-bear. Robin's hair was all wrong, wetted and combed with a parting instead of all tumbled and curly and he held Pauline's hand and didn't immediately run to me. I thought he was a traitor.

'Granny brought it but I *choosed* it,' he said proudly. When I hugged him I could smell Pauline, her face-powder and perfume.

'I'm coming home the day after tomorrow,' I said.

'And the baby?'

'A few days more, she's out of Special Care, they just want her to gain a couple more ounces.'

'You're coming home *without* her? What about feeding?'

'She prefers formula,' I said. Richard was annoyed that I wouldn't persevere with breast-feeding, 'Breast milk is designed for babies,' he said. 'It's what I tell all my mums.' 'You feed her then,' I said. 'I've heard its possible, if you take female hormones and let her keep sucking.' He gave me his long suffering look.

I tried again but Billie just didn't like it and nor did I so we gave up. It meant that Richard could get up in the night with her, and that suited me.

\*

It did get better. When Billie learned to smile and gurgle I started to quite like her. Robin loved her. I think he knew I didn't and was puzzled. He didn't feel betrayed. She was his favourite toy. He talked about 'my baby' at nursery and drew pictures for her bedroom walls. I had to stop him lugging her out of her cot and carrying her about by her head. And she adored him, more than anyone. Her eyes followed him and her smiles were, more often than not, directed at Robin. She grew fatter and pinker. People said she was pretty. Her hair grew fluffy and brown, my colour. Some people even said she looked like me. I took pictures of the two of them. I went to the park every day and to the Baby Clinic every week. I had lunch with friends. Family life was all right. Billie cried at night a lot. She was colicky and fretful from sunset to sunrise like some sort of vampire, but Richard coped with most of that. It made him too tired for sex which suited me.

By the autumn, things had settled down. Richard was vague to me. I did everything you have to do if you have children. Oh the house was a mess but I was not *bad*. Richard suggested we hire a cleaner, but I didn't want anyone to see the mess or know about it. Sometimes I went blank. Once I just lay down on the kitchen floor and couldn't get up. My face was pressed against the door of the freezer and I could hear it humming and I was comforted by the thought of all the food in there frozen stiff, white and frosty and safe, all suspended from the rotting process. Billie was crying in her pram in the garden. Robin was playing upstairs. I just lay on the floor and went through the contents of the freezer in my head: ice-cream, lollies, fish-fingers, chips, peas, sweetcorn, spinach, broccoli, bread, haddock, free-flow mince over and over. I could see and hear what was going on but I could not move and I could not get my mind out of its groove. I felt nothing. I don't know how long it was before Robin came downstairs and said: 'Mummy, Billie's crying.' He stood and looked at me for a minute, then went into the garden to rock the pram. Billie was crying harder and harder. The telephone rang and stopped. It was only the sound of our next-door neighbour, Jan, talking to Robin over the fence, asking him where I was, that broke the spell and enabled me to move.

At Christmas Pauline came to stay. When she'd gone, on New Year's Eve, I got very drunk. I was drinking with relief because Pauline had gone home, because the terrible year had ended, that I could look *forward* now. And I felt odd, I hardly recognised the feeling, a heat in my lower belly, a sort of voluptuousness. I seduced Richard who was drunk himself and, having been both on-call and on-duty with Billie every night over Christmas was stultified with exhaustion. I took off my tights and knickers and stood in front of him, slumped on the sofa as he was.

'Inis!' he laughed nervously. 'What's going on . . .' We had hardly made love since Billie's birth. I undid his trousers and climbed on top of him. 'Help,' he said, 'Oh Inis . . .' I didn't do it for him but for myself. It was quick and good.

'Happy New Year,' I said. 'I'm sorry I've been such a cow.' He pulled me down to kiss him but I didn't want to be kissed. He stank of whisky. He had been helpless. If he had done that to me while I was drunk and drowsing, taken off his trousers and climbed on to *me*, I would have called it rape. Therefore I could not blame him, not even slightly, when two weeks later I woke feeling sick, checked my diary for the date, secretly bought a testing-kit and saw the little stick turn pink.

# AFTERNOON TEA

Trixie hears a knock at the door and heaves herself out of her chair. On the television a young woman is showing her how to stencil grapes and strawberries on her walls, something she would never do in a million years, yet its nice to watch the neat slide of paint, the lovely fruity frieze appearing. She's been in a trance, half of her watching, half of her miles away. She sighs. It will only be Inis with her bits and pieces: washing-up liquid, lavatory paper, carrots. She opens the door, planning to take her shopping and get straight back to her programme, but Inis practically barges her way in.

'Got your stuff,' she says. The dark roots of her hair are plainly showing and she looks pale and seedy. 'Shall I put it away for you?' She stands in the room with the carrier-bag.

'No,' Trixie says, 'no need. I'll do it later.'

Inis's eyes stray to her letters on the table, as they would. *Want to look*? The stencil item has finished now and there's that nice coffee advertisement. But still Inis stands there in her horrible skimpy black trousers all bagged at the knee. They make themselves look such frights, these days, the young.

'Would you like a cup of tea?' Trixie asks reluctantly.

'Thought you'd never ask.' Inis laughs and flops down into a chair. 'I'd better have a look at your leg first. How is it?' Trixie rolls down her stocking and Inis, sniffing, kneels down in front of her and peels off the tape that secures the lint. 'It's still a bit wet,' she says. 'I'll bathe it for you.' The graze is shrinking, the skin thick and dark round the sticky place. There will be quite a scar. 'All right?' Inis asks. Trixie nods. 'Let me put the kettle on,' Inis says.

Trixie rolls her stocking up. 'I think I can manage that.' She presses her lips together and goes to put the kettle on. She should be grateful but somehow she isn't. Inis is being kind, she reminds herself, she is being a good neighbour. But now she'll miss 'Economy Cook' – feed a family of four on £15 a week – she likes that, watching them stretch mince with lentils and grind dandelion roots up for coffee. It reminds her of the war, not that Trixie had to worry, money sticks to money she thinks with a guilty shiver, spooning tea into the pot.

Inis comes and leans against the kitchen door-frame, but Trixie keeps her back to her. 'I can't get my heating right at all,' she says. 'It's getting worse, the radiators are hardly even warm. And I think I'm getting a cold.'

'I manage with my electric-fire,' Trixie says. 'Never had central heating and I'm not starting now.'

'No . . . well it's what you're used to,' Inis says. 'Actually, Trixie, I've got a favour to ask.'

*I'm sure you have*, mouths Trixie. 'Just a minute dear.' She arranges the tray very slowly, the embroidered cloth, only a little splashed, the sugar bowl, the milk jug, a few biscuits on a plate. As she does so she practises saying no to whatever it will be, though she can't imagine. *No dear, I don't think so, not this time.*

'I'll carry it,' Inis says, muscling in. 'And shall I pour?'

'Let it brew a minute.' Trixie sounds quite sharp, for her.

'It's nice out,' Inis says. 'Have you been in the garden?'

'Yes dear.' She watches the way Inis's eyes skim the room, what is it she's looking for?

'Actually, could I go to the loo?' she asks, such a bolt from the blue it quite takes Trixie's breath away. 'I've come straight from the shops.'

'Yes dear,' Trixie says, 'of course you can.'

Inis goes up the stairs and Trixie's heart thuds at the sound of another person moving in her house. The cheek, the downright, bare-faced cheek. As if she couldn't pop discreetly back next door like any decent person. What is it she thinks she'll see up there? Trixie paces about agitatedly, her nails slicing the palms of her hands, listening to the movement, the running of the taps, the flushing sound . . . then a pause a little too long, what is she doing, looking in the medicine-cabinet or what? Then the door opening and another pause. Is she looking in the bedroom, is that it? Potato soup with home-made *croûtons* followed by jelly trifle, a filling meal, nourishing and cheap, but Trixie cannot even look at the screen. She cannot contain herself another minute, she goes to the foot of the stairs, ready to call out but Inis is on her way down, her face quite bland.

'I do like your landing wallpaper,' she says. 'Very old. Original perhaps?'

The raging cheek of her! *Very old* indeed! 'I'm sure I don't know,' says Trixie.

'Shall I be mother?' Inis says, all perky as you like and then suddenly a flinch like she's been stung.

'Yes, do,' Trixie says.

They sip the tea in silence. Inis's shoes need a polish, her fingernails are dirty. She keeps sniffing, Trixie practically expects her to wipe her nose on her sleeve. *Why don't you blow it*? she longs to ask. Inis eats three biscuits and drops crumbs down her sweater. 'Time for my quiz soon,' Trixie hints.

'Oh yes,' Inis says, politeness personified all of a sudden. 'I won't keep you, only I wanted to ask . . .' Trixie holds her breath. 'Those photographs, remember we talked . . . I thought if I could get a few of you in the garden and around the house, candid shots, nothing posed, you needn't dress up.'

'No dear, I don't think so,' Trixie is amazed to hear issue from her lips.

Inis's face falls, it is quite comic the way the smile drops from her face so that you almost expect to hear it smash on the floor.

'But I thought . . .'

'I know what you thought.'

'You said . . .'

'I know what I said, but I've, well let's just say I've reconsidered.' Trixie is practically enjoying herself.

Inis finishes her tea and puts down her cup. 'It's just that I've got this project all mapped out in my head now and . . .'

'Old ladies are ten-a-penny,' Trixie says. 'You'll have to find another one.'

Inis stands up. 'OK then.' She's all sag; her knees, her elbows, her neck and Trixie feels almost sorry. 'Don't get up,' Inis says. 'Bye.' Trixie sits still a minute until she hears Inis's door bang and then she turns up the volume on the television.

Inis pauses outside her front door, her key in her hand then changes her mind. Bloody Trixie, what's got into her, awkward bag. You'd think she'd be pleased to have someone interested. And it's not much to ask, after all the shopping, the help . . . the worry of having a needy neighbour, just a few shots, nothing posed or forced. Old women may *be* ten-a-penny but you can't just go up to people in the street and anyway, it's Trixie's face she wants, not just anybody's. *Trixie's* expressions, Trixie herself.

She wanders round the shops. So many gift-shops selling cards, inflatable guitars, candles, key-rings, amusing mugs, incense. Billie's birthday is in two months. She sets her jaw. The baker's window is full of gingerbread pigs and teddies. Every woman on the street is pushing a buggy. She should go home but why? What for? Still, there's nowhere else. She shivers, realising that her throat is sore. That's all she needs, a cold.

In front of her is Trixie's friend, Mr Blowski. She catches him up.

'Ah, Inis, good-day,' he says, touching his hat. He at least seems pleased to see her. 'I go to see Trixie.'

'I've just been,' she says.

'How is she?'

'Oh, you know.' Inis moves her hand from side to side.

Mr Blowski nods sagely. 'And you Inis, how are you?'

'OK.'

'Yes?'

'Well, I'm getting a cold – and there's something wrong with the heating, the boiler bowing out I think, oh you know. Life.'

'Yes.'

'Fed up, to tell the truth.' Inis laughs. They have reached her house, and Trixie's.

'I tell you what, I look at your heating. Sometime quite handy, me.'

He goes into the kitchen. Inis is ashamed of the cup rings and crumbs on the yellow table, the loops of spaghetti in the sink, the wet tea-bag on the draining-board leaking thick brown.

'What a mess,' she says weakly, as if surprised.

'My God, you need electrician,' Blowski says, squinting at the boiler. 'Something buggered.'

'Yes, well.'

'You ring landlord?'

'Ha!'

'I know electrician, my good friend Oscar, he fix it up, no sweat.'

'Oh don't worry,' Inis says, 'It'll be spring soon.'

'You joking? Anyhow, what about next winter?'

'Oh . . .' Inis shrugs. She hasn't thought as far ahead as next winter but of course she won't be here, the thought is unimaginable, that far ahead still to be looking at the same white walls with the ghosts of roses. 'Like some tea or something?'

'No, I have tea with Trixie, thank you,' Mr Blowski says. 'You find her . . . ?' he mimics Inis's hand movement.

'So-so,' Inis elaborates, 'a bit . . .'

'Unlike Trixie?' Mr Blowski looks excited.

'What? No, I wouldn't say that, just a bit . . . low.'

'Ah. Well, I say goodbye for now. Another time, a cup of tea, yes?'

Inis comes to the door with him. 'She was watching her quiz, but it'll be finished now.'

'Oh, I'm late, me,' he says. 'Goodbye.'

'Bye.' Inis shuts the door and stands with her arms wrapped round herself, shivering, listening to him knocking on Trixie's door, before she goes upstairs.

# COMPOST

I heard them. She is a sneaking bitch. First she wants photographs. Why I ask? Photographs. Does she want to identify me or what? And then there is him. Blowski. She had him in her house. I heard them, clear as day. I heard them saying goodbye. He does not come when I want him and then he goes to her first. What does she do for him, give him, what does he want from her? What do they say about me?

Then he came knocking at my door, I ask you. A tom-cat prowling, that's Blowski, my bloody charming Blowski, see what he's brought me to, swearing now, yes bloody, bloody, bloody, Blowski. Did I answer it? Did I heck. Left him on the step. Oh he stood and knocked and even called, I heard his voice, 'Trixie, you all right?' Lifted up the letter-flap to call it. Who does he think he is? Who do they think they are? What are they up to?

I don't know where to put myself or what to do. I hurt. I want to go out but I can't go out because I might fall. My leg is sore, she made it worse with her tender ministrations. Something is battering inside me as if it wants to get out. I am in pain. I should pray, oh yes because God is there, He is still there for me. I have my faith, I do, I do, I do. I must put my faith and trust in God and stop this nonsense.

But what is it that they say behind my back? What do they say?

Stop it Trixie. Solace in your garden: seek it. Your own miracle. Where you are in control.

*

Trixie tips her kitchen compost tidy of tea-leaves, peelings, old lettuce into her compost bin and straightens up. She breathes in the musky scent of flowering currant, admires the pink clashing against the yellow forsythia. She can feel the sun on her back. Another spring has sprung and here she is yet.

She heard Inis's door banging shut some time ago. Soon she should be back with the money and shopping. She didn't want to entrust Inis with her bank book. She contemplated going out herself. It's not far. There's no ice or slippery rain. But since her fall she can't face going out. She can only be at home or in the garden. *You're closer to God in a garden, than anywhere else on earth.* And there *is* God in the creamy primroses, in the pale pink flexing of an earthworm, in the clash of currant and forsythia.

If only Inis would set to and sort her garden out. She'll have to have a word. It's nothing but an eyesore that Trixie has to turn her back on to enjoy her own. The mattress has grown dark speckled patches of mould and there are hairs where a cat settles itself down every night. Already the dandelions are pushing up their dark toothed leaves and before you know it the fluff will be in the air, getting its roots in her own fertile soil.

Trixie agonised long and hard about whether to give Inis access to her bank book, but in the end there was no choice. That blasted Blowski hasn't turned up again or she would have asked him – though she doesn't ask him favours as a rule. And she's out of money. She gets a hundred pounds out of the bank at a time and ekes it out on food and what-nots. Everything else is paid straight into and out of the bank, simplicity itself. She keeps the cash in the top of the piano, covered by the cloth and the fruit bowl and the photographs, quite secure.

She put her finger in the Bible in the end, letting Jesus decide whether Inis was to be trusted. After an irrelevancy: *They shall not drink wine with a song,* her inspired finger alighted upon *Devise not evil against thy neighbour, seeing he dwelleth securely by thee.* She took that as positive and, comforted, signed the authorisation slip and put the book and shopping-list through Inis's letter-flap. But her heart sank as they hit the doormat. She could have taken it the wrong way. It could have been a warning that *Inis* devises evil against *her*. She wants to tick Jesus off for being so cryptic.

She could have knocked and asked for the bank book back on some pretext or other. But what could she have said, all of a flutter as she was? And now it's too late. The die is cast. Despite the sun, she shivers.

# FREEZER

'I cannot have it,' I said.

I was surprised that he did not object. It was hardly spoken about, hardly acknowledged as real. He never mentioned that it was my fault, no contraception, what on earth had been going on in my stupid head, none of that and I was grateful. What *had* been going on in my head I couldn't begin to contemplate. There was a week when I was sick in the mornings, as discreetly as possible. I felt awful, hateful, full of poison, leeched, parasitised. I never thought of it as a baby. It was an illness, something I wanted to recover from quickly. I did not want to have to think.

Richard took me to a clinic to be counselled. In a small windowless room that stank of air-freshener, we sat side-by-side on plastic chairs, holding hands. The woman was very earnest. She wore a big purple sweater down to her knees and long Indian silver earrings. Her iron grey hair was cut very short. There were little broken veins in her cheeks that matched her sweater.

'I can't have it,' I said.

'Right.' She leant towards me. 'Would you like to tell me why?' She squinted sympathetically.

'I feel so sick . . . I've got two . . . I just can't.'

'What would happen if you *did* go ahead with the pregnancy?'

'I . . . I don't know. I couldn't. I can't cope with anything else, any more . . .' The woman blew her nose on a child's handkerchief with a nursery rhyme on it. Suddenly I wanted to laugh. I looked hard at the hairy green carpet tiles.

'My wife hasn't recovered from our daughter's birth,' Richard said, 'either physically or mentally.' I shot him a look. 'Sad as this is for us both, I really consider she's not strong enough to proceed with the pregnancy.'

The pregnancy, the pregnancy, like a sort of animal, children's drawing, blob on legs, like the gonk I used to have, I'd forgotten about that gonk until then. He used to sit on my bookcase, a knitted gonk. Mr Humpty. I wonder who knitted him?

'Right, fine.' The woman was happy to transfer her attention to Richard, rational Richard, Dr Goodie Two-shoes who knew exactly what to say. 'The usual procedure would be for me to explain the process of termination to the client, but I'm sure you . . .'

'I don't want to know,' I said. 'I just want it out. Like a tooth.' I wanted to laugh again. This time Richard gave me a look.

'If you wait in the waiting-room she can see the docs, make an appointment and Bob's your uncle.' She smiled warmly at Richard and her earrings tinkled.

What I wanted was to be put to sleep then and not to have to wake up till it was all over. The examining doctor was black and cheery. He was kind, his fingers gentle. He kept his eyes on my face as he delved inside me, pressing down on my abdomen with his other hand and whistling 'Waltzing Matilda' through his teeth.

'Seven weeks,' he said. 'I'd wait another week or two . . . can be dodgy so early on.'

'No,' I said. 'No, as soon as possible.'

There were two days to wait. In those two days I hardly spoke or even thought. I was like a robot woman, going through the motions of life with my mind frozen up. Richard tried to explain what they would do to me but I shut him up. He drove me through the snow to the clinic. Soft sticky flakes clung to the windscreen wipers. When we got out of the car I caught a flake on my tongue and felt it vanish.

Richard looked sad but I felt quite cheerful now that at last it was happening. I was put in a room with three women all dressed in white gowns, long socks and their own colourful slippers. They were quiet for a moment when I came in, then two of them resumed their conversation. The third a very young and pretty girl never said a word. She stared blankly at the wall ahead of her. I thought I should try and talk to her, to comfort her. But the other two wouldn't stop chattering, steering resolutely clear of the reason they were there. It was as if they were at a party, or in a departure lounge; trembling on the edge of something, furiously bright.

'Are they Marks and Sparks?' one said, nodding at the slippers of the other, and they were off into the subjects of shops and weather, holidays and horoscopes, talking and talking with never a gap, never a gap for the truth to get through. They even laughed, going on about some rubbish on television the night before. Rubbish that I'd watched too, filling my own head with it so I didn't have to think.

'I could have wet myself when the door opened . . .'

'And there *he* was, with that look on his face . . .'

'. . . and his bicycle clips on!'

'*Shut-up*!' I wanted to shout.

A big tear rolled down the young girl's cheek.

One by one we were removed. My time was 10.30 but it was 11.15 before it was my turn to go. I was second. The young girl went first. There were a few moments of contemplative quiet while we listened to her slippers slapping away from us on the polished floor. Then the two started up again. I felt sicker than ever because my stomach was empty. I flicked through a *Woman* magazine, avoiding the pork recipes, the advertisements for food and nappies – it didn't leave much.

Then it was my turn. I did not think about what I was doing.

The nurse was kind; the anaesthetist didn't meet my eyes. 'False teeth?' he asked. 'Crowns?'

'No.'

'Right then.' He tapped the back of my wrist.

'You'll feel a little prick.' The nurse looked at him and tittered. 'Then count to ten.'

It was all very brisk. I got to six and thought I wouldn't go to sleep. I noticed a dead fly inside the flat white glass light fitting. I woke to the sound of a voice.

'Inis dear . . . wake up now . . . all over.' For a minute I thought it was my mum. Once she came to the dentist with me when I had gas for an extraction and she was so kind. She drove me home, tucked me up on the sofa and we spent the afternoon eating strawberry ice-cream and watching a soppy film. But it was not Mum. I could not think who it was or where or what. Then I knew. For a second I felt violently relieved. It was over. I was wheeled back to my bed. The other beds were empty.

'You sleep it off,' the nurse said, 'then we'll find you a spot of lunch.' I lay on my stomach with my face in the starchy pillow. Between my legs was a fat wad of sanitary towel, in my belly a dull, comforting pain. 'All over, darling,' said my mum's voice, 'all better now.' And then I went to sleep.

Lunch, powdery grey soup and fish-paste sandwiches, was a subdued occasion. The young girl was not there. Maybe she didn't go through with it, I thought, found myself hoping. Changed her mind at the last minute, because you can do that, right up to the last second it is a matter of choice.

After lunch it was time to return to the lounge and await our escorts home. Richard was the first to arrive. When he walked into the room, he did look dear to me, his curly hair wild around his head, his eyes anxiously seeking mine. I was proud that he belonged to me.

'All right?' he asked.

'Fine.' I stood up, my knees wobbly, and he helped me on with my coat.

'Well, so long,' I said to the others.

'Good luck,' they said.

Outside it was not quite dark. I was surprised. It was like coming out of a dark cinema in the afternoon and being dazzled by daylight.

Richard kissed me in the car and gave me a yellow pot chrysanthemum. 'I love you,' he said. I squeezed his hand. 'Thank you.' I held the plant to my nose to inhale its cold florist's smell. 'I love you too,' I said and at that moment, I did.

'Do you?' He flicked me a look as he nosed the car out into the middle of the road. 'Good. Now you just relax. Everything is going to be fine. You just see.'

It was three weeks later that I started crying, three weeks later that I left them all behind. The night before I'd had a dream. I had had a little baby, a boy, just like a baby Robin. I had put him down to sleep in a room, in a strange house. It was like I imagine an army barracks to be, breeze-blocks, khaki paint on the doors. I heard him crying and I tried to go back to him, but I could not find the room. There were long branching corridors full of identical doors. I ran up and down trying door after door but either they were locked, or the rooms empty, or full of brushes and brooms. All the time I could hear my baby crying for me. Then I ran to find the caretaker, I went out of the building and into a town, a seaside town. Bonny was sitting on a corner with a collecting tin round her neck, collecting for widows and orphans. 'Go back,' she barked when she saw me. I ran back to the house – but it had gone. There was only the outline of where it had been on the grass and a big tree standing by. The crying had stopped. The baby had gone.

I'd woken sweating and shouting. Richard held me. 'It's all right,' he said, 'It's only a dream.' I let him hold me, my ear against his chest, listening to the thud, thud, thud of his sensible heart. But with an awful draining away of my spirits I recognised that it was not *only* a dream.

I cannot believe Richard has not found me. I know he promised, when I rang him up, well I gave him no choice, but still he knows I am at my wits' end. Who knows what I might not do? A woman who leaves her children could do anything. After that, anything is easy. Or perhaps I haven't properly left. I sent them another card on Saturday, a Mondrian – whom I can't stand but Richard likes. The cards I have sent will be postmarked Sheffield. He might have been to look for me, for all I know. I haven't even changed my name. What kind of bid for freedom is that? He could at this very moment be cruising the streets of Sheffield peering at all the women with long brown hair. Ha!

'It's not a failure to accept that you need help,' he'd said to me a few days before, when I thought I was all right, maybe a bit quiet, things were going on in my head but not so that he'd know. I kept the freezer filled so full you could hardly shut the door but I couldn't use anything out of it. It had to be kept full. If a single fish-finger was used I would worry until I had bought a new sealed pack. I bought fresh food every day, better for you anyway. Richard was appreciative. He thought it was a sign of stability. But it was only that I could not bear the panicky gap in my mind that something missing from the freezer made. No doubt it's half empty now, half packets of things, loose peas rattling round, empty frozen air. But that is no longer my concern. Here I have no freezer. I eat in cafés, or content myself with biscuits and toast. It is such a relief to have no dealing with food, with the planning of meals, the lurking doubts about nutrition, of finicky children, of varied diets. A relief to be free of food.

And anyway I didn't want help. Only space. He knows that. 'Mummy needs space,' he said to Robin once to explain my mood.

'And I need a spaceship,' Robin retorted, making me laugh. The last time I remember laughing.

Richard's given me space and time. Generous to a fault. Or maybe not. Pauline will be well settled in by now, in her absolute element. One hand in my freezer, the other clasping my children's hearts. They will be well cared for, successfully lied to, no doubt. *Mummy's having a little holiday.* They will be fine. If they never saw me again I think they would be fine. I am not indispensable. That should be a relief.

I must go out. It is sunny today, like spring. The sun shines through the thick splashed dust of the kitchen window. I only have winter clothes with me, jeans, thick leggings, sweaters, boots. I can't contemplate buying anything else. I must go out for some air and to fetch Trixie's things. I feel terrible, a splitting headache and my nose all blocked. But I promised I'd go to the bank for her, and fetch some shopping. All I want to do is sleep. But I will go out first and get it done.

# CROESUS

Does she think I was born yesterday? Face all pasty innocent. Bleach, bin-bags, tuna, cheese. How much can that come to? Of course, she'd conveniently lost the receipt, *of course*. I didn't want to make a scene, not unless I was sure. I didn't make a scene. But how much *could* that little lot come to? £2 top. And when I counted the money, there was £94.45. Which would make the shopping £5.55 which is simply not possible. She has robbed me. I have been robbed by my kindly smiling neighbour, robbed and swindled and taken for a fool.

I knew, I knew. Somehow deep down I knew her for a cheat.

I said nothing. I thanked her and counted the money out, slowly. Oh I saw the sliding of her eyes, panic that's what it was, panic at having been rumbled. I could have faced her with it, I should have. Instead I said nothing. *Turn the other cheek* was in my head. Her eyes kept straying to the kitchen but if she thought I was going to make her a cup of tea she had another think coming.

I counted out the money again, emphasising but not querying the total. And the cheek of the girl, oh it quite took my breath away.

'Surprising how it adds up, isn't it?'

Ha! The brass-plated cheek.

She hung around, though I gave her no encouragement.

She blew her nose on a bit of lavatory paper. 'I've got a stinking cold,' she whined. I put the purchases away very pointedly but left the money on the table, plain as day, an accusation. Was she expecting me to let her see where I put it? That's it. Now I've given her my bank book she'll know I'm loaded. Rich as Croesus. Lucky she doesn't know the half of it.

'Can I help?' she sniffed.

*Help yourself more like.* She wandered round the room, peering about, fiddling with my things. Looking at the photographs on the piano, as if to say, I know this is where you keep it. Though how can she know? Nobody knows, not even Blowski whom I would trust with my life.

'Is this you?' she asked, indicating the picture of me as a child in my stretched dress. *Why? What's it to you.* I didn't reply.

'Well, I'd better go,' she said. 'Just put a note through when you want something next.' And she was off leaving a sort of smell in the air of avarice.

I made myself a cup of tea and tried to settle to the Good Morning programme. The couple on the sofa looked like puppets nodding and grimacing. Somehow I couldn't take it in, not like I usually do, couldn't get myself absorbed.

You see I was quite devastated by her treachery. I'd rather a thug brandishing a poker made off with every penny. At least that's honest, it's what it is – robbery – not the insincerity of a swindler masquerading as a good neighbour. *My ship's come in*, she will be thinking, *loaded old woman on tap*, *candy off a baby*, all that. Or maybe she thinks if she ingratiates herself successfully enough I'll leave it to her. 'Have you any family?' she asked me, oh, early on, when I still took her at face value. Well I see the way the land lies now.

Oh she generates unease. I've never felt it before, not so clearly. Why does she live all alone and why is she so quiet? What I would not give for a bit of normal noise, even something to complain about, a radio loud at night, a row with her boyfriend though there's no such person on the scene, sometimes I wonder if she isn't of the other persuasion –

well she's hardly feminine – but then I haven't seen any women there either.

It's revenge that's what it is. It came to me while I watched how to lengthen curtains by adding a strip of contrasting fabric above the hem. Rather attractive. I would have been good at being poor. Revenge. I would not let her take my photograph and now this! Oh I'll never be able to settle, not enjoy my television, never settle, never sleep tonight.

It's not the money it's the treachery. She is a viper, a vixen. It's easier for a camel to go through the eye of a needle I know, and yet, and yet, there's Proverbs too . . . I cannot forget Proverbs . . . *riches certainly make themselves wings; they fly as an eagle towards heaven.* But it is not that, not that no. Personal gain is the last thing on my mind. I am not thinking of myself. I am thinking about the eventual destination of the money. I am thinking of the Salvation Army. She must have stolen a couple of pounds, at least. Not much, but it's not the amount so much as the principle. Someone who would *cheat* an old lady of two pounds would cheat her of two hundred or two thousand or two million.

Stop, stop, listen, sing:

> *Angry words, O let them never,*
> *From the tongue unbridled slip!*
> *May the heart's best impulse ever,*
> *Check them ere they soil the lip.*
>
> *Always cheerful, always cheerful.*
> *All our words let love control;*
> *Always cheerful, always cheerful,*
> *Constant sunshine in the soul*

Yes, Jesus, yes. But it is so hard. Oh I will not rest today, will not.

# BOY

If she does not let me out I will

If she does not let me out

I will

She will be sorry

If she makes me angry . . .

I am a danger if I come out and I am angry

How can I out?

If she does not let me out I will

# FREE LUNCH

Something I started to do after I had Billie, was steal. At first it was accidental. There I was in Sainsbury's, with Billie in her sling and Robin in the trolley-seat kicking his legs and fidgeting. Exhausted, I unloaded the mass of groceries from the trolley and pushed it through the check-out – genuinely overlooking the bag of disposable nappies that hung from the hook on the front. I noticed the nappies, after I'd paid, while I loaded all the stuff back into the trolley to wheel out to the car. I opened my mouth to say . . . and then shut it again. After all, the check-out assistant had overlooked it too.

Driving home I felt a sudden rush of triumph, exhilaration, glee, I'd got away with something. I sang 'My Old Man's a Dustman', which made Robin, strapped into his seat in the back, laugh, but also, I saw in the mirror, give me a very Richard-like what's-got-into-her sort of look.

I didn't tell Richard about the nappies.

And after that, I did it almost every time. There'd be the nappies which were a cinch and I'd always start off by taking an apple or a packet of crisps for Robin to eat while we went round.

It gave me such a sense of freedom. Such a *buzz*, my heart flittery-fluttering, all my senses heightened, the colours of the packages on the shelves glowing neon; the smell of baking bread bringing juices to my mouth making me hungry for the first time in ages.

Robin began to love shopping trips because they made me

so light-hearted and generous. I wonder if it's affected him permanently? When he's grown-up will he love supermarkets, subconsciously remembering the jolly times we had? Maybe he'll be a pervert, haunting the aisles, turned on by wire trolleys and plastic carrier-bags.

Shopping was the highlight of the week and it rubbed off even on to Richard. I used to go on Friday afternoons so the check-outs would be busy, the workers worn out and flustered. Because I was in a good mood I'd buy generous treats for the children, and for Richard and me. Things that were easy to cook and great to eat, salmon steaks or Peking duck that only needed a minute in the microwave, ready-prepared salads that Richard disapproved of – if he found the packets – and expensive bottles of wine. So we all looked forward to Fridays.

The stealing was the focus for me; the shopping just a useful by-product. One technique was to put a bag in the trolley and conceal items under that, or slip small things into my handbag or pocket. I got a lot of make-up that way: lipsticks in all sorts of unsuitable colours, I wasn't fussy. I didn't want the things, I wanted only to get them for nothing.

*You don't get owt for nowt this side of the grave*, my dad used to say, echoing his Yorkshire grandad. And Richard took the same line: *there's no such thing as a free lunch*. It cheered me up to prove them wrong. I never felt bad about the stealing. I didn't think of it as a problem, it was more a sort of hobby, a way of bringing excitement into my life, making Friday technicolor in a black-and-white week. Some people hang-glide or bungee jump for their kicks. I just stole.

But then I did something else. My neighbour, Jan, was a good friend. Probably my best 'mummy' friend. Her Lily plays with Robin and I suppose Tamara will play with Billie when they're older. Jan is a knitwear designer and she makes me feel terrible. She can't help it. She makes me feel inadequate.

I could have confided in Jan instead of running away.

I bet she's hurt that I didn't. She would have helped but I didn't want help. I only wanted to know why she could cope when I couldn't.

Jan is tall, slim and beautiful in a classy ageless way; she's talented and industrious; she's stylish even under pressure; she's tidy; she's sexy – I've seen even Richard's eyes linger on her bare shoulders at barbecue parties; she's a wonderful mother who never raises her voice and she's in love with her handsome architect husband. I like her very much – but I also hate her.

Jan was the person I saw most often before my . . . before I left.

'Sure you're all right?' she'd say sometimes, looking at me quizzically with her slanting green eyes. 'I could always have the kids for an hour . . .' I sometimes wondered if Richard had told her that he thought I couldn't cope. It's the sort of thing he would do, enlist support. Well sod that, I thought. I didn't confide in her because she was too perfect. If only she'd just put on a few pounds, or bawl at the children, or let her hair get greasy or her house plants die.

But I can hardly blame my frailties on her.

And one day, in her bathroom, I saw a marcasite brooch on the shelf, a beautiful one, a little curving lizard with the most delicate splayed feet. She wore it often and I'd always admired it. I don't know what made me – but I took it. I slipped it quickly in my pocket before I could stop myself. And then, and this is most strange, I forgot it, forgot I'd taken it. So there was none of the triumph I felt after Sainsbury's. There was no point.

Two days later I found the brooch in the pocket of my jeans when I was sorting out the wash. I was aghast, remembering the scene, my quick hand stealing. I felt sick when I saw it. I didn't want it. I could never have worn it, anyway, it was so much hers. Next time I went round I dropped it on the gravel front path and pretended to find it. Pretended successfully, I'm pretty sure. I don't think she saw through me.

'Thank you,' she said, hugging me. 'I'm so relieved. It's valuable you know, an anniversary present from Steve – used to be his grandmother's. I'd looked everywhere. Must have been this scallywag.' She ruffled Lily's hair.

'Weren't,' Lily said, and Jan raised her eyebrows at me and grinned. So it was all right. But still.

It was in trying to prove Richard wrong about the free lunch that I spoiled everything. I thought just for the secret kick of it, I'd serve him a free dinner. I thought how delightful it would be to watch him eat it, watch him eat his own words.

He loves steak. I wouldn't choose it myself, but this was to be his dinner. Grilled rump, mushrooms, a spinach salad and a robust wine, something quite special.

Billie flopped asleep in the baby-carrier on my back. I let Robin walk round as long as he behaved and pinched him a banana to eat. Everything was very smooth to begin with. I slid the spinach and mushrooms under the bag in the trolley. Then I piled the legitimate stuff on top – even the nappies, I thought I'd pay for them for a change. The wine I chose carefully, hesitating between French and Australian and ending up with Chilean Merlot because it had the nicest label. I was wearing my kagoul with its long map-pocket in order to conceal the bottle in there. It just fitted. I left the steaks until last. I selected a well-sealed pack that wouldn't bleed, and slid it in my handbag.

A supervisor was standing at the end of the check-out as I went through. 'Can I help you pack, Madam?' he said. He did so very methodically, clearing his throat and stopping a couple of times to blow his nose on a crumpled tissue. He lifted the bag out of the trolley to reveal the spinach and mushrooms. 'Whoops!' I said. 'Nearly got away with them!' But he didn't smile. I was very cool but it was as if electricity was pulsing in my veins and my ears were ringing with tension. I was conscious of the weight of the wine slanting across my heart, sure he could see the bulge. When I had paid, the superviser said, 'Is that everything Madam?'

'Yes,' I said.

'Are you quite certain?'

My mind darted. I wavered. 'What?' I said. 'What do you mean?'

In the manager's office I wept. Poor Robin was confused but Billie didn't notice a thing. 'I'm so sorry,' I kept saying. 'I don't know how I could have been so silly . . .' They had found the steak in my bag, despite my carefulness, leaking blood on to the cotton lining. But they hadn't found the wine. I kept my kagoul on. 'I didn't realise what I was doing . . .' I said. Robin's frightened face was the only thing that made me feel really bad. Someone cuddled Billie and gave Robin a tube of Smarties.

They didn't call the police. The manager, though stern, was kind. He was one of Richard's patients, he said. And he and his wife had small children, he understood the tizzy women got themselves in on shopping day, he'd give me the benefit of the doubt this time. But he did ask me not to shop at Sainsbury's for a month or two. And made it clear that another time the police would be involved.

So it was all right. But all the coloured fizz had gone out of the day. We ate fish-fingers with the kids that night, washed down with orange squash. Richard never asked me why. I'd got away with the wine but couldn't bear to look at it. It's still in the cupboard under the sink at home, behind the shoe-cleaning stuff – unless Richard's found it.

I will never steal again.

It's too corny to say I've learned my lesson. It isn't that, it's just that it's spoilt for me now. It was my game, my secret gamble. Now it's wrecked.

# INHERITANCE

Not quite a year after I'd left home to join the Salvation Army, my father died. If I had known he was to die so soon, I might have waited. And then perhaps things would have worked out better. But he did die, suddenly and unsaved. I'd always presumed Mother would go first, there was so little life in her.

Auntie Ba had been to see me shortly before. I'd sent her my address, and she'd called in after she'd been to visit my mother. Proudly, I sang to her; together we sang 'The Raggle-Taggle Gypsies'. She hugged me and said, 'I always knew you had it in you. There's never been a girl in the family yet that couldn't sing. Look, I know what Charles's attitude is to . . .', she gestured at my new uniform, 'but let me tell you Trixie Bell, *I* am proud of you and so would your mother be if she was in a fit state.' She tried to persuade me to visit my parents. 'They miss you, whatever your stubborn father says.'

'The only way I can *be*,' I replied, 'is separate from them.' She nodded sadly. 'Perhaps one day,' I said. Sincere or not I am not sure.

And then there was the letter. Father had been taken seriously ill with a stroke, although he was only fifty-five. He had collapsed on to the floor during Sunday afternoon tea and Mother had done nothing. It had been Louise's afternoon off and she had only found him, found them, when she came in next morning: Mother sitting wet and cold in her chair by the ashes in the grate, Father stretched out stiff on the floor. I have a picture of them frozen like that lodged in my head, clear as a snap-shot. The letter made my heart beat so violently that I had to sit down. I did not know what to feel. I sat on the edge of my bed, the letter shivering between my fingers, waiting to be hit by emotion. Sorrow, I expected, and guilt. Perhaps relief. But there was nothing.

I wore my uniform to the funeral, not mourning for that is not the Salvation Army line. To wear mourning would be a negative reflection on the providence of God. Mary said she'd come with me but I did not want her there. I wheeled my mother into the church in a chair. I don't know if she realised what was going on. I don't know what went on behind those dull eyes. There were no tears. Her hands gripped the arms of the wheelchair so hard that her knuckles stood out like yellow marbles. She had caught a chill on the night of Father's death sitting in her soaked dress, stiff and still all night, and the only sound that came from her was a sound like rustling paper that was her breath. I sang the hymns loudly and proudly, thinking that perhaps Mother might hear me, that I might reach her. Now that *he* was gone I felt fonder of her.

The coffin was draped with the firm's flag. The church was full. Aunt Harriet, my father's sister from York, had turned up and organised the funeral tea. The house reeked of boiled ham and in the kitchen were basins of water crusted on top with white fat.

Auntie Ba only came to the church for the service. She stood beside me in the churchyard, one hand in mine, one on my mother's shoulder and watched while the coffin was lowered. Since Mother was incapable, I flung a handful of soil on to the coffin lid, a dry rattle of grit. A little sigh of something like satisfaction came from Mother and I looked at her sharply, but there was no expression. I saw the eyes of the other mourners upon me waiting for tears, for a seemly show of grief, but there was no feeling in me. I tried to imagine my father under the coffin lid, a scowl on his face, fists clenched, dead eyes glaring furiously up into the dark.

Auntie Ba left then. Her older daughter, Bea, was about to give birth and she was preoccupied with that. Naturally she wanted to be there to greet her first grandchild. I stood by Mother's chair receiving condolences.

'When the time's right,' Mr Bolt, Father's manager said to me, embarrassed by his own forthrightness but unable to resist his curiosity, 'we'll have to hear your plans.'

'Plans?' I said.

'For the business.'

'Oh, I'm not to inherit,' I said. 'Nothing to do with me, Mr Bolt.'

'Then whom?' he said.

I shook my head. I really had no idea. Father hadn't been one for having ties with people. Aunt Harriet was married to a wealthy man and there was no particular fondness between my father and herself. He certainly wouldn't leave a scrap to Auntie Ba or her family. There was no one else.

When the solicitor read the will the following day, I found that I was wrong, Father had not done what he'd threatened. He had not cut me off. I was to inherit everything. Whatever he had not been, Father *had* been a good businessman. He had recently turned over most of his capacity to the manufacture of rubber tyres, and despite continual labour problems, business was flourishing. I was suddenly a very wealthy woman. There were two conditions attached to my inheritance: one; that I, personally, take care of my mother for the rest of her life and two; that the Salvation Army was not to benefit, in my lifetime, from my wealth.

I lay in bed that night staring at the flowered curtains and realising that they were *mine*. That this was *my* house now. That I had money to burn if I wanted. I was young single and rich. It was so like Father to attach those conditions to the money. A last spiteful jab of his finger from beyond the grave. But I was more worldly than I had supposed. I accepted the conditions and thus the inheritance.

Next morning, according to the solicitor's advice, I became a sleeping-partner in the business, the major shareholder. I wanted nothing more to do with the business. I knew nothing of it. As a girl I had not been considered worthy to be told anything about it; as a woman I chose not to learn.

I walked back to Curry Street to see my friends. I didn't mention the money but told them that I was moving back home, temporarily, to nurse my mother. When I returned I walked round every room, except the mirror room, touching the things that were mine, though still imbued with my father's essence. Apart from Louise, I was once more alone with my mother. I sang hymns to her.

'Look Mother, listen, I can sing!' Every morning, though it was late summer and fine outside, Louise lit the fire because it was a dark room that didn't catch the sun except on summer evenings, and Mother's stillness made her cold. We sat one on either side of the hearth. I had my song book with me and I sang hymn after hymn. Louise joined in the well-known ones sometimes, as she moved about the house. When I didn't know the tune I made it up. I sang until my throat ached and my mouth was dry.

Mother sat unmoving while I sang at her, while I tried to make myself love and forgive her. Anyone else I could have forgiven anything, but this was my mother. Her face was yellow-white and the lines looked dark in the shadowy firelight. Her hair, which had turned silver, was pulled back from her face, I did it for her every morning like that, brushing hard and wrenching it back tight like she used to do to me, but still little curls escaped and fizzed out round her forehead.

'I forgive you,' I said once but the words jarred in the air like a lie.

'The Reflective Punishment,' I went on. 'What Father did. What you let him do.' But it was no good. I couldn't make myself mean it. God has the power to forgive all sins but I am not God. The more I tried to forgive her the more my voice retreated. I heard and felt it weakening. 'Jesus bids us shine with a pure, clear, light . . .' I sang and my voice withered to a dull flat thing, and my tongue was thick.

'I wish I could leave,' I said, and even my speaking voice was changed, was hesitant and childish. I could never bear to say my name when I was a child and a stranger asked it. Trixie Bell. It sounded so silly and fanciful like a fairy name but I was not a fairy child, nothing like, so I always mumbled. Now I mumbled again. I almost expected her to say, 'What?' and lean forward irritably, jerking her chin, 'Speak up girl.'

The brown curtains were drawn against the bay-window. I remembered a little girl sitting behind them, her knees drawn tightly to her chest. I wanted to leave the house that moment. I knew I must put my mother to bed and then I would have to go out. I could go and visit Mary. I might catch the end of the meeting. I needed a breath of fresh air, of friendship, of God. I was scared. It was ridiculous but I was scared of my helpless mother. Silently, I prayed. The fear was nonsense, nothing.

The back room had been converted into a bedroom for my mother since it was too hard to get her up and down stairs. Louise helped me get her through there and we sat her on the commode. She did nothing.

'All right?' Louise asked. 'Can you manage, only I'm meeting Roddy tonight.' Despite Father's prediction, Louise had found herself a young man, as plain and steady as herself. She was quite preoccupied with him, and had become unusually sloppy with the cooking. Not that Mother noticed, and I hardly cared.

'You go and have fun,' I said.

Mother had grown very light. I realised I had not fed her. I thought I'd get Louise to scramble her some eggs in the morning and make sure she ate them, every scrap. Her chest was rattly and she panted a little as I moved her.

'Tomorrow we'll have the doctor back,' I said. I spooned a little water into her mouth and then some of the thick black linctus that had been prescribed. Some of it went down but most of it ran stickily down her chin and on to her chest. While

I undressed her, I tried not to breathe in the smell of her body, something familiar gone stale. She was burning hot. I tried not to look at the flat skin bags of her breasts. Or, rather, I did look, with compassion. I was still wearing my uniform and it seemed to be the only thing holding me upright, reminding me of what I was now, a grown-up soldier for the Lord not a child.

I lay Mother on her side in bed. She was bent into a sort of sitting position. I covered her up. I don't think the sheets were damp, that is just an idea that has crept into my head from somewhere. I looked down at her, her poor old face, the skin thin and slack. I considered kissing her. 'Goodnight Mother,' I whispered and then I pinched her. I don't know why. But I pinched her. Hard. I pinched the flesh on her wrist. Only once. It was hot and loose. She made not a sound. I turned out the light and left the room.

I did not go out that night. I could not bring myself to face anyone. I went early to bed and lay sleeplessly gazing at my uniform that hung on the back of the door. It looked like a dwarfed me: the waist of the skirt inside the shoulders of the jacket, the bonnet hanging on a hook above, tipped down to hide the empty face. I was afraid I would have an absence and there was only me in the house. Me and Mother. I could not rid myself of the memory of her skin between my fingers, hot, loose, ill skin sliding between the pads of my finger and thumb. I pinched my own wrist but the skin was firm and warm, wedded to the flesh beneath.

I lay all night with the lamp lit beside my bed, watching the shadows, listening to the night. I did not want to sleep. I wanted to make sure I stayed with it, stayed myself. I averted my eyes from the dwarfish mockery of myself on the back of the door that wagged and nodded its head knowingly when I did look. I thought I should get up and make a pot of tea, sit and read the Bible until daybreak. I could go and sit with Mother, turn her so that she did not get sore, read soothing Psalms to her. But I did not go to Mother.

I thought I should give up the money in order to be free. When I thought Father had cut me off I had felt relieved and free. It was the happiest time in my life, looking back I believe that to be true, so why could I not give it up again? Regain that freedom. I do not know, though during the creeping hours of that long, long night, I almost vowed to do so.

I fell asleep towards dawn and I had a Benjamin Charles dream. The struggle, the suffocation, the kill. I woke as always sweating and whimpering but not in bed this time, not in bed but in the sitting-room, the brown curtains pulled back, my face pressed against the window so that condensation wet my face and my fingers scrabbled squeakily against the glass as if trying to get through, to get out, trying to be born out of the place where I murdered Benjamin Charles. Only it was not murder, of course it was not, Auntie Ba said it was not. I was only an innocent baby and anyway, I loved him, I would have loved him, my brother, the one I was meant to be, I loved him so why would I kill him? It was not me. It was not my fault.

I went back to bed and this time, since it was nearly day, I slept quite calmly and peacefully. I was woken by a knocking at the door. Louise put her head inside.

'Trixie, are you awake?' she asked.

'What is it?' I could see that she was distressed.

'It's Mrs Bell . . . I went to do her fire first thing and . . .'

'All right. I'll come.' I climbed out of bed and put on my dressing-gown.

Louise stood by the door wringing her hands together. 'I think, I don't rightly know, but oh Trixie, I think she's passed on.' Her voice ended in a wail. My heart pounded with excitement and terror.

Mother was lying on her back, her head flat on the sheet, her pillow on the floor. I drew back the curtains. In the soft morning sunlight her face was blue and her eyes wide open.

'Go and fetch the doctor, Louise,' I said. I put my hand on my mother's cheek. Last night her skin had burned, now it was barely warm. I picked up the pillow, lifted her heavy rolling head and settled her. I went to the window and opened it wide. The sunshine smelled of the start of autumn, a blackbird sang from the birch tree on the front lawn.

I turned back to Mother. On her wrist was a pinched up ridge of skin. I pressed it flat with my thumb. I pressed down the lids of her eyes and knelt by her side, praying. When I opened my eyes again, one of hers had opened too, as if she was winking at me. I left the room.

Another funeral. Smaller this time. Less fuss made. Auntie Ba came again and stayed with me for two days. She was sad, of course, wept, reminisced about a person I never knew, a jolly girl, always joking, who loved to dance and sing. 'Quite the little actress,' Ba said. 'My brother used to call her drama queen. Melodrama, more like. But she was funny. She was fun. I wish *you* could have known her as a girl.

'I don't *entirely* blame Charles for squashing the life out of her,' she said. 'Her mother . . . she was taken similarly in middle-age . . . Maybe it's something hereditary. I do hope not.' She looked at me. 'I don't know . . .' She trailed off, then took my hand and squeezed it.

'I hope I did right by you as a child,' she said. 'Sometimes I wanted so much to take you home with me. But I thought best leave well alone. Separating parent from child . . . well it's not natural is it? Not that Charles would have let you go. Quite a one for appearances, your father.'

We travelled to King's Cross by taxi. 'You're a rich young woman now,' she said, as we kissed goodbye. 'You look after yourself.' She hugged me tight. 'Life is a trial . . . but there is happiness too. She smiled to herself and I knew she was thinking of Bea's new baby, Gregory – quite a little character already, she said. It was new life that preoccupied her rather than death.

'You are . . . all right?'

'Yes,' I said. I thought she meant was I grief-stricken, was I coping with my double bereavement. Afterwards I remembered the look she gave me. Perhaps she was asking me more. But at that moment I *did* feel all right. I was sad but I was free. I thought now the absences had to stop completely and forever because now, my life was my own.

'You've got your new friends, at least,' Ba said, leaning out of the carriage window. 'They'll be a great support. Will you stay at home?'

I shook my head.

'But it's such a lovely house . . . and you could put others up . . . that nice girl, Mary – I didn't say at the time but those lodgings of yours . . .' she shuddered and pulled a face. The noise of the train filled the platform, clouds of steam swept back as the train began to creak forward.

I walked along beside the train. 'Maybe,' I mouthed, then blew a kiss and stood and watched it depart, thrilled to the core by the chugging roar, the taste of steam.

I walked all the way back to Holloway deep in thought. It hadn't occurred to me that I could bring my friends into my parents' – my – house. But I could see the sense in it. It was a big, spacious house. To confront my fear of it with my faith and my friends, to fill it with joy and song might banish the shadows and reflections of my childhood more soundly than simply running away.

And it would be one in the eye for my father.

# WOMAN WITH A CROW

I suppose I will go home. Of course I will have to. Of course there was never any question that I would not. That is why Richard hasn't come looking for me. He knows me. He allows me space. Even from a distance he is always right. Always bloody right. Which is better than always being wrong.

I haven't worked today or for the past few days. Restless, ants in your pants, my dad would have said. Wandering round the shops, I found a couple of pounds in my pocket. Lovely, that surprise. Like winning something. I'd been thinking fondly of Richard and I wanted to buy him a special card. I chose a reproduction of Picasso's *Woman with a Crow*. Against an intensely blue background a sad-faced woman holds a crow to her breast, her long fingers cup it most tenderly and her lips are against its black head as if she might kiss it. When I saw the card in the shop, I started. It seemed to apply to me somehow, as if it was a message. I am afraid of rooks and crows. To tell the truth I don't know the difference between them, but it doesn't matter, they stand for the same thing. They are all black, like scraps of the darkness that I do not understand come free, flapping like old gloves or rags and in raw voices crying out my pain. They are the badness in me which I should accept like Picasso's woman. A sad face, hands that are strong yet tender holding a piece of darkness close to her heart.

It is that dark part of me that Richard doesn't know. But that is stupid, how can he? How can I blame him for that?

Good grief. I think I must be feverish. I've written the card to Richard and put my address. No message other than that. I wanted to say *I love you* but my fingers would not let me write it, I am not ready. Before I go home I need a bit more time. For what? It is just a sense I have. For a sort of finishing off.

Trixie was weird this morning. I delivered her her shopping and there was a sort of atmosphere. Almost as if she doesn't like me. I do like her, feel a sort of sympathy for her. But I do not know her.

I like to look at other people's houses, the inside of them, they are so much more expressive than people themselves of their state of mind, of the inside of their heads. Once when I was babysitting for Jan I spent an evening searching for dirt and found none. Not even dust on top of the wardrobe or under the bed. I felt grubby just looking. Trixie's bathroom made me sad, narrow and clean, smelling of damp and something she'd washed her underwear in. Above the bath hung a row of peach silky bloomers and thick brown stockings, pointy-toed, swaying in the draught from the window. All perfectly blameless. She has hard lavatory paper, I didn't think anyone would use that from choice, slippery, useless squares out of a box on the wall. NOW WASH YOUR HANDS is printed on each sheet. Why that should have made me feel so melancholy, I don't know. I don't know what to do. What can I do? She is not my responsibility. The idea of leaving is difficult, but I have to go. My children need me more. Or at least, I need them.

This is an awful cold. My head feels stuffed full of something dry and hard; I can't think straight; I'm shivery; when I lean over there's a deep dizzy pain in my sinuses; when I lie down, I cough. I want to be rid of the cold before I go home. I've bought lemons, honey, whisky and I'll stay in bed today and maybe tomorrow too. The heating is barely working and it's got colder again. That's why I hate this time of year, early spring or so you might think, you might just relax a bit, open out a bit – then blink and it's winter once more. I bought a hot-water bottle when I was out and it's rubbery and comforting to cuddle against my chest and sniff. Lemon pips float on the surface of my hot toddy. Now I've written the card to Richard, even though I haven't posted it yet, he's on my mind. How I have despised his strength. Oh he is annoying, no one could deny that, he is smug, he is never wrong. And I – I am often wrong. I act hastily. I give things up. What have I ever completed? It is just like me to leave my children. Just what you'd expect. *Lacks application* my school reports used to say. And what have I ever achieved?

There is this flight. If you can call that an achievement.

And my photographs.

# SHELTER

Not a sound from her. Not a door's bang, not a creak, not a stir. Is she ashamed? I haven't had a wink of sleep. I knelt on the floor last night and prayed, never mind my throbbing shin. I put on my uniform and sang my songs loud and clear, right through the wall for her to hear. I sang 'Oft Our Trust Has Known Betrayal' and 'Surrounded By A Host Of Foes' – not only a message to her but also a plea to God to help me, to put my mind at rest so I could simmer down and watch my programmes, or get some sleep.

In bed, awake, I tried to soothe myself with a good memory. There are few enough of them. Good memories. Why doesn't my Blowski come? He is a selfish, neglectful old blighter sometimes. I want to tell him what has happened. I want him to know her in her true colours.

The weather has had a change of heart; the cold has returned; the frost is like iron on the soil and buds are shrinking back into themselves. The petals of the flowering currant are blighted with the frost. And where *is* Blowski? It is too long since I saw him and in two days it is my birthday. He always comes on my birthday. If he did not come, I could not bear it.

I did take up Auntie Ba's suggestion and open up my house to my friends. For the first time in my life I had friends. It was hard to know *how* to have them. I could hardly accept the open smiles, other people's belief that what I seemed to be was what I was. I was overwhelmed. I did not know how to *be* with many, most of them. I was very shy and although I had found my singing voice and loved to sing more than anything, I still spoke too quietly and people had to ask me to repeat myself and when I repeated whatever I had said it sounded weak and hardly worth the saying. So I was not much of one for conversation. Mary was my real, my best, friend. Mary Bright. Just the right name – she had a bright face, quite ordinary but beautiful when she smiled or sang because it glowed like a rosy lamp with the light inside her. She was only six years my senior but it might have been twenty. She was mature at twenty-eight, capable and trustworthy and she liked me. Really, she did like me. And her liking was the first thing to make me like myself a little.

It was Jesus that guided me to the Citadel that day when I first met Mary and Harold, of that I am convinced. Harold was a friend too. He was Mary's fiancé. It had always been expected that they'd marry. They grew up together, the children of Salvation Army officers, he a year Mary's junior. They were the two people I loved best in the world, apart from Auntie Ba. Apart from Jesus, of course.

Mary and Harold helped me after my parents' death, prayed with me every night. I confided in them the problem of my inheritance. We decided that I could contribute to the Salvation Army by keeping the house. Mary stayed there and paid what she would have paid in rent to the Army and there was room for others too.

I was well nigh happy. The first thing I did was fix a red and gold Salvation Army badge in the centre of the mantelpiece, the first thing anyone would see when they entered the room. The house filled with my new friends, trooping up and down the stairs, laughing, singing, making a wonderful racket. Furniture was shifted so the rooms looked different. I was all right when the others were there but if I was ever alone I could hear the rustling of my parents' disbelief, the creak of their outrage. Sometimes when the others were there and I felt strong inside I almost wanted to laugh at their helplessness in the face of what I was doing. But that was spite and I had to ask God's forgiveness for the pleasure it gave me.

Mary chose the room with bars on the window. I had not

been inside it for years. An almost bare room with an oval mirror hanging over the empty hearth.

'Why the bars?' Mary asked as she walked round. I stood with my back to the open door. She walked to the window and touched them. 'It's like a prison cell.'

'I don't know,' I said. 'Don't choose this room, it's gloomy, there are nicer rooms.'

The mirror hung on the wall like a wide oval eye. I tried to keep my own eyes away from it.

'I see what you mean,' Mary said, 'it does have a melancholy feel, but with a bit of fresh paint, some flowers . . . it's got good light. If we get the bars removed from the window, I can't be doing with them. I like it Trixie and we can leave the bigger rooms for others. I don't need much space. I'll ask Harry about the bars.'

She went to the mirror and looked at her own face. Just an ordinary unselfconscious look. I let my eyes travel to her reflection. I held my breath. Her face looked quite normal but vague. She gazed at herself as she continued speaking, saying the room needed airing, needed a fire lighting in the grate, probably the chimney sweeping, and my fast heart skittered. As she spoke and moved slightly, the glass warped her face, pulled her mouth askew. Even Mary, it even did it to Mary. She seemed not to notice, turned away, went back to the window and peered out.

'Nice view of the street . . . plane trees . . . lime . . . Yes, Trixie, this will do me very well.' She turned back to me and smiled. 'It's a good house,' she said. 'When can I move in?'

'Now,' I said, 'as soon as you can, as you like.'

'Tomorrow, after the meeting?'

'Yes, let's go down, I'll make some tea.'

Louise had left after my mother's death, left to marry her young man, so the kitchen was mine and I liked that. I liked the kitchen best of all because it didn't feel like my parents' territory. It had a warm and wholesome air. Mary and I drank our tea sitting close to the range.

'It's cosy,' she said, and I was proud.

I really wanted to burn all the furniture, rip down the curtains, roll up the carpets and start again. But the house was well furnished, the curtains and carpets had years in them. Mary wouldn't hear of it.

I did take down the lace curtains and I did open the windows, chipping away at thick layers of paint, to let air and light into the house. I took down the mirrors from the walls and stored them in the cellar. I removed some of the paintings. The one I loved, the two girls picking flowers, I put in my room by my bed so that I could gaze at it as I fell asleep and on waking. The sun shone from the frame as if the picture was a window opening on to another world, a happy childish world. Even with my new friends, even with my love of God, with music inside me, even with my parents dead, I would still have climbed through that frame, if it had been possible, to be one of those girls, bare-footed, with buttercup and daisy-chains in my hair.

Because, although I had had no absences since my parents' death, although I was as near to happy as I have ever been, there was always the fear. The fear of what I was. The fear of being found out.

But for a long time everything was almost as it should be and I grew gradually less afraid. I wore my uniform proudly. I thought about other things, my new life, my new concerns. For the first time I was looking outwards at the world and at the suffering of *other* people. I worked long hours at the shelter on Bothwell Street. It was miserable stinking work but I never took a single moment for granted. I never stopped being grateful for every normal minute that passed.

The shelter was a terrible place, like a barn, a place I could never have slept in. But we kept it clean, we charged a few pennies for soup, tea, bread and cheese, the chance to wash, a bed for the night. There were seventy beds in the one dormitory, too close together I thought, so that the men's breath must have mingled as they lay in bed, but more space would have meant fewer beds, and the beds were always full. We always had to turn men away.

The poor wretches turned up at six o'clock each evening with their handfuls of greasy pennies to pay for their night's lodgings and were able to wash, were fed, were able to rest in reasonable comfort. But it was their souls that benefited the most. For gambling was forbidden, and gambling is the chief downfall of the poor man. It is a temptation I can understand. It seems a chance for a sort of magic to happen – for sixpence to become six pounds, then sixty, perhaps six hundred and for life to be transformed. That is the temptation of it, a false and wicked temptation because of course it never works like that. It is a vice. It is one of Satan's traps. So gambling was banned from the shelter. On the wall under a portrait of General Booth was a sign in red lettering, the only splash of colour in the room:

HELP KEEP THIS HOSTEL FREE FROM
THE DETESTABLE EVIL OF GAMBLING.
ANY MAN FOUND PLAYING CARDS OR
OTHERWISE GAMBLING WILL BE EJECTED
AND NEVER AGAIN ADMITTED
UNDER ANY CIRCUMSTANCES.

Gambling gives false hope. Our concern was to replace this false hope with hope for another kind of transformation, equally magical but good and sure and lasting. To this end we prayed with the men and sometimes we sang hymns. And sometimes we did save a soul, though many of the men's eyes were empty and lightless, blocked off from God's love, sometimes we did find a spark and wherever it was found it was kindled.

> Oh, the drunkard may come,
> And the swearer may come,
> Gamblers, all sinners are all welcome home.
> If you will but believe and be washed in the Blood,
> For ever and ever you shall dwell with the Lord.

We sang that at open-air meetings, aiming to reach out to those that had ears to hear. We sang outside pubs. Harold and I. One time. It was the beginning of the end although I could not see that then.

I am cold.

I cannot stop this blasted remembering.

Thank God for my television. Coco-Pops. *I'll have another bowl of Coco-Pops.* I like that tune. Properly catchy. Coco-Pops are something I've never had but they look like a cheerful start to the day. *Something cheerful, always cheerful, Constant sunshine in the soul.* Something new to try. I will have to go out.

*I'll have another bowl of Coco-Pops.*

Concentrate on the memory. It will come. Get it over with.

All right then.

I did nothing wrong. There was attraction between Harold and me. Nothing happened, oh no. One day we were singing outside a pub, The Cross Cat. Mary was not there, she'd gone to visit a relative. It was the day after an absence. They had started again. I thought no one had noticed any difference. I did not want to know about the absences. I ignored them, pretended nothing had happened.

A man was staring at me. I took no notice at first, people always looked. We were there to be noticed, and some men did take a fancy to a young woman in uniform, it was well known. In the pubs on Friday nights when we sold *The War Cry*, dreadful suggestions were made and we took no notice. But this man persisted, looking at my face and then with a long, lazy, almost licking look at my body, at my uniform rather. He wore a Panama hat and a long light trench-coat. He waited until he'd caught my eye and smiled and shook his head at me in a horrible, *knowing* way, that made me feel sick. He had a crude scarred face. I averted my eyes, made myself smile at a little cluster of children who'd gathered.

'Oh the drunkard may come,' we sang. I tried, I fought against the shrinking of my voice. It was as if I was shrivelling under his eyes, my voice, my self, to nothing. The round eyes of the smallest child were full of the ribbon on my tambourine. I kept my eyes on the children and at the edge of my vision, at last I saw the man move away. I turned slightly then, watched him enter the pub. But he looked back at me, caught my eye before I could escape his, shook his head and touched the brim of his hat. The door swung behind him and he was gone. There had been something so *knowing* in his manner that my voice died altogether and I shuddered. Later Harold walked me home.

'I saw the way that man looked at you,' he said, quite delicately, 'and I saw your reaction.'

'I was frightened,' I admitted, 'the way he was looking.'

'He's not an acquaintance . . . not a former acquaintance?'

I walked faster. 'Certainly not.'

I wanted to be away from Harold, away from everybody. I wanted to shut myself in my room and pray. On the floor of my room, I had scattered sharp gravel to kneel on during prayer to stop myself from going off again, to keep me conscious of and in my skin. The consciousness of the pain prevented the fearful drift. For this reason, I almost liked the pain of the gravel biting into my knees.

'Trixie, I have been wanting to talk to you.'

'Do you think Mary would mind you walking me home?'

'Mary would not mind.'

'What is it?' I asked.

'I don't know how . . . I've prayed for guidance. I've spoken to Mary about my feelings. Trixie, you must have guessed . . .'

'No!' I hurried so that he had to lengthen his stride to keep up with me.

'I love Mary as a sister and a friend. I have not looked at another woman – hardly looked – before in my life. But you . . . I know you feel it too. Trixie, I am excited by you. I could love you in another way. The way God meant a man to love a woman.'

My heart went cold. 'And you've said this to Mary? Harold! How dare you?'

'She understands.'

'I don't care! Mary is my friend. Is that why she's gone away?'

'No . . . not entirely . . . she is worried about you – your activities. Oh she is innocent. Innocent where you are not.'

'What do you mean?' I stopped and faced him. I pressed my lips together to prevent them from trembling.

'If you will marry me, you will be saved. Mary will stand aside. If you will not marry me, then I'll marry Mary.'

'Poor Mary.'

'Mary is strong. She would wish us well.'

'I don't believe it.'

'Trixie there is a wildness in you, something dangerous. There is talk . . . If you marry me you will be safe.'

I began walking again, fast and then slower. The idea began to settle on me like a soothing cloud, a temptation.

'Let me come in with you. We can pray together for guidance.'

I let him come in and made him tea. I remembered the day when my feet had first carried me to the Citadel, when I had seen Mary and Harold together and wanted to *be* Mary, to be with him. Now I had the chance to do that.

We did not pray. I was filled with dread that Mary might have seen me in an absence, spoken to me when I was not there. I was weak, tired, confused by Harold's closeness. He held my hand gently in his own. His hand was beautiful, long fingers, little dark hairs curling on their backs. To have another person so close, a person who cared, who loved me, wanted to hold me, hold me for the rest of my life was an overwhelming temptation. His mouth was wide and kind, the skin on his chin and cheeks shadowed bluish with the stubble underneath. I almost gave in. I said I would tell him tomorrow. The idea was so big and pressing in my mind that everything else got pushed aside and I could not think straight. When he left he kissed me on the lips. A long, deep kiss, not holy, a kiss that left me breathless.

'I am not blind to your eyes, Trixie. I know the way you look at me. Do not deceive yourself,' he said as he left, and I shuddered after I closed the door on him. If he had not said that . . .

Something in his eyes, his tone of voice, reminded me of the knowing eyes of the man who had looked at me so . . . so intimately, so greedily. I had thought of Harold as good, as sent by God but the way he spoke those words made me doubt him.

As I knelt on the gravel and prayed, the thought came to me that he was not of God, he was the Devil in disguise. A good disguise. Oh with his smooth tongue he had nearly tricked me. Even that thought didn't remove the temptation. Lust. It was that that he felt for me and not for Mary, lust not love. And though that knowledge shocked me I felt an answering stir. But he loved her. He could never love me because I am not loveable, I am not even a whole person, so how could he love me? And when he got to know me, when he discovered the deep flaw in my soul, then what? Then he would regret leaving Mary and I would be despised. I would have lost everything.

So next day I said no. Because of Mary, I said, because Mary is my friend, because I do not love you, is what I said. Because of the lust in your eyes that excites something bad in me, because I cannot let you know me, is what I thought.

If I had married Harold where would I be now? Sometimes I wonder if that was my one chance, if I had been fooled by a sort of double bluff – the Devil made me see evil and lust in him when there was only goodness and love. Perhaps I would have had children, two girls and two boys. No, not boys. Not babies at all, oh no, no, no. I could not bear to be near a baby. I'm worn out with these everlasting memories, going round and round in my head, what if this? what if that? questions, questions and no answers. Never, ever, an answer.

Time for my quiz: Countdown. I like this. You can make answers to this. I keep a pad by my chair with a pen attached, to save a scramble every afternoon, and I try to beat the contestants at their own game, and sometimes, on a good day, I do.

# ADA

My love for Frank. Oh ... you cannot imagine. The sight of
Frank made Trixie shudder. Poor Trixie who knows nothing. I
do love her, of course I do, she is my ... she is my ... I have
responsibilities. I have work to do. There is the boy I have to
keep him in. Somebody has to.

That boy is a monster.

Frank killed people but he killed them according to the rules
because criminals do have rules. The rules are more exacting
than the ones they cross. Break a rule, get the knife. Simple.

No, I do not agree with killing but, a funny thing. His killing
hand on my body it made pleasant gooseflesh.

Can you explain?

One day, a hot windy day. We were in torment. Trixie was trying
to move her Salvation life into our childhood home. Trying to
deny the strengthening me. I was feeling bad, knowing I would
hurt Trixie with my love for a bad man. The boy was weak then,
it was me that was the other mover.

The country, Epping Forest. He drove me in his Armstrong-
Siddeley black and shiny as a stag-beetle. We drank beer outside

a pub in the sunshine. We walked past a hedge full of blossom. Bees hummed and bumbled. The grass was long and soft about my ankles. I had hardly seen him outside. Under the shadow of his hat I saw his skin was scarred, little bluish zig-zagged lines on his cheekbones. He had thin crooked lips but eyelashes like a girl's.

Up against a tree.

'Let me love you,' he said.

I looked around. There was nothing and no one, only green trees swaying and creaking and childish white flowers like stars in the grass. He lifted my skirt and moved aside the lacy edge of my knickers. The tops of my thighs were a shocking blue-white in the sunshine.

Trixie's thighs too.

'Not here,' I said, aware of the hardness of the tree trunk against my back.

'Where?' he said.

'Mine,' I said, thinking of Trixie, thinking, can I? Can I? I knew if I could stay *me*, stay away from Mary then I could bring him back. 'Tonight.'

'You're on,' he said. He took off his hat and put his head down. I saw for the first time that his hair was thinning on top. I thought he would kiss my thigh but instead he nipped the flesh between his teeth. A sharp nip. When he stood up, he smiled. I think it was the first time I'd seen him smile a whole smile. It revealed the sharp ivory of his narrow slanted teeth. Rat's teeth I thought, and the thought was not repellent.

# FEVER

Two whole days and nights in bed. I think it must have been flu or something, worse than a cold anyway. I was so ill, time just hung in the room around me and didn't pass and my dreams were like stale tastes in my mouth when I woke. I staggered to the lavatory once or twice, and to fetch water to drink. I oozed tears into my pillow because there was no one to look after me. My mum used to wipe my hot head with a cool flannel when I had a temperature, bring me fruity drinks, change my hot rumpled sheets for smooth, cool ones. Richard would bring me medicine and cups of tea and try to keep the children away. But there was no one – and it was my own fault.

Something strange, I remember, a bit like a dream. I got out of bed, feeling ghastly. I went to fetch a glass of water from the bathroom. Before I got back into bed, I pressed my hot forehead against the cold window. It was either early morning or early evening, anyway, barely light, but Trixie was outside in her dressing-gown. I thought she was looking at her plants but then I saw that there was a cat in her garden, a big black-and-white Tom, he prowls round my garden too, a nice cat. As I watched, Trixie leant down as if to stroke him and then, with a quick movement, caught him by the tail and pulled so hard she jerked him off the ground. The cat's scream was frightening, but what was worse was the sound of her laugh as the cat ran off. A *sort* of laugh, horrible, jeering. If I hadn't seen with my own eyes I wouldn't have believed Trixie could do such a thing.

I was very feverish.

Maybe it *was* a dream.

Today, though, I woke with a clear head and the aching in my muscles almost gone. My stomach was hollow, my skin all shivery and mottled, but still I feel much better. I looked at my parchment face and greasy hair in the mirror. I ached for a bath – but the boiler has completely packed up. I thought I'd ask Trixie if I could have a bath at hers.

There was nothing for breakfast, only a bit of stale bread, an inch of thick milk in a bottle, so I had to go out. Everything was sparkling, so bright it hurt my eyes. The fag ends and dog turds in the gutter were stiff and whiskery with frost. My legs felt hollow and weak. I was walking along the main road to the supermarket when I saw a little boy running ahead of me. He had blue padded trousers and a red jacket just like Robin's. His hair was dark, he was the same size. Just for a splinter of a second I thought he *was* Robin and my heart leapt. The little boy was running towards the busy road. It looked as if he wasn't going to stop. I didn't stop to think, I leapt forward and grabbed his hand. And he turned, surprised. And it wasn't Robin, of course it wasn't, quite the wrong face, a nice little boy but not my son. His mother hurried up and caught his hand from mine.

'I thought . . .' I started to say but she did not care to know. She gave me a tight suspicious smile and whisked the boy away – and who can blame her? If someone had grabbed my Robin like that I would have reacted in the same way. I thought how I must look, pale, haggard, greasy. I could have been a mad woman for all she knew. The episode left me feeling faint. Instead of the supermarket I went into a café and sat in the window drinking coffee and forcing myself to swallow a toasted tea-cake.

Through the window I watched the procession of mothers and babies, mothers and children, pregnant women. It was as if someone had put a breeding spell on Sheffield. I seemed to be the only woman under the age of forty without a child in tow or brewing.

Then I walked back home, feeling exhausted, dispirited, so flattened that I forgot to post Richard's card. I'd had it in my bag but the boy had distracted me, wrenching me painfully into a moment of motherhood, responsibility, reminding me of the panic of protective love . . . I'd meant to buy a stamp and post the card but my surge of energy had evaporated. All the way home my hand kept clutching at the empty air.

I felt disgusting, ugly, smelly, caked in the cold residue of my fever. I needed to bathe and then to sleep. I knocked at Trixie's door. I was scared of her reaction. But I really needed a bath. There was no one else I could ask.

The door sprang open quickly, surprising me.

'Inis init?' Trixie laughed as if this was a great joke. 'Come in, always thought it a funny sort of name, funny *peculiar* that is. In is.'

I followed her in. She looked and sounded different, the whole room seemed different, though it was dark, the curtains were pulled against the sun and the light all came from the silently flickering television screen and the orange bars of the fire. As my eyes grew accustomed to the gloom I was amazed to see that she was wearing lipstick and a raggedy chiffon dress sprinkled with shiny black beads. And the room smelt overwhelmingly of rank perfume. A huge perfume atomizer, with a silky black bulb to squeeze, stood on top of the piano. For a moment I thought it wasn't Trixie at all but a sister, perhaps a twin. Where's Trixie? I almost asked, but *she* knew *me*. And anyway, I could see that it really was Trixie.

'Sherry?' she picked up a bottle of Harvey's Bristol Cream. 'I've been longing to offer you a sherry. Never mind tea.' She sniffed. 'Old woman's drink.'

I opened my mouth to object, to explain what I wanted but already she had poured me a glass and pushed me quite firmly into a chair. All her movements had changed, as if she was a smaller, lighter, younger person. I didn't have the strength to refuse.

'You've caught me unawares,' she said. 'Only half ready, unprepared.'

'I'm not well . . .' I began but she seemed not to hear.

'It is an anagram of I sin,' she said, 'your name. Has anyone at any time pointed this out to you?' I shook my head. 'And Ada is a palindrome. A.D.A. Identical read backwards or forwards. Anna is another and Hannah another, the longest I've been able to devise with my feeble . . . ,' she tapped her forehead, 'is redivider. Whether that's a bona fide dictionary word I couldn't say, nor do I care if you want the truth. It is, in any case, a word.'

'Well yes.' *Ada?*

'If you can divide something then you can redivide it. And if you redivide something you must become – however briefly – a redivider. Yes?'

'Yes, I suppose so.'

'Oh don't worry, my dear, I've had plenty of time to puzzle these things out in my miserable *waiting* existence.'

She swallowed down her own sherry and topped it up. I sipped mine. It was very sweet.

'I didn't think you drank,' I said. 'I don't know why, for some reason I didn't think you would.' Particularly in the morning, I thought.

'Yes well, one can never tell can one? Thing is, it is my birthday.'

'Oh Trixie, you should have said.'

'How old do you think? Go on, guess . . .'

I hesitated. Truth is, she could have been ninety. 'Sixty-five,' I offered, ridiculously, but she crowed. 'Not far off, not too far off.'

I felt as if I couldn't breathe, what with the heat and the perfume and, I suppose, a sort of shock. I couldn't take Trixie in. I sipped at the sweet sticky sherry and my stomach lurched with alarm.

'Thing is, Trixie,' I tried again, 'I've been ill, there's no hot water . . .'

'You do look a perfect fright,' she said, 'take a tip . . .' She lifted a curly black wig from a shadowy place on the floor and fitted it over her sparse white hair. 'There . . . my natural colour,' she said patting it into position. 'Why does she have no mirror hanging? Jet black, almost blue-black.'

'Who?' She only patted and preened. 'Is anyone coming?' I asked. She looked so festive, the black beads and the nylon hair glistening warmly in the orange light from the electric-fire, her arms bare and withered under the ragged chiffon sleeves, her mouth an approximate, passionate slash in her white face.

'There's you,' she said and my heart sank. I wanted only to crawl away. I had given up the idea of a bath. 'And possibly a certain someone else,' she said mysteriously. In my pocket I could feel the edge of Richard's card. I thought I must get a stamp and I must send it.

'Yes?' I said, politely. 'Mr Blowski?'

'The very same, if he can get away from his infernal vegetable. Brenda I mean, of course.'

'Trixie!'

'Oh that name,' she said.

'I would have got you a card, a present.'

'Don't be silly, I don't need presents when I have your presence.' She cackled.

'But I can't stay long. Trixie, I've been ill, in bed for two days . . . no heating. I've been really ill.'

She was not listening. 'Back to your photographs I suppose,' she mused. 'How about a photograph of me . . . a birthday portrait?' She posed, pouting, hand on her hip.

I hesitated. 'I thought . . .' I started – but what a gift. After the disappointment before. If I demurred she might easily change her mind. And she looked so . . . striking.

'I love to be photographed,' she almost purred, 'go on Inis, as a present to me, a reminder of me as I am today.'

'Well, yes, thank you.' I put down my sherry and went to fetch my Leica. My house was so cold, the lens misted in

Trixie's warmth. I used a wide-angle lens, cruel maybe, but the distortion was what would make the shot. I felt bad, taking advantage. She was so drunk I was sure she didn't know what she was doing. She was like another person.

When I got back she had opened the piano and was picking out a tune and singing: *Eadie was a lady, though her past was shady. Eadie had class . . . with a capital K.* The piano's sound was soft and plinky and slightly out of tune but her voice was fabulous, so different from the strident, hymn singing voice I'd grown used to, that had threaded its way into my ill, half-dreaming state. It was low and husky, almost gritty as if with yearning.

I didn't want to use flash, I didn't have time to organise lights – I thought she might change her mind, so I simply drew back the curtains and let the bright sun spill into the room and hoped for the best.

She seemed hardly to notice me as I photographed her, she was so involved in her song. I shot her at the piano and then followed her when she forgot it and began to sway around the room, the light catching her brilliantly, hands flattened over her belly and hips, head thrown back, eyes half closed.

When she'd finished she pulled the curtains again, and pressed more sherry on me. I'd started to feel quite drunk. It was something like a dream, like an extension of my feverish state, Trixie done up so glamorously – while I'd been gone she'd applied, crookedly, a pair of black eyelashes, and I suspect another drench of perfume. I sat down with my drink and then suddenly Mr Blowski was there at the door, his arms full of white lilies that flickered blue and tangerine in the television and firelight.

'Good day,' he said, and his eyes seemed to light up when he saw how Trixie was.

'Blowski, my Blowski,' she exclaimed, enveloping and kissing him, crushing the flowers between them. 'What a delightful surprise, and lilies . . . oh, my dear, my most favourite flowers.' Mr Blowski disentangled himself, his face was smeared with red. Trixie took the flowers from him and pressed her finger deep into the white horn of a bloom. 'Rude flowers,' she said, 'don't you think?' She held them out towards me. 'Suggestive flowers.'

Mr Blowski looked quizzically at me. I hardly knew where to look. I thought he must be embarrassed.

'I thought they were sort of symbols of purity,' I said, feeling most foolish. Trixie threw her head back and laughed. 'How quaint,' she said. 'Blowski, don't you think she's quaint?'

'I've been commemorating the occasion,' I said, amazed at how pompously my words were coming out. I indicated my camera. 'Trixie's birthday, I mean.'

He smiled. 'That nice,' he said. 'I never said: how do you do?' He held out his arthritic hand and I shook it gently.

'Snap us together,' Trixie begged. 'Do a nice picture, the two of us together.'

'All right?' I looked at him.

'Whatever the lady say.'

We drew back the curtains again and I took pictures of their two old passionate faces gazing into the camera, of them embracing, of them with the piano, Mr Blowski playing a little despite the pain in his hands, Trixie singing, her hand on his shoulder, her red mouth opened to the ceiling, her eyes closed. I took them out in the garden, to be sure of the light and took a roll of close-ups, the two faces, gazing at the camera's lens with touching seriousness.

Then I went home and left them alone. I made myself another cup of lemon and honey and, before I went to sleep, gazed at the big glossy rectangles that were my husband and children, my own loves. I slept heavily for several hours and woke dry-mouthed and ravenous. I could not think for a whole minute where I was. It was getting dark.

I was all ready to go out to post Richard's card and to buy food when I remembered an extraordinarily vivid dream about Trixie. Then I saw my camera lying where I'd discarded it by the bed and realised that it hadn't been a dream at all.

Not my dream. It had been more like wandering into someone else's.

# BOY

I see through the crack of her sleep but I cannot come through
I can do anything I am a boy
If I could come
It is not fair
Some nights her sleep gapes her open but she is heavy
It is not fair
The world is for boys and I am
I am a boy I really am
I can do boys' things
She is too heavy
I used to come out when she was small
I used to come out and be bad
Stealing, all that
Hurting frogs and cats
Smoking Father's pipe
A worse thing one time – and then no more
But I don't feel bad
Babies are only weak
I see through her but I cannot come through
Now I am very angry and
She will be sorry

# SNAKES

I do not want to be in the house, although it is chilly out here. I must go in. The frost is melting and the sun is just warm. Under the earth are roots, shoots, seeds. It is a wonder to me every time a seed grows, how the little specks that could be crumbs or dust are full of life. How can a person deny God when square yards of glory, of colour and fragrance will grow from a packet of dust? I sniff the air, not winter air, it is the beginning of spring. There is promise in it, generosity. Early this morning I opened all my windows to dispel the stench of winter that is like stale perfume, sickly sweet. The hyacinths are finished. When the ground has thawed I'll plant them by the fence. Next year there will be hyacinths again and the year after and the year after that, spindlier and spindlier until they are single flowers, blue or white bells. And none the less beautiful for being simple.

That woman next door is peering out of her window. I can feel her eyes on me. What does she want of me? What does she want?

Every birthday that passes, every year I think I won't live to see another. Eighty-four years. Yesterday was my birthday, though I know nothing of it, oh I must not dwell on that, not dwell. But what is it that she knows looking at me like that, bold as brass? I will not turn but I know she is there, that she is staring and grinning all over her face. Every spring I think I've seen my last crocus, tulip, daffodil. Every time I tip waste into my compost bin I wonder, will I still be here when it's ready to dig into my soil? Each Christmas when I fold up my little tree and sweep up the silver strands from the carpet, I think I'll never get it out again. But there you are, that's old age for you. You get so tired of it. It's so repetitive.

I will not open to her today. Open the door I mean. There is nothing I need. It is always a mistake to let people in. Let them know your business. I must pull myself together and go out. Then I won't need her. Get my own bits from the shop, the post-office. Do my own banking. But, I am scared of falling. If I fall what will become of me? Who will know me? Who will come close then? I do not want to do harm.

Oh I am chock full of nonsense today.

Dear Jesus, let me remember yesterday.

All those cups of tea she's had, all those biscuits, and then cheating me of two pounds, slut with her dark roots growing through. No, no, I must not set myself up as judge. I am cold. I must go in. It makes me seethe the way she shovelled down my biscuits, the cheek of her. *Amazing how it adds up!* How could she do that and look at me with those innocent eyes. I rue the day she took that house, better the butcher's rumpus, better the emptiness than this. She will drive me mad. Water is running from her drain. She might come out. I must go in.

I do not want to be in there, in that mess. How it gets in a mess I don't know. Things conspire against me. What nonsense. I do not know myself this morning. I am out of sorts, that's all, Trixie do not panic. My head aches and my limbs. How can a person stand in a lovely garden surrounded by new growth, the sun almost warm on her hair, and still feel angry?

If I was not so stiff, I would kneel down here and now and pray.

You do not have to kneel to pray.

I still have my faith despite all and everything, I still have that.

I have never in my life knowingly done wrong.

I have never knowingly hurt another person.

I do not understand why my mind is turning back on itself, turning inside out. I cannot look forward. Well that is old age for you. What is there to look forward to? Come on Trixie Bell, get the house tidied, a cup of tea inside you, the television on. Season hard on the heels of season, winter hardly over before the nights are drawing in again. I cannot look forward or outwards, only back. And for that I must blame *her*. No, no, that sounds mad and I am not mad, only confused this morning, only worn out. I will not let her further in. For her own sake as well as mine.

A baby slug crawls across the grass, a tiny sliver of life, feelers so delicate. I should pick it up and pinch it in half before it has a chance to grow and breed and destroy my plants. But I haven't the heart today. Let it live for today. See how tender hearted I am?

My house smells of perfume, my body feels sore, ill-used. I am stiff. The space that is yesterday is awful. It reminds me of other, past mornings when I woke filled with dread. In my house, my parents' house, with Mary there too.

I thought that was all over. I thought I'd never lose a day again. Like then, back then also I thought all that was over.

It is not fair. Jesus, Jesus, it does hurt. Why have I been cheated of my life? Cheated from inside and from out.

One morning back in that house I woke with my head crashing. When I tried to lift it, the room spun round. I thought that I was really ill but then I looked back and saw the hole in my memory. I lay still, my heart chugged like an old motor starting up. I closed my eyes and swam in sickly oily darkness where swirls of coloured light floated away until I was afraid that I was dying and my soul descending to Hell. When I opened my eyes the light pulsed unbearably. I tried to pray. I lay absolutely still looking at the ceiling through my eyelashes, thinking about getting up to pray, but the thought itself took away all my energy.

I gradually became aware that there was something in the room with me, something sweet and repulsive. It turned my stomach. It filled my nostrils, it beat in nauseating waves even in my ears. *Jesus, Jesus, help me*, I begged silently. I was afraid of what there was beside me in the bed. I could feel something soft and cool against my skin and the stench was an evil sweetness. I needed to drink, to cleanse myself, to drink at the well of the Lord, to cleanse my head, my sticky body, my soul with water from His crystal spring but oh it all sounded like nonsense. It made me sick.

I slept again. I heard a knocking at the door of my room. I could not open my eyes. I was deep in such a sticky drowse. The heavy scent was like a sleeping drug. I heard as if through water the door opening and someone moving about. I smelled the fresh and rainy scent of Mary. I heard a gasp, I heard the clearing away of something, the clink of glass. I heard her light my fire. Then she was gone and it was quiet.

Jesus was wagging his finger at me. I saw it behind my eyes where the dark was – not black dark – velvet red. I saw His finger, pale, disembodied, wagging. And I felt his finger on my body, waxy warm and soft. I felt it against me. I do not want to understand the feelings, the swelling urge that caused me to lift my hips against the weak finger that wagged and fluttered where I wanted it to press. And oh the scent in my nose and the rhythm of Jesus's finger, wagging at me because I was so wicked such a wicked woman. My heart was beating with the need for Jesus to come right into me, enter me, fill me with love. Then I was taken with a kind of fit, that was strange and nevertheless dismayed me with its familiarity and I cried out with the painful pleasure.

When I opened my eyes I saw that I shared my bed with white lilies. On the pillow when I turned my head, a bloom gaped at me, a rude blurt of white and wax tongues, at their centre a damp, sticky, three-lobed thing, six stamens steeped in yellow dust. The petals were slightly crushed, bruised at the edges to brown. The smell was sweet and rotting. When I pulled back the sheet I saw my naked body and the lilies, the flowers and the tapering leaves stuck to my body, crushed between my thighs and breasts. I felt sick. I got unsteadily out of bed, the walls billowing like curtains, and pulled the flowers off my body and out of my body. I stood shivering by the fire that Mary had made. My skin was imprinted with the shapes of leaves and stems. I washed in cold water and dressed, thankful to button my body away in the plain thickness of my clothes.

I knelt and prayed. I thanked God for sending me the pain that smashed in my head, the sickness in my stomach to punish me. I tried to banish the memory of the silly wagging finger of Jesus that had so inflamed my morning dream.

But it wasn't fair. It isn't fair. I am a good, pure woman. I am. No intention in me is other than good.

I was afraid of what Mary had seen, of what Mary knew. Of what she'd tell Harold.

I threw the ruined lilies on the fire where they hissed and curled like snakes.

Another morning, soon after, I woke filled with dread. Dread wrapped round me like a cold sheet. I was not over the other shock. I had prayed night after night on my knees amongst the gravel until I was exhausted – but the more exhausted I was the more my sleep turned into absences and the more frightening the evidence of the absences when I awoke.

I got slowly out of bed. There was something wrong with me. Trembling, I lifted the hem of my nightdress. High on my thigh was a small patch of gauze. Blood had seeped through, stuck it to the wound, some sort of wound on the inside of my thigh. I fell to my knees and prayed. I asked Jesus to forgive my body for what it had done, whatever it had done. I begged him to free me from the Devil. I had dedicated my life to Jesus, I would do anything, anything if only I knew what He wanted. What more could I do?

I could not remember the night before. I remembered the morning and some of the afternoon, but I could not remember the night.

When I removed the gauze from my thigh I found a thick black scab, hairy with stuck threads. It was the size of half-a-crown and as thick. I did not touch it. I could not bear to imagine what this body had done. I left the scab and put on the uniform and I did my work. My face, my smile, the same as ever. I looked sinners and fellow soldiers in the eye and all the time above the top of my thick lisle stocking there was the wound that burned as if the Devil had branded me with a fiery horn. All day my fingers longed to go to the place and touch. All day I prayed and fasted to punish my body.

In the shelter that evening, I sat with a dying man. He was not more than fifty but his body and mind were pickled with strong drink. His skin was red and coarse, traced with the hectic purple of broken capillaries, his nose was swollen and strawberry-pitted. Between their lashless lids his eyes were watery blue. I tried to look at him with compassion, tried not to smell the sour reek of his breath and skin, not to mind the dampness of his hand that clutched mine as I prayed for him. I sat with him almost all night. I prayed and softly sang to him. He seemed to like the childish choruses. Perhaps a memory from his childhood stirred in his dying mind, a memory from the time before Satan with his tobacco, his spirits, his gambling, his traps of flesh, had won his soul away from God. He opened his mouth and I swear he said 'Jesu', that is the last word he said, I am almost sure it was that, as he slipped into his last sleep. And only I knew, as I walked home through the last of the night, that as I had prayed for his soul the Devil had been there in me, in the burning under my skirt, the hairy, devil-print on my thigh.

That day I really lost heart. It did not happen all at once; it was the beginning of a peeling back, as if the petals of a chrysanthemum – that many filaments of hope – were peeling back, falling and dying, one by one.

I did not touch the place. I did not let my fingers travel there. I lay with my hands outside the sheets and prayed for the soul of the dying man. I knew I should not let myself sleep, that that was weak. I should have spent the rest of the night on my knees in the chilly room. But even while thinking that, I did fall asleep and my dreams were filled with choking horror: the taste of a man's flesh, hot compression, an obscene stuffing of the senses. When I woke I got out of bed and fell straight to my knees, terrified of the heat in my body, of a strange wet heaviness. It was late and the sun laughed through the curtains with the Devil's glee.

'My dear,' said Mary coming into my room. 'Are you not well?'

'I have slept so late!'

'I came in and looked at you,' Mary said. 'I did not wake you. I thought you ill, your face flushed, tossing and turning, muttering. And yesterday you appeared so pale and strained. I noticed that you did not eat. And then up all night . . .'

'I'm all right.'

'Get straight back into bed and I'll bring you tea and toast,' she said. She knelt down to light the fire. 'You must rest this morning. And that's an order.' She sounded kind enough but she had not looked me in the eye and I was hurt by that. I wanted her to look at me in the old loving, approving way. The burning place on my thigh pulsed.

'I should get dressed, I should return to the shelter.'

'Later, Trixie. Mr Petit died this morning, peacefully an hour after you left him.'

'Oh . . . I should have stayed.'

'You should have done no such thing. You were up nearly all night. Nobody could have done more. Trixie, I believe you won a soul for Jesus last night. God doesn't require that you make yourself ill in His service. What earthly use would that be?' She stood up and brushed her skirt. 'There, that's lit, now I'll fetch your breakfast.'

Before I returned to bed I shook out my rumpled sheets and blankets as if shaking them free of the sinful dreams and as I shook, a crust, black as a beetle's shell, jumped on the white sheet. I flicked it on to the floor as if it was a poison thing. I picked it up in the folds of a handkerchief and threw it into the flames. When I dared to look at my thigh . . . oh I cannot express how I felt, how my voice welled in my throat sour and sick as curdled milk. For there, on the top of my thigh, on the whitest, smoothest part was a red rose, risen and inflamed, a crude and ugly tattoo, a picture of a red rose.

I thought it was a sign. A sign that I was damned. It is there still, an old rose now, creased with the folds of my old skin, an old brown-red rose, the Devil's stain.

# ADA

*Call me romantic,*
*but still I maintain,*
*I was born to lo – ove.*

When Frank said he wanted to make me his, how could I refuse?
A ring, he said, a ring you can take off. He took me to be tattooed.
I did think of Trixie, and afterwards I was sorry for the terrible
shock it gave her but . . . well maybe I thought, why should it be
only Trixie's body? Maybe I, too, like Frank, maybe I wanted to
make my mark.

I remember it was night, Frank drove me to the place. It was a
narrow shop in Golders Green. The tattoo man stripped to the
waist and I gasped and Frank laughed at me. He pinched my
arm with his hard fingers. 'Let's choose,' he said. I had gasped
because the man seemed more dressed in his coloured skin than
he had in his plain shirt. His skin was hairless and every inch
from his wrists to his collar-bone was covered in the tiniest of
tattoos.

'My showcase,' he said. It was as if he was wearing a most
elaborately patterned garment, woven neat and smooth as skin
itself. There were alphabets and elephants, flowers of every kind.
A tree grew from his navel, the roots disappearing below the waist
of his trousers, the branches spread across his chest laden with
every kind of bird and fruit. Adam and Eve stood beneath the

tree and a serpent with a red eye curled around the trunk. Eve held an apple in her hand with a bite taken from it. The more I looked, the more I saw. He turned around, there, on his back, was an eagle like the big eagle on Frank's back. He rolled his shoulder-blades and the bird seemed to fly and all around it trembled other creatures: rabbits, tortoises, wolves, lions and unicorns.

'What's it to be?' he asked. I thought for ages, touching the warm skin beneath the designs. I liked the eagle, I thought perhaps an eagle like Frank's but tiny, but he said no and decided for me. He chose a rose, red to signify our love.

I had to sit on a chair and lift my skirt. My thigh looked so white, the purest thing in the room. The man knelt before me, between my legs and swabbed the place, the inside of my thigh above my stocking-top with a disinfectant that left a yellow smear. Frank stood behind me, his hand a weight on my shoulder. I closed my eyes, frozen in a mixture of fear and excitement. The tattoo man had cold fingers and he smelled of smoke and hair-cream. On top of his head, the hair was slick with grease. His breath came out in little sighs and grunts as he concentrated on his task. He pressed his fingertips into my flesh to keep it taut. I bit my lip against the pain of the needle. When I opened my eyes and looked down I saw the blood risen in lines of scarlet beads. I felt faint and sweat rose on my upper lip. I could hear a buzzing in my ears, but Frank was behind me, he made me strong. He lit a cigarette and a drift of ash fell on my skirt.

That was near the end.
Next time I saw him it was through Trixie's eyes.
Next thing I knew he was dead.

# SWIMMING

I sin, she called me. And is it a sin to leave one's children? I posted Richard's card last night. Walking back past the telephone-box I hesitated, itching to ring to hear their voices, but no. Now I have sent the card I must wait. There are things I must do. I'm going to buy some brown hair-dye so I don't look too strange and shocking to the children. I'm going to put a mud-pack on my face and shave my legs. I look a sight. But I am almost better. I went to the Lateshopper last night and bought a frozen lasagne and a custard tart, also a can of Guinness, since that's supposed to be good for you. And I bought a birthday card for Trixie, an old ladyish sort of card, red roses and curly gold writing. A sentimental verse. I slept well and woke early, full of nervous energy. By now, Richard's card will have been collected, it may even have been sorted, it may be on the train to London already. Tomorrow morning he should get it. Perhaps tomorrow I will ring.

When I woke early this morning, I drank a mug of strong coffee before I went up to my darkroom. I sat for a couple of hours watching Trixie float into existence over and over, the drunken Trixie, lipstick smeared, wig askew, eyelashes coming unstuck so they curled up like little grins, independent of her lids. And Mr Blowski's serious monkey face, his chaotic white eyebrows and the dark lip prints on his withered cheeks. The photographs made me smile and then laugh, and that is an almost forgotten sensation, a bubbling tickle in my diaphragm, the air jolting staccato from my lungs, a smile on my face to match Trixie's.

I'll ask again if I can photograph her as she usually is, her everyday self. She enjoyed yesterday's session so much, I'm sure she'll agree. I want to put the photographs side by side, such a contrast but both true. Two facets of the same woman.

The laughing made me want to see my children more than ever, it freed something in me, something natural that is love. But I must have will power, I must be strong. If I move too soon it might all be ruined. I am unfurling a tendril towards them and it could easily be withered. What if Pauline answers the phone? Because most probably she is there in the space I have left. I would be, am, grateful to her, but still if it was Pauline who answered the phone I don't think I could speak. I would have to put the phone down without a word and she might guess it was me. It might make things worse. No, I will wait for tomorrow night, for the card to have arrived, for Richard to be home.

When Richard answers the phone, what will I say? 'Hello stranger!' or 'Guess who?' or 'Surprise, surprise!' No, no, no. Flippancy is inappropriate, though he would know it was fuelled by anxiety. He would understand. Still, better to say, quietly, with no inflection. 'It is Inis', or simply, 'It is me.'

Sometimes Robin picks up the receiver first, he loves to answer the phone. 'Who are you?' he always says. If it was Robin it would be all right. 'It's Mummy,' I would say. Oh God, I've almost forgotten his voice.

When I went down for a refill of coffee, I saw Trixie in the garden, the usual Trixie in her brown nylon housecoat, her white hair all flat against her head. She was moving very slowly and stiffly. Hungover, I expect. She was moving like a sleepwalker. I should have gone out and said hello. I don't know whether to show her the wonderful photographs of her birthday, what will she think? Surely she would love the one of her and Mr Blowski together, radiating fondness. They are the best work I've done. I can't wait to show Richard, to explain to him that something good has come from this terrible thing . . . something good for me at least. But is that selfish?

Why wait? Why telephone? Why not go straight home? I could be there in a few hours. But my heart squeezes, panicky at the thought. I am not ready. I have to clear up the loose ends. I have to explain to Trixie, and I don't *look* ready. I can't go home feeling like this. I want to look good and be good. Maybe I'll go to the hairdresser's and get my hair done properly, dyed chestnut, my own colour, trimmed. I wonder what Richard will say, I like it short – but he's always loved my hair long and when I've talked about cutting it before, he's sulked.

So what about the colour! Me, a peroxide blonde! What would he say to that? There's this woman, one of Richard's patients, always up at the surgery with this and that, and worse, always calling him out at night for nothing, for the most trivial things. And he always bloody goes, like a spaniel or something obedient. I wouldn't have gone, I would have told her where to get off, but Richard was conscientious. *What if*, he always said, what if this time it really *is* something. So he always went – but one night he came back in a filthy mood. She'd called him out with some story about her ears, and when he got there he found it was because she couldn't get her earrings out. At 3 a.m. *Ignorant fat peroxide blonde*, he called her.

I loved it! I loved him for that, for letting that slip. Dr Right-On Goodie. I lay beside him grinning into the dark, long after he was snoring.

Looking at the prints of Trixie's old face made me think of my granny who died when I was ten. I loved her. She was the one who took me to the kennels when I was seven to choose Bonny. The children should grow up with a dog. Why don't *we* have a dog? I can't think. When I get home I'll take Robin to get one, a black labrador, like Bonny, or a golden one.

I remember when my granny died. Hers is the only dead body I have ever seen. In death her breasts had slid down her sides under her nylon ruffle-neck blouse and her mouth was set in a smirk. I thought how awful to be dead and have people stare at you, come up close and stare at you like that, right up your nose even.

Richard is always seeing bodies. Mostly old, but sometimes not. Once a child with meningitis whose mother failed to call him out in time, a little girl who died. He was depressed after that, depressed and angry in turns. That was when I was expecting Robin. I was good then, I was supportive. For a time, maybe the only time, I was the strong one.

I said to Richard, how awful to be dead and have people staring at you up close when you have no defences. He laughed. But you are *dead*! he said.

If I had not left I would have hurt my children.

I said, 'If I die before you, don't let anyone look at me, have my lid nailed down so no one can look.'

When Billie was crying, the day before I left, I caught myself looking at a pillow. I caught myself thinking how easy it would be. How easy to shut her up.

Nobody would ever have guessed because they trusted me. Just because I am her mother they trusted me.

For weeks before I left, the newspapers, the radio, the television screamed stories at me, about people who hurt their children: fathers, stepfathers, mothers, others who beat their babies, scalded them in hot baths, threw them down the stairs, burned them with cigarettes, poisoned them, starved or strangled them.

Mothers like me. It was a warning.

I can't plunge back in until I'm ready. I am nearly. The thought of plunging reminds me of the seaside, the way my parents would both run down the pebbly beach and hurl themselves into the cold brown sea, right under, and come up spluttering and laughing, my dad's hair all sleek with wet, my mum's yellow swimming-cap with its white rubber daisies glistening and Bonny's head bobbing between them.

'Come on Inis,' they'd call, 'don't be a baby,' and Bonny would yap but I could not go right in at once. I had to go forward one step at a time and let the water rise up my thighs, tip-toeing up from the waves. I thought if I dived straight in my heart would stop with the shock. If they splashed me I ran out again, they had to leave me be, let me take my time.

Robin is just like them. With his water wings he is a slippery daredevil diver, he terrifies me, but Billie clings and cries, her chubby legs clamped round me, her skin marbling in the cold water. Perhaps she *is* like me.

I wonder if Pauline has taken them swimming.

Even thinking about it makes me cold.

# IVY

If Mary had not been humiliated by Harold's feelings about me, if she had not been jealous and bitter, then she would not have been real. Because she was a woman and not a saint. What a fool Harold was to believe otherwise! Did he really think he could tell her he loved me, desired me over her, that he wanted to ask me to marry him and when I said no, that she'd go back to him herself like a grateful little lamb and we could all remain the best of friends? He was an utter fool.

It was not me that ruined our friendship, that ruined everything, my life included, it was Harold. It was not my fault. I did my best but when Mary came back there was this formality, this awkwardness between us that had not been there before. I never met Harold's eye. Mary rarely met mine. She came less to my room. Soon after Mary's return their engagement was announced. They seemed happy together.

I felt like something dirty and devilish, a temptation overcome.

Something else too, another disappointment. I'd made an application for officer training. I'd talked to Mary and Harold about my plans. 'Are you sure, Trixie?' Mary asked. 'Of course I am, why?' I was surprised she was not more encouraging. But I was turned down at the first stage of application. There was no explanation. The disappointment was crushing. I could not understand, I worked as hard as anybody, harder, I lived my life in holiness as far as I was able. I prayed every morning on waking and after each meal. At 12.30 each day, like Salvationists everywhere I paused to ask God's blessing on The Army all round the world. I worked till I was fit to drop in the shelter, glad to help the degraded souls; I sold papers; I collected money. I attended several meetings every week, always staying behind for the prayers. I lived simply, frugally. I did everything I could do and it was not enough.

But whoever knows what God has in store for them? What tests he will devise. I should not question His wisdom but I cannot help it, sometimes I cannot. Sometimes I scream at Him, I shake my fist, I shake my tambourine. I scream and I cry, *It is not fair. I tried. I tried and tried but I could not be good enough. Dear Jesus listen to me. It is not fair.*

What tests. A few weeks after Mr Petit's death in the shelter, there was a letter, a blunt-pencilled note rather, from a Mrs Petit in search of her husband. She had been told by someone, I've no idea who, that her husband had been at the Bothwell Street shelter. She'd been turned out of her home with her three children, the youngest a babe in arms, the oldest only four. She was using her last remaining resources to try and trace him.

There was no address, no means of replying. But she said she was coming. I was glad. I felt I had let Mr Petit down, leaving him to die alone. I thought I could make up for it. I imagined a large soft woman, down-at-heel and shabby but good at heart. I planned to win her soul for Jesus.

'She must stay with us,' I told Mary.

'Yes,' she said, 'it will be good to have children in the house.'

We moved some furniture round to make things comfortable. We bought cots for the babies and brightened Mrs Petit's room with ornaments and flowers. They could have slept in my parents' room. I stood by the locked door where the wardrobe was, trying to steel myself to go in. But could not. Mary did not ask questions, I think she sensed my fear but did not intrude. Oh she was good. I wish, I wish, I wish. If wishes were horses the devil could ride. So we left the room and the wardrobe inside it where it was.

I hate it, hate it, that wardrobe. But still, when I moved up here, when I sent for my stuff – because I could not show my face there after what followed – I sent for the wardrobe too. I had the removal men put it in the attic, though they had to saw it in half to get it up the narrow stairs and reassemble it up there. They thought I was mad. I saw the way they looked at me. They thought I was a mad woman, but I paid them for the job, they almost doubled the price when I insisted that they get the wardrobe into the attic. 'What do you want to go keeping this for?' they said. 'And all the junk inside?' It was full of the things, the same old things. Truth is, I don't know why I kept it. I just could not let it go. It was a reminder of something. Father's punishment. Why should I want to remember that? No, not that. It was more like a part of me. And a reminder of Benjamin Charles, my brother. If he had lived . . . oh how different my life would have been.

Mrs Petit arrived at the Citadel at the end of a meeting. It was a hot night, July, still light. As soon as I saw her I knew who she was. Mrs Petit, Ivy, was a tiny woman, under five-foot tall, bird-boned, sharp featured – and heavily pregnant. Her babies looked incongruously huge with their round heads, chapped red faces and hair fine and colourless as dandelion clocks.

The oldest child, a girl, held the second, a boy, by the hand. A third slept in the pram, packed around with bundles and clothes. Pots hung from the pram handle and at the foot of the pram, most prominent, was a Bible.

'Welcome,' I said. She looked round the hall. Her eyes were sharp and narrowed.

'Where is he?' she asked. 'My husband, Mr Petit, where is he?'

'I'm sorry,' I said.

'Sit down, do,' Mary said indicating a chair.

'Sorry?'

'Mr Petit passed away.'

The baby woke up and looked at me with startled eyes.

'We're so sorry,' Mary said. 'Do sit down, would you like a drink of water, you or the children?'

Mrs Petit ignored her. 'He's passed on?' She brought her knuckles to her mouth. 'The *bastard*,' she said.

Mary flinched. She knelt down to the level of the children. 'I'm Mary,' she said to the little girl, 'What's your name?'

'I'm Jean and he's Arfur,' said the girl, 'and him in the pram he's Colin.'

'Beg your pardon,' said Ivy, 'excuse my language . . . but what am I supposed to do? He never was no good for nothing. Now he's gone and died!' She said this as if it was the most outrageous of a string of outrageous acts. 'What am *I* supposed to do?'

'We have a room for you,' Mary said, 'all prepared. You can stay with us till we fix up something more permanent.'

'Where's our daddy?' Jean asked.

'He's with Jesus,' Mary said. 'In the sunshine.'

Mrs Petit looked sardonic. 'I could do with getting these to bed,' she said.

'It's sunny *here*,' Jean said.

'In the permanent sunshine. Heaven.'

'What's pernananent?'

'For ever and ever.'

'If he's gone then,' Mrs Petit said, 'where's his things?'

'What things?' I asked.

'His gold watch, his chain, his good boots with the money in the soles.'

'When your husband arrived here he had none of those things,' Mary said. 'He had nothing but what he stood up in.'

Mrs Petit's face flushed. 'We haven't come all this bloody way for nothing,' she said. 'I want his things, that were promised me. "Ivy," he always said, "whatever becomes of me, you must be sure to have my things." Three little bastards to feed, and another one coming. Every one of them his, though he might argue but what they wasn't. But they're his spit, don't you think, his bleeding spit.'

I looked at the white-haired, red-faced children, tried unsuccessfully to recognise a likeness.

'Come,' Mary said. 'Let's get you back and put the children to bed. Then we can discuss other matters.' She took the handle of the pram and we set off. I held two sticky little hands in my own. We walked slowly along, the tired children dragging their feet, accompanied by the clanking of pots and pans against the pram's frame.

'I see you have a Bible among your possessions,' Mary said. 'Do you read it?'

'Oh yes,' Mrs Petit seemed to collect herself. 'Every night, don't I Jean?' The girl nodded blankly. 'Only how I'm going to manage on thin air . . . and this little one never to lay eyes on its father at all . . .' She patted her stomach and started to cry.

'Come now,' I said, 'It will be all right, you'll see.'

Ivy Petit settled in, but she was not grateful. Do you want gratitude? I asked myself and the answer was no. I was not really being generous, only trying to make amends. Maybe I was trying to show Mary how good I was, because I missed her love. It was as if a cloud had dragged across the sun and blotted up its warmth. So whenever Ivy was rude, or took advantage, I tried not to mind, I tried to meet her nastiness with kindness as if each mean word had antiseptic qualities that might cleanse and heal me. Which they did not.

The woman seemed to fill the house, her and the children. After she had rested for a day or two, I asked if she'd like to help keep house to pay for her keep. I was only concerned for her self-respect. I thought her coldness was pride. To accept charity is hard. It is hard for the taker not to hate the giver. But when I suggested it she was affronted.

'I've come all this bleeding way,' she said, 'to find my poor old man gone, not cold in his grave. To find his valuables what was promised me gone missing . . .' and she gave me, as she said this, a most accusing look. 'And now I have to work . . . in my condition . . .' Her voice took on a whining quality, her eyes filled with tears. 'Me, a poor, grieving widow with all these mouths to feed.'

I tried to like her and forgive her. But the truth is, I failed. The truth is, I thought her a miserable, deceitful, leech. The only time she showed any sign of grief over her husband was when work was mentioned. The truth was . . . no, my suspicion was that she had never set eyes on Mr Petit but that she had somehow heard of the man's death and decided to claim him. Even if I am wrong, even if the children were his children, I don't believe there ever was a watch and chain. There never was any money. He was a habitual drunkard and no man who has drunk himself into such a state of wretchedness still has valuables to his name. If he hasn't sold or pawned them for drink they will have been stolen. If there is honour among thieves there is none among drunkards, no honour, no dignity, no pity. But I don't believe so-called Ivy Petit knew him anyway, she called him Jim – though in our records his name was George. When I asked little Jean about her daddy she knew nothing. 'Where is he?' was all she would say. And Ivy's stories varied, she tripped herself up. One day her husband had been a grocer swindled out of his shop; another day he'd gambled it away. One day he was a good man and she managed to squeeze out a tear in his memory, another day he beat and forced himself on her. Some of it may have been true. But I believed nothing. There was no sincerity in her greedy, darting eyes. And never a thank you after all we did for her, hardly even a smile.

I know that these are not Christian thoughts, not charitable nor forgiving. Whatever else was false, the truth was that she was poor and homeless and had three children to support and another on the way. Her lies and cunning were her means of survival, the tools of her trade. If she survived by weaving, then balancing upon, a tissue of lies who was I to despise her for it? At least she knew what she was doing and why.

There was something else too. Ivy had a narrow, slanting way of looking at me, accompanied by a mocking smile as if she saw right through my uniform and godliness. As if she knew me for a sham. And this I could not stand.

'I'd push off,' Ivy said. 'I'd go now if you give me what's rightfully mine.' Mary and I exchanged glances. I picked up the poker and stirred the glowing coals. Although it was August, it was a chilly evening and we had lit a fire. Ivy sat in the chair my mother used to sit in, but whereas my mother had been so still you could almost forget her, Ivy fidgeted and fretted so that no one could rest.

'He had nothing,' Mary said, as she had said, patiently, over and over again. 'He arrived here in filthy corduroys. No linen even, no stockings. His boots were worn through, lined with newspaper, only fit to throw away.'

'And why should I believe you?'

'Because it's the truth. We have no interest in stealing.' Even Mary's voice had developed an edge of irritation when she spoke to Ivy. 'And anyway, where do you think you'd go?'

Mary looked exhausted, she'd just put the children to bed, while Ivy had sat staring into the flames. Apart from the odd snap or slap, Ivy had practically ignored her children since she'd arrived and Mary had taken them over. I could see in the way she spoke to them, played with them, scolded them kindly, a sort of rehearsal going on for the day when she had her own. When Harold was there, he watched her with a look of such enchantment on his face that I had to leave the room.

Ivy was hunched over the mound of her stomach, twisting a strand of her hair nervously round a finger so tightly that the tip of it had gone a dark, fat red. I knew very little about pregnancy but I thought she couldn't possibly get much bigger. Mary had arranged with a midwife that she should be confined at home, and all talk of moving her to somewhere more permanent had ceased until after the baby was born.

'What are you gawping at?' Ivy asked me suddenly.

'I was only thinking about the baby.'

'Cup of tea?' Mary asked.

'Not for me,' I said. 'I think I'll go up.'

'If Jim had been alive,' Ivy said plaintively, 'it would of been his birthday today.'

'Oh, my dear.' Mary went over to Ivy to embrace her, but Ivy flinched away.

'Don't give me your bleeding pity nor God's *love*,' she almost spat. 'Just give me what's rightfully mine and I'll go.' Mary stepped back.

I went upstairs. Her ingratitude made me seethe. I had given her the best room, fed her, put up with her children for weeks – and for what? To be abused, to be made uncomfortable in my own home. I knelt on the gravel by my bed and prayed to God to help me forgive her.

In the night, I was woken by Mary's fist on my door, her voice: 'Trixie, Trixie my dear, are you awake?'

Ivy was in labour. She had woken Mary a few minutes before. Mary was already dressed to go out in her bonnet and cape.

'I'll go and fetch the midwife,' she said. 'There's no rush, it'll be hours yet – but best be on the safe side.' Her voice bubbled with excitement. 'You keep her company while I'm gone.'

She touched my hand and smiled. It was the first real tenderness she'd shown me since the Harold episode and I thought I was forgiven.

I took a few moments dressing, a moment or two for prayer, not long. I was not prepared to find Ivy as I found her, sitting bolt upright against the bed-head with her knees open and up under her – my – long nightdress. Her hands were twisted in her hair and her face gleamed with sweat.

'It's coming,' she gasped.

'Not yet,' I said, 'Mary said it'd be hours.'

'I tell you, it's bleeding coming.'

On the sheet was a streaky wetness. She gasped and gritted her teeth, I could hear the faint grinding along with her moan.

'Oh Christ,' she groaned, 'Oh Christ get this bastard out of me . . .' Then her face darkened as she bore down.

I did not know what to do.

'Mary will be back soon with the midwife,' I said.

'Aaaah . . .' I thought she would tear the hair from her head. She slid down further on to her back, I tried to get her hands out of her hair, but in the process some of it came out and was left tangled around her fingers. I hovered uselessly by the bed. 'What shall I do?' I asked.

She pulled her nightdress right up and I saw that her private parts were stretched open. I put a hand on one knee. I was surprised by its coldness. She was trembling violently. I picked up a blanket to cover her but she fought it off.

'Aah . . . aaah . . . aaaah!' her voice rose from a moan to a scream and she grasped my hand and squeezed with her bony fingers until I wanted to cry out myself. Then she began to push, her face swollen and dark. I was awed by her strength. Her eyes were closed and veins in her neck and forehead bulged.

She stopped and looked at me for a moment, then she laughed. 'You've gone white as a bleeding sheet,' she said. 'You're no more use than a chocolate tea pot. Oh Christ . . .' and then it started again.

'Jesus, Jesus, let it be all right . . .' I muttered, I couldn't think of a coherent prayer. I kept one hand on her shuddering knee, the other gripped in hers as she pushed down, her belly like a boulder, squeezing and contorting with the force of the contraction.

'Water . . .' she whispered and I gave her a sip, helping to support her small head. Her hair was damp. I kept looking at the door, hoping that Mary would come with the midwife.

Then she grasped my hand again and began to push, making a low deep growl. One hand went down between her legs and I saw her stretching wider open like a slow grin spreading, and heard little sticky ripping sounds and then, crammed against the lips of her opening was something crumpled, soft and blue. I saw a wisp of colourless hair and realised it was the baby's head.

'It's coming!' I said.

'You don't say.' She paused, panting, before the next contraction was upon her. I was excited now, as if somehow *I* was achieving this, helping to achieve it. At the next push more of the head came out and I thought Ivy would split in half, with the great blue upside-down head jammed half in, half out. But then, at the next push it seemed to swivel and the head was born. Ivy was making little animal cries and gasps.

'What do I do?' I said. 'Water? Is there anything . . . ?' but she did not answer. She squeezed her eyes shut and with a wet gush the shoulders, then the rest of the little blue wax-caked body came slithering out. The room filled with a hot, wet, bloody, womanish smell. The cord seemed a terrible twisted thing, pulsing and snakeish. I was trying to lift up the steamy, slithery baby just as Mary came in, followed by the midwife.

'Beat us to it, Angel,' the midwife said. 'Hot water, towels . . . I could murder a cup of tea.'

'Trixie, oh Trixie, I'm sorry.' Mary put her arm round my shoulders. 'I never dreamed it would be so quick.'

'It was fine,' I said, 'perfectly fine.'

'You've done well.' She kissed me on the cheek.

I went downstairs feeling almost as if I had been blessed, feeling light-hearted, quite silly with joy and relief, with a ridiculous sense of achievement. My hands were greasy from the stuff that had coated the baby's skin. As I boiled water and gathered towels, I could hear the high mew of his new voice and alongside it, Ivy's complaint.

For two days there was an atmosphere of celebration in the house. I thanked God for answering my prayer. Sharing the experience of birth with Ivy had brought us closer, I thought. I felt that I understood her and though that is not the same as *liking*, my dislike was not so strong. She was quieter, exhausted by the birth, softer somehow. She'd decided to call the baby Harold, after Mary's Harold, when he brought her a parcel of clothes for her son.

I was fascinated by little Harold's newness. His cloudy-blue eyes, when they squinted open, seemed filled with impossible knowledge and wisdom. When I held him in my arms and sniffed the soft skin of his scalp, the smell made me ache, I don't know what the smell was, only skin and hair but it was more like new-baked bread . . . no, more than that, it was almost a spiritual smell as if something was permeating from him along with his warmth, something like the smell of Heaven.

And then. Oh this is the worst thing. Why do I torture myself with this memory?

Many of the Salvationists from our Corps visited the new baby and gave him gifts. He was like a little prince, surrounded by admirers. Mary, Harold and I sat round the bedside on the second evening and sang. Ivy's children, all freshly bathed with their white dandelion-seed hair standing up like haloes round their heads, sang with us the verse Mary had taught them. Ivy looked almost beautiful in the soft light, with the baby, wrapped in a white shawl, in her arms. *Jesus bids us shine with a clear, pure light, like a little candle burning in the night.* Harold's voice was so tender and low, and Mary's so sweet – but mine was reluctant. I don't know why, as if I was choked, too full of emotion to sing. Harold and I had hardly looked at each other since his proposal but on that night, our hands touched as I passed him a cup of tea and our eyes met for a stinging second.

And then a wickedness came upon me, just for a moment, only a thought, come from Satan, but I thought I would have him, I would snatch him out from under Mary's nose. Have him, how I do not know, whether to keep or just to use, I really do not know. It was only a second's evil thought that intruded into the song, but I was so ashamed. *In the world of darkness, so we must shine, you in your small corner, and I in mine.*

Ivy didn't like to have the baby sleeping in the same room, she could not sleep she said, hearing him snuffling, waiting for him to wake up and cry. So on that night, after she'd fed him, we tucked him up in the pram in the hall where he'd wake Ivy only when he was properly crying. I stayed for a moment after Mary had gone upstairs rocking the pram to make sure he was settled. I bent over and kissed the top of his downy head, breathed in that heavenly smell. And then I went upstairs to bed.

I cannot bear to think this, I cannot bear to remember. Move Trixie shift your bones, do something.

Our Father, who art in heaven.

Oh no no no.

What is it that is wrong, dear Jesus what is it?

The next day, the baby was gone. Just gone. I woke in the early morning to the sound of a scream downstairs. I stumbled from my bed and hurried down. Ivy was in the hall in her outside clothes and the pram was empty. She stood by it, pointing and wailing. The little blankets were flat as if there had never been a baby and when I put my hand in, the sheets were cold.

All was confusion. The police were called. We were all questioned over and over. That was a terrible day for we all feared for the life of little Harold.

Who would take a baby, a newborn baby? Who would steal him from his mother?

The house and the garden were searched. And on the evening of that day, while the police and the Salvation Army were still searching, questioning, trawling the river, Ivy made her accusation. We were sitting round the fire, Ivy wrapped in a blanket was staring into the flames. She had not spoken for an hour. Mary, Harold and I had been talking in low voices and praying.

'We must eat,' Mary said, for we had not touched a morsel all day in our fright and confusion. Nobody answered but she got up and went out to the kitchen. When the door had shut, Ivy turned her head slowly and looked at me.

'You took him,' she said. 'You took my baby.'

'Ivy!' Harold stood up. 'We are all with you in your suffering but you cannot make wild . . .'

'She took him.' Her voice was calm. She gave me a still, cold, narrow look.

'You simply cannot say such a thing!'

Mary came back into the room with a tray of bread and cheese and tea.

'What is it?' she asked, feeling at once the atmosphere, seeing the way looks travelled like blades across the room.

'She took my baby,' Ivy said again. She lifted her bony index finger and pointed.

'Ivy,' Mary put down the tray and went across to her. 'I think it's time for bed. I've got the drops the doctor brought to help you sleep.'

'She must apologise,' Harold said.

'It's all right,' I said. 'She's not in her right mind . . . Ivy, it's all right.' For that moment I was filled with love and compassion, not hurt by her accusation. I walked across and took her pointing hand in my own. 'It's all right,' I said.

She spat at me. So quickly that I hardly understood the puckering of her lips, the jerk, until I saw the little ball of white spittle on my sleeve.

'Ivy!' Harold was outraged. I stepped back, wiped my sleeve on my skirt.

'First she stole my Jim's things,' Ivy said, subsiding, tears coming to her eyes, 'his gold watch, his money, his good boots . . .'

'There was nothing,' soothed Mary. 'And Trixie would never . . .'

'Then she even took me bleeding baby . . .'

'Let's get you to bed,' Mary said. Together, Mary and I coaxed Ivy up the stairs, gave her her sleeping draught and stayed with her until her eyes closed.

Of course it was a lie, or a sick fantasy, but Ivy did continue to accuse me. Of course it was not true. That doesn't need to be said.

But one thing shocks and shames me. A coincidence only. On the night of baby Harold's disappearance, before being woken by Ivy's cry, I'd been dreaming. I'd put on my dressing-gown and stumbled downstairs into the chaotic intolerable day and all thoughts of my dream had been driven from my head. But it had hung over me like a bad taste, the flavour of dread. It was only later that night, after Ivy had fallen asleep and Harold had gone home, only as I knelt on the gravelly floor by my bed to pray for the baby's recovery, that it came back to me, with a swift, sick shock the dream I'd had the night before. I had dreamt about Benjamin Charles. It was the dream I'd had since early childhood, the hot, cramped, slithery struggle in which I killed Benjamin Charles who was not separate at all but was a part of me.

It was coincidence only, that that dream had come to me on the night of baby Harold's disappearance, coincidence, or the Devil's work, but it hurt me. It made a terrible, secret wound in my mind, my memory, I don't know, in some hidden, fragile part of me. Maybe my soul.

Ivy left. Baby Harold was never found, and one morning she was gone and her children with her. She stole a few items – silverware, a clock, Mary's purse. She left her Bible behind and I don't suppose she missed it. She fled before the truth could be discovered. The scale of her evil. She was fully dressed that morning, the morning of the baby's disappearance, dressed and in her boots as if she was going out. Or had been out. Why was she dressed so early in the morning? The house was quiet after her departure. And though she was searched for, she was never found. She never went to another Salvation Army Corps for help or we would have heard. What she did and where she went remained a mystery.

And after her departure, the weather changed. Not the weather so much, it remained fine, but the atmosphere. The sky was as blue, the leaves as green, but in the air, scarcely detectable, was a faint tang of decay. The sensation of something nearing its end. Not only summer. They changed towards me, everyone, even my friends, especially my friends.

Nobody said they believed Ivy's accusations because they were preposterous. The woman was a liar and a fraud. She had never set eyes on the poor dead drunkard, of that I am certain. There never was a watch and chain, there never was a good pair of boots with money in their soles. Every claim she made was a lie, every accusation. A woman like that could sell her child. Why was she dressed, why was she fully dressed so early, if that was not the case? Where did she get enough money to spirit herself and her children away? Can anyone tell me?

That was my reasoning. The only explanation I can think of. The only rational thing. And others agreed, the police even, agreed that it was an explanation. And nobody suggested anything else, not to my face. But *what if Ivy didn't sell her baby, what if the woman was telling the truth for once in her life? What if Trixie Bell stole the baby? What if* . . . Nobody said it, nobody even thought it, of that I am quite convinced. And yet . . . and yet the weather changed.

Mary was even more formal with me after Ivy's departure than before. There was no spontaneity, no warmth. She spent most of her free time with Harold. They talked endlessly about their wedding, and Mary about the children she would have, almost as if they existed and sometimes I felt they did, in spirit, they were there already clinging to her skirt, trailing up the stairs behind her, awaiting only the bodies she would give them.

One afternoon. A coal fire in the grate, the curtains half drawn against the lashing rain, the lamp lit. The three of us harmoniously together for once, drinking tea and making toast on the fire.

'It's like winter,' I said.

'In the winter we will be married.' Mary smiled at Harold with her eyes. 'In our own little house.' They had found a small place in Islington that would be free in December. 'Trixie, you must come and look at it. We like to walk past don't we Harold? If it stops raining we could go this evening.'

'Not this evening,' I said quickly, 'I've got things . . .' I trailed off. In truth, there was nothing.

'Well, another day then. She must come, mustn't she Harry?'

He nodded. He looked like a giant sitting on the low stool by the fire, his knees bent up, his hands with their long fingers too big for the cup. I liked to look at his hands. I'd like to have stroked the little black hairs on their backs. He smiled at me but it was a snatched away smile. His eyes were dark under the flop of black hair and I could not read them.

'Oh!' My toast had blackened in the flames.

'Give it to me.' With a knife, Harold scraped away the black crumbs. 'There.' I took it and as his hand touched mine I felt a jump of something live . . . something that could have been love given half a chance but was only regret and sorrow. For a second I hated Mary, sitting there, so rosy and smiling and confident. She had him now, for sure, and quite right. She would be a good wife, a good mother. While I could never be either, never, that I knew.

'Trixie,' Mary cleared her throat and looked at Harold for support and I knew that something was planned, that they had something to say. 'Harold and I have been talking . . .' She looked at him, waited for him to take over, but he was unprepared, opened his mouth in a rather stupid cod-like way. 'You have not given testimony lately, Trixie,' Mary continued, 'you are silent at the meetings.'

'I . . . I have not been strong,' I said. I don't know what I meant.

'We both love you, you know that . . . in Jesus Christ,' Mary continued. 'Our duty has been to help you in your fight against sin.'

I nodded. My mouth had gone dry, I could not swallow. But my hands were wet. I could not make myself ask what she meant, what sin?

'We've talked and talked and prayed, haven't we Harold?' She appealed to him again, more irritably. He sighed, cleared his throat almost apologetically before he began.

'We're concerned about your . . . behaviour.' He blushed and I thought *you may well blush*, remembering, as I'm sure he was remembering, his behaviour, the way he had kissed me. 'About your commitment to God and the Army.'

'How can you say that!' I burst out. I could not bear it.

'But Trixie,' Mary said, 'though you work so hard and profess such dedication . . . you don't speak up at meetings and you . . .'

'Yes?'

'Harold and I both have knowledge of you that . . .'

Harold looked into the fire and rolled bread-crumbs between his fingers.

'That?' I prompted. I could not bear the hesitation. The fire crackled and snapped.

'That we cannot . . . you know that cases of gross misconduct must be reported to the C.O. That it is likely that your name will be removed from the Roll . . .'

'You can appeal . . . you can request a court martial hearing,' Harold said. 'Trixie you must understand our position.'

'My *friends*,' I said bitterly.

'No Trixie, don't . . .' began Mary.

'I took no baby,' I said, fiercely, 'I know what they think, what they are saying. But I harmed no child.'

Mary looked startled, darted an uneasy glance at Harold. 'No, it is not *that*. We don't believe *that* or else we . . .' her voice trailed away.

Harold struggled up from the low stool. He stood towering over me. 'Do you inspect your soul and your actions every week, Trixie? What are the questions you ask yourself? Ask yourself the questions, Trixie. What are the questions?'

The rug in front of the fire had an uneven fringe, grey where it had once been white. I kept my eyes on the fringe as I recited:

'Am I guilty of any known sin?'

'Well?'

I shook my head and the shaking seemed to dislodge a shower of soot to blacken my heart.

'Do I practise or allow myself to indulge in anything – in thought, word or deed – that I know to be wrong?'

Again I shook my head. Mary gazed at me sadly. But it was true, I did not, do not *know*.

'Am I the master of my bodily appetites so as to have no condemnation?'

They waited for my reply but I was silent. Their eyes were hot on my down-turned face.

'You are not telling the truth,' Mary said softly. I got up and went to the window where it was cooler, I put my cheek against the cold glass. The rain had stopped and the sky was pearl between the thinning clouds. 'I have seen you Trixie, I have seen what you do. And you know it.'

'I do not know.'

Mary sighed. 'Trixie, we cannot hold our heads up as Salvation Soldiers and overlook or condone ... we cannot ... do you understand our position?'

A thrush had picked up a snail and was smashing it on the stones that edged the path. A ray of sun came out and the garden glittered.

'The rain has stopped,' I said.

'Turn round Trixie,' Harold said. I turned. He stood beside the Salvation Army badge that I had so proudly and hopefully fixed to the mantelpiece. He looked hot and damp standing by the fire. Suddenly I thought of my father standing there, just where Harold stood in front of the hearth scolding or scorning me and I knew he was still there. And my mother sitting vacant in the chair beside him.

'We have prayed. We have weighed our friendship for you in the balance with our integrity, our duty ...' Harold continued.

'It's all right, I understand.' I experienced a sudden draining away of light and energy from my head as if I would faint. I sat down.

It was at this moment that I knew I had to leave. The Army was my life but my life was a sham. The Army had given me every bit of self-respect I'd had. It had been like a uniform. The uniform was my self-respect and sometimes I almost believed in it myself. The uniform *was* me. I was a black bonnet of official dimensions with a scarlet band and ribbons not exceeding 2½ yards in length; I was a navy-blue serge speaking jacket with a stand-up collar; I was a black serge skirt; a crimson shirt, a white linen collar. I was a pair of plain black shoes, for patent leather, brown or white leather must not be worn. That is what I was.

But I was a sham. Ivy knew me for a sham. I searched my heart over and over, every night I had searched my heart and could find no trace of badness, hardly a trace. Just like the times when I was forced to stare in the mirror searching for evil as a child, I found none. I was only good intentions, no evil desires, no vices. But I could not answer the questions in the negative, not definitely because there was a sort of clamouring inside me that I could not hear; there was knowledge in me that I did not know; there was guilt for deeds I never did or had even heard of. I could not give testimony at meetings, I could not pray aloud. The Spirit simply wasn't in me. I was all confusion. But it was not my fault.

I had pledged my life, my self to Jesus and he did not want me. What more complete rejection could there be than that?

I had never really been Saved. It had all been pretence.

Like my father said, a monstrous charade.

How was I supposed to stand it? I felt not only that my heart would break but my body too would smash – with the hurt and the pressure of the silent clamouring – like a vase, a mess of glass, water, petals.

A weak beam of sunshine found its way into the room.

I stood between the window and the hearth and I felt my childhood was still there skulking in the corners, fluttering in the shadows and the curtain folds, still there. And still there in me too.

I hated that house. I did not want it. Mary and Harold could have it. Why not? What they did with it did not concern me. I didn't want the house and I did not want my body either. I had had enough of myself.

I felt almost happy. I tidied myself up, polished my shoes, put on my bonnet, tied the ribbon firmly under my chin. I left that house. The air was soft and kind, a clean-rinsed summer evening. The sun sent silver shafts to the earth that once I would have linked to God's love or some such stuff. But it was only sun shining down on a late summer's evening, only a physical phenomenon. Its beauty was meaningless. I walked very fast along dirty gleaming footpaths. I walked as fast as I could, my skirt flapping around my legs. I walked towards the river while my resolve was strong.

# ADA

I should have kept us together.
Poor Trixie but . . .

Frank was killed.

Nobody told me, who would tell me? I saw it in a newspaper.
UNDERWORLD GANG BOSS MURDERED.

I did not know what to do. I could not. What could I do?

It was not even me that saw him last but Trixie. She was with
some Army songsters, singing outside The Cross Cat. Frank
walked past her. He didn't look at Salvationists as a rule, dug
his head down into his collar. But somehow this time he did. He
looked up and saw Trixie and hesitated. I could read his eyes
even under the shady brim of his hat. He thought it looked like
me, remarkably like me, but that it could not be me. Not his
passionate Ada, not in a Salvation Army uniform, not shaking
a tambourine.

No, I do not know what he thought.

Through a filter I saw him, through the filter of Trixie's eyes.
Poor Trixie was shaken by his look. How I wanted to reach out
for him, go into the pub with him, to take him home like I had a

couple of times, sneak him in past that interfering Mary. How I wanted to make love to him, my whole body tingled inside Trixie's, frightening her with the feeling. But all I could do was mouth the stupid hymn. I was helpless. But the music died in Trixie with the shock of it with the force of my longing, lust, love, frustration.

I was helpless.

When I saw in the newspaper that he was dead, my Frank, I . . . I was not.

That is all. I simply lost my strength to hold us together and we went into a spin and the boy, he . . . I was not in control. I let go of the reins in my weakness. It was my fault.

Trixie was in despair because Mary knew about my doings and thought it was her. What a laugh! Trixie drinking and making love to a gangster in the most interesting of ways. Trixie enjoying herself. Ha!

And then Ivy coming, and that baby, and me, in my torment, in my grief, letting go, letting the boy break through. I let us down. Trixie. I should have held us together.

Because that boy is a monster.

That boy will kill.

# SOAP

Trixie was out in the street. I have never seen her out in the street before. I went to knock at her door and saw that it was ajar and that the room was empty. I walked out to the front and there she was, hesitating beside the road as if she was about to cross. She put one foot forward and then drew it back again, as if something was coming – but there was nothing. She wasn't wearing her coat, she had no bag. Across the road outside the greengrocer's back entrance, cauliflower leaves littered the path. I went to Trixie and caught her arm.

'What a mess,' I said, just for something to say.

'Compost,' she said, shaking me off.

'Oh!' I was relieved. I'd thought she looked demented. 'I'll fetch them for you.' I crossed the road and picked up the thick curved leaves. 'Here.'

She took them without looking at me.

'I was coming to see you,' I said.

'For a cup of tea?'

'I wouldn't mind . . .' She turned her back on the road and walked back up the passage. I followed. 'Thank you. And I was going to ask a favour.' We went into her house. It was freezing cold, the windows all open, no trace of the sherry, the flowers, no sign of the day before. 'I've bought you a card,' I said, 'sorry it's late.'

She opened it and smiled tightly. 'Roses. Very nice,' she said and stood it on the mantelpiece.

'Pretty aren't they?' I said, 'I know you like flowers . . . gardening.'

She turned her back and went into the kitchen. She was in a strange, tense mood. I listened to her fill the kettle and light the gas. She started humming. To the tune of 'What shall we do with the Drunken Sailor' she began to sing, pointedly, as if to me. '*What shall we do with the Sneaking Judas. What shall we do with the Sneaking Judas?*'

'Want any shopping?' I asked.

'I'm not a prisoner,' she said quietly coming back through. I didn't think I'd heard her right.

'Sorry?'

'I'm not a prisoner. Don't think I don't know your game, keeping me locked up. I know your sort.'

'What? Trixie . . .'

She subsided a bit.

'Trixie, that's just nonsense,' I said as gently as I could. Clearly, she was distressed. 'Why don't you sit down and I'll make the tea? Let's shut the window shall we, it's very cold in here.'

'You can shut the window if you like,' she said and went back into the kitchen. I did so and sat down. The television was switched off for once and I could see my distorted reflection in the curved screen.

'I came to ask you something, and tell you something,' I called. She clattered about in the sink and the kettle shrieked. She carried the tray through, pale tea slopping on the biscuit she had placed in each saucer.

'Thank you,' I said. 'I do look a sight . . .' I nodded at my reflection and she flinched. She looked very upset.

'Are you not well?' I asked.

She bent down and switched the set on. There was an advert for Flash and one for insurance. 'I'm going to get my hair done,' I said. 'There's a place along the high street where you don't need an appointment, and I thought I could get a load of shopping in for you . . . you see . . .'

'I don't know what I want,' she said.

'Whatever it is I'll get it for you.'

She laughed: a dry, squeaky, disused sound.

'Peace of mind,' she said, 'can you get me that? Just an ounce or two, just a slice.'

'If you could buy it I'd have some for myself,' I said. I reached forward to touch her hand but she jerked hers away.

'I wanted to ask you a favour,' I said.

'Spit it out then.' Her tone was suddenly sharp. 'What is it, money?'

'No! Trixie, what a thought! I wondered, you know my heating's gone kaput ... I wondered if I could have a bath here. I'd pay you for the hot water, of course. You see – I'm going home.'

'Home?' she said. Her face went dreamy, her voice childish.

'Yes.'

'Home on the range?'

'Sorry?'

'Where seldom is heard a discouraging word?'

I smiled. 'Sort of. Back to my children.'

'Children!' She started. 'Children! You never said anything about children.'

'Two,' I said, 'a boy, four, Robin, and a little girl, Billie. She's nearly one.'

'A baby,' she said, pulling her fingers to make them crack.

'Yes.'

'Now you see me, now you don't,' she said, putting her hand over her eyes and removing it, almost teasingly. 'Where is he then?' she asked in a sing-song voice. 'If you've got a baby, where is he?'

'She – I know Billy's usually a boy's name. They're in London, at home, with my husband.'

'London? What part?'

'Bromley,' I said. 'Do you know London?'

'Do I know London!' She sat on the edge of her chair.

'Bromley's not London. Not what I call London.' Her face seemed to be changing, the muscles sliding beneath the skin. I was alarmed, I thought she might be having some sort of stroke or seizure. Her face flickered, that's it, flickered between its usual lax tiredness and a sort of concentration that was like a skew-whiff face-lift, the muscles tightening and bunching, the cheeks rising. She smoothed back her sparse hair as if there was a great cloud of it. 'Do I know London she asks!' I recognised the Trixie of the day before.

She leant forward conspiratorially. I sipped my tea which was weak and cool. 'And what have you done with the baby?' she whispered. 'You can tell me, *I won't* tell. Have you done away with him?'

'Trixie!'

Her face changed again. I was beginning to feel dizzy. It was like being in a room with several people. It was unsettling. I was so glad I would soon be home.

'Oh, that name,' she said, 'that tiresome name. I thought I said, my name is Ada, palindrome, you know. A.D.A. Same either way.'

'Ada . . . yes you did say. My children are both with my husband. I'm going back. That's why I want to get smartened up a bit.' I thought it best to be normal, not to react to her strangeness.

'You *do* look a fright,' she agreed. 'He won't look twice at you like that you know, it's perfume they like, men, perfume and tight clothes. Silky black clothes. Oh, and lace. Did you run off with another man? Was it an affair of the heart?'

'Nothing so exciting,' I said.

'No?' She looked me up and down.

'I just . . . Oh I don't know, Trixie, Ada, I can't explain. So could I, do you think, *could* I have a bath, just a quick one.'

'You could get a plumber in,' she said.

'I know, but it would take ages and cost . . . and I'm leaving. But never mind, it doesn't matter. I can go without.'

'No, no, no . . .' She stopped to think. 'Of course you must have a bath. The tank is full. Now?'

'If it's convenient. Or later . . . it's just that I've had this flu and I'd like to freshen up before I go to the hairdresser's.'

'Now will be fine,' she said.

'Thank you. I'll get my stuff.' I stood up.

'Stuff?' A woman in a skin-tight white dress was silently singing, her eyes smouldering at the camera. 'That would suit you,' she said, 'a dress like that. Something to show off your figure. They don't last forever you know, figures.' She ran her hands complacently over her solid midriff.

'Not my style. I'll fetch a towel and soap.'

'Don't be silly. There are piles of towels, rich thick piles of towels, too fat to shut in the drawers, white towels, blue and red, any sort of towel you want and soap, bars of it, heaps of it, pink soap, white, Imperial Leather, Pears, Camay, all the big-name soaps.'

'Oh, well!'

'Up in the attic. Where I store things. Go up in the attic and choose.'

'No, I can't.'

'Go on . . . go up and take your pick.'

I hesitated. My own towels were damp since there was nowhere warm to hang them. And I could hardly be bothered to go back. Also, I was curious. I wanted to see what Trixie's attic was like.

'Thank you,' I said. 'I'll do that.'


I was surprised that she used the attic, the stairs were very steep. There was a lock on the door at the bottom but the key was in it. The stairs were dim, narrow and uncarpeted, dangerous for an old woman alone who could so easily slip. There was a thick, musky, musty smell that made me sneeze violently. In the light from the dim red bulb that dangled from a frayed flex I could see the hairy clumps of dust gathered at the corners of each stair.

At the top there was a small, bare landing and another door, also locked, also with a key. I opened the door and gasped with a mixture of shock . . . delighted surprise . . . I don't know. In the centre of the room was a double bed, rumpled sheets, shawls, pink and black silky underwear, crushed flowers tangled with the sheets – Mr Blowski's lilies by the look of them. The room was lit by one small dusty skylight. Chairs were heaped with chiffon and satin; Trixie's beaded dress was on the floor; black and red feather boas were draped over dusty mirrors. So many mirrors! And on the dressing-table was a powdery jumble of make-up, perfume bottles, hair-clogged brushes, lipstick-smudged hand-kerchiefs, sticky wine glasses. High-heeled sandals littered the floor and stockings were everywhere, one hung from the lampshade like the spectre of a leg.

My heart was beating unnaturally. I felt disconnected. This attic was not like the rest of the house, as Trixie last night was not like the usual Trixie. Again I had the feeling that I was intruding in someone else's dream. A sweet, stale chill hung in the air. I shivered and felt my skin prickle into goose-pimples. I looked round for the clean towels and the heaps of soap but found none. It was such a mess. There was nothing clean. I stood gazing at my dusty reflection in the dressing-table mirror. My heart nearly leapt out of my mouth, as the door suddenly banged and there was Trixie with her back to it. She was wearing the wig again though she had not changed her clothes and her crimson smile was immense.

# BOY

Nearly out sometimes
Like a boy's arm sticking out of a cave
The cave is an old woman
It is not fair
If she does not let me out I will . . .
How can I?

I am bad because boys are

Big
Because it is for boys, all that, bad and that

I am stuck in Trixie
A danger and a disgrace

Baby boys are weak like girls are
They are supposed to be boys but they lie about in blankets
and suck milk from ladies' titties and cry

One day I will out
Making me angry, keeping me inside as if I am nothing
When I am more than her
I am the boy

Watch out for me
Watch out

# RIVER

Terrible things. My head like a merry-go-round. I must calm myself, collect myself, must collect. Yes, pull myself together. Hear me Trixie? Pull yourself together. Things going on, an absence . . . if it was an absence.

Look, perhaps it is just old age, just absent-mindedness, just ordinary. Now I can think that. I am old, an old woman, memory leaking like a sieve. Ha! It's almost funny. I'll forget my head next.

The memory leaking like a sieve, seeping out all the time like some sort of wound staining my days.

Should I have a bath? The water is so hot it's growling in the tank. A long, hot soak. But the bathroom is so cold. When the water is warm you never want to get out, you lie there until you wrinkle, you lie there till the water is nearly as cold as the air and then, when you get out, you are so chilled, you just cannot get warm again, not properly warm, not for hours.

Now, if I brought a towel downstairs, I could air it by the fire first. But having a bath is such a terrible palaver, what with the undressing, the running of the bath, getting in, washing, getting out, getting dry, getting dressed, cleaning the bath. Oh it makes me tired just thinking of it. It's a night's work, having a bath, and for what?

It might soothe my headache away, ease my stiffness. Maybe later. Soon it will be time for 'Countdown' but before that there is nothing I want. Oh I don't know, I don't know where to put myself. My throat is sore as if from shouting or talking and talking and my heart is beating hard. Oh there is such a crashing in my head, a commotion, almost as if a voice is crying out from the very roof of my skull, 'Let me out.' If only I could, I say, if only I could.

The River Thames is a strange and filthy beast. I was always afraid to get too close. From far off it is just water, an opening, pleasing among the bridges and buildings. I did think, once, that the river was like God's love, deep, eternal, *whiter than the driven snow*. But close to, it was grey and brown, khaki. There was a stench of I don't know what, oil, something sulphurous almost, something rotten. It was not that my faith in *God* had deserted me, it was my faith that He could save *me*. There was a flaw in my soul. I was unsalvagable. I was lost.

I went down beside Hungerford Bridge and sat on a stone. There was a place where small boats were moored, used to be, in the shadow of the bridge. The river's cold got into me and I shivered. The water sloshed against the stone platform. I had never looked at the river so closely before. In the distance it seemed a beautiful thing. It seemed to belong to the city, to be tame. It ran between the houses, roads, warehouses, under the bridges as if in obedience. But that evening, in the mood to end it all, I saw my mistake. The city was obedient to the river, designed around it.

The pagan idea came to me that this river was itself a sort of God. It was nature. Not tame, not there to serve commerce, not there to provide a lovely view. It was nature and it had the power, if it wanted, to rise up and swallow ships and towers, wash the bridges away, drown the buildings and the people in them. It could destroy. I could see that, smell it on its breath. The water was muddy and carried fragments, lashed them against the side of the platform. Sometimes the curve of a wave would break against the stone like a seaside wave, splashing my skirt with dark spots. I saw paper rubbish, bits of wood. I saw a tiny shrunken thing that might have been a drowned kitten, very new. I saw flowers floating past, a stream of them as if someone had flung them, one by one from a bouquet: rose, rose-bud, rose-bud, rose; green ferns like feathers; and a puff of babies' breath. Not old flowers but fresh: snow, sunshine, flame. I thought it was the end of love, a spurned gift. The River carried them away like an offering.

I imagined myself in the water. I would go up on to the bridge, climb the rail and drop. I knew how cold it would be. I felt already the slapping shock of it, the gasp. I knew my body would struggle, for not all of me wanted to die, oh no, not all. I knew that my clothes would grow heavy, my skirt thick and wet around my thrashing legs. A shout might even come from my mouth, a cry for help, but it would be in vain for I could not swim and the River was greedy, it licked its lips, all those grey tongues against the stone, slavering for such a gift, a warm woman, an unsaved soul. And into my shouting mouth would rush the water, into my nostrils. I would breathe in water and my mouth would fill with oily feathers, flower stalks, I would float and be wound about on my voyage to the sea with ropes and strings and slippery weeds. Dead kittens would tangle in my hair. And there would be silence.

I climbed the steps on to the bridge. There were people about, it was a fine evening. I listened to the traffic and another sound, I almost laughed. Very distant, by some acoustic fluke, I could hear a Salvation Army band, I swear I could. I stood looking at the low orange sun on the waves. A barge passed under the bridge pulling a series of wide flat vessels packed with timber. It looked neat and toy-like. St Paul's dome shone dully in the distance ahead of me. My mouth, I found, was moving, mouthing the words of the chorus I thought I could hear, so faint and distant:

> *The Cleansing Stream I see; I see;*
> *I plunge and lo! it cleanses me;*
> *It cleanses now, it sets me free,*
> *O praise the Lord it cleanses me.*

Was Jesus having a laugh at my expense? Did I think that? Did the band happen to be playing that tune? Was there a band at all? In my memory there was and that is all I have. You cannot catch it by its shoulders, memory, shake it, force it to tell the truth.

My memory tells me I heard the chorus, shaped my mouth around its words, smiled slightly, bitterly, at the coincidence of deed and musical accompaniment, climbed over the railing, and glancing down to check that no boat was directly beneath me, jumped.

Jumped, everything white before my eyes, feeling no emotion at the precise moment of jumping. What did I think of? Babies. Baby Harold and Benjamin Charles swaddled together in a soaking shawl.

The babies would have been in my mind as the water engulfed me but instead there was a split second of air and flight and then a jolt, a rip, a scream. A scream from outside or from my own mouth, I do not know, but there followed other shrieks and running feet.

My skirt had caught on an iron projection, ripped but stuck in the thick hem, so I dangled head down, most of the skirt about my head, the rest caught up behind me. I screamed again, this time it was surely me, my frustration, and then a terrible mad laugh fled from my mouth. It was as if the life inside me gathered into a ball in my chest, around my heart, and hurled itself out and I was sick, sick even as I shrieked with laughter, hanging there my legs all on display, my underwear, my stockings, even perhaps my tattoo, all visible to the people, crowding round now, on the bridge. I choked as the acid from my stomach stung the lining of my nose, I struggled to get free, to drop, but someone had grabbed my shins by then. I was untangled and hauled back over the railing, on to the bridge and a sort of safety.

The past is pressing in and the present flickering in and out. Oh I am not myself. A bath, later I *will* have a bath and an early night. Just now I can't shift myself from beside the fire, from in front of the television. I don't know what to do with myself, holes and gaps like empty windows with draughts blowing through.

Pray Trixie or sing, drown it out, drown out the voice in your own skull that cries *Let me out*. Jesus is with me. I must believe it. I do. I *do not* feel alone. He did forsake me but He is here with me now. In my eyes, my body, my mind. And in my memory. And it will all come out tonight, now that the stones are rolled away and now that it is started. Like a reckoning.

# THE ROSE TATTOO

I don't believe this. I don't know whether to laugh or scream. Scream I think, now that the time is passing, it is a joke gone on too long. She has shut me in her attic. Not a joke at all. I can't make sense of her or it. I am not exactly frightened, but it's bizarre the way she's acting. She's gone off her head. So I *should* be scared. If she was a man I would certainly be scared. It is absurd and it is bloody freezing up here. I thought it was cold in *my* house. I'm only a few feet away from my own attic, my darkroom.

I think she brought Mr Blowski to bed last night, I think they rolled together in the flowers, dark red sheets and white lilies. They are so old and . . . it doesn't bear thinking about but . . . Richard and I have never had such an exotic, erotic time of it.

And what she told me . . . I don't know what to think. Well it's true, there's proof, the mark on her skin. She came back upstairs when I'd been here maybe an hour, locked the door, put the key in her cardigan pocket, stood with her back to the door, her arms folded.

'Trixie, please let me out,' I said.

'Since you want to know,' she said, quite fiercely.

'Know what?'

'Since you will not keep your nose out I will tell you.'

I shivered. Her face was frightening.

'Since you are so fascinated. Curiosity killed the cat.'

'Please let me out, now, I want to phone my husband.' I'd

decided I wouldn't wait, I'd ring him at work, I'd get him somewhere. After all he is a doctor, other people can get him when they want him so why not me? 'Trixie, please . . .'

'My name is Ada. A.D.A.'

'Yes . . . Palindrome, I know.'

She snorted. 'Oh knows it all does she . . .'

'Trixie . . .'

'Trixie is a waste of space with her watery tea and her television, forever banging away at that bleeding silly tambourine, forever singing, if you can call it singing, "Oh Jesus, Jesus!" as if her life depended on it.'

'Yes.' I sat back down on the bed. I thought if I let her talk, it would be over and she would let me go. I wanted to ring Richard to ask him what to do, she was obviously *completely* off her head. He'd know what to do.

'And you think I'm Trixie! Are you absolutely blind? She stopped and looked at herself in the dusty mirror. 'Oh I see . . . yes, I am wearing Trixie's dress . . . I don't have the choice . . . hardly have a chance . . . Do you think I would wear a sack like this from choice?'

She struggled to unbutton her brown cardigan but the buttons slithered between her hasty fingers.

'I am Ada,' she said, peering closer at the mirror. 'Can't you see?' She rubbed a space clear in the dust. 'See, it's Ada.'

'Yes,' I said, 'I do see, but I don't understand.'

'What is there to understand? Oh the weather!' She looked up at the skylight, rain had started falling, making a fidgety sighing sound. 'How I long for the sun. I swear I have Mediterranean blood in my veins . . . you can see it in my lovely skin, and my eyes . . . almost black . . .' She pushed her face into mine and I gazed into the watery blue.

'Yes,' I said, 'I see.'

'Oh the stories I could tell you! How I have longed to tell you!' She wandered round the room as she spoke, her breath white in the air. She wrapped a purple feather boa round her shoulders and I thought I caught, in the look she gave the mirror, a snatched impression of what she saw, a sultry, sulking beauty – but when she turned to face me again there was the same puffy old face.

I had a painful surge of longing for Richard. I felt lost in her mind, nothing real, it was as if her craziness was contagious. I did want to hear, but in safety, on my own territory. 'Trix . . . Ada, I need to go and make a phone call. It's urgent. I'd love to hear your story, but I must make the call first.'

'Why? Why now? Who is it you have to phone? The police, isn't it? Oh no. That you will not do.'

'Why the police?'

'Then who?'

'My husband, my children.'

'Oh yes . . . the so-called husband and children. Can't you do better than that? Suddenly there is a husband and children.'

'I told you before.'

'I've thought it over. It's a lie.'

'I do have children, two.'

'And I'm the Queen of Sheba.' She came close and put her hands heavily on my shoulders, pushed her face into mine so that I could smell her powdery skin, her sour breath: 'I have listened to you, Inis. I have listened to every word you ever spoke to Trixie and you never mentioned children, not a husband or children. Don't give me that rubbish. Husband and children, Ha!'

'I ran away from them,' I said, 'and now I want to go back.'

'To call the police,' she said. 'Was I born yesterday?'

'Why should I want to call the police?'

She paused. 'Oh the rain, the rain, it is breaking my heart. Like soft little fingers against the glass, don't you think? Scrabbling. No. You are a cunning bitch. I think you are a queer, that's what. Else why cut your hair like that? You're no more a mother than me. But you needn't think I would look at you . . .'

'Tr . . . Ada!' I almost wanted to laugh. 'Look . . . if you don't believe me, come to the phone-box with me. You can listen. I will *not* phone the police. You can talk to my husband if you like, to Robin, he loves to talk on the phone. Then you can tell me your story.'

'As if I am begging you to hear my story!'

'Well not then, I don't mind. But I do need to phone.'

'Do you think I'm stupid?'

'No, no, I don't think you're stupid.' Trixie is an old woman, heavy but not strong. I knew I could easily force her to give me the key. I could see it in her cardigan pocket, the glint of it just peeping over the top. But I would wait, I did not want to hurt her. There was no need to panic. I tried to quell my exasperation. 'Just tell me, why you think I'd want to call the police.'

'Think you can trap me like *that*.'

'What do you want?' I asked. 'You can't keep me here against my will.'

'No?' Her face became dreamy. She pulled out the tapestry stool from under her dressing-table, and lowered herself on to it. For a moment I thought she was Trixie again, but no. She stared at me but with her eyes focused somewhere beyond. I decided to be patient, to be kind. She was confused, 'senile dementia' was what Richard would say, or else she was simply mad. Whatever, I thought, best to be kind.

'I would love to hear your story,' I said. I shivered and pulled the red chenille bedspread round my shoulders.

On her face was a faraway smile. 'I never had a husband of my own, but if only you had seen my lover,' she began. 'His hands were . . .' she stretched her own hands out and looked at them in awe. 'His hands were . . . he could encircle my waist with his fingers. Where is he now . . . oh these people who vanish because I can't hold on to them. His fingers were long and strong. Manicured nails with the moons so perfect . . . Sharp nails, hard hands. He was a cruel man, yes, but he worshipped my body and let me tell you that is a rare thing, you don't need to tell me that no one has ever worshipped yours, not like that . . . but mine . . . Ah well it's such a pretty body, if it wasn't so blessed cold I would show you . . . oh no . . . not with your inclinations.

I can see you think I'm vain, but there are worse things, my dear, than vain.'

She cupped her hands over her breasts and ran them slowly over her body as she spoke. 'Shoulders smooth as ... I don't know what, breasts like little pink-beaked birds that's what he said, don't you think that's poetic? Legs, long and slender. I always wear silk next to my skin, it is the only thing, my dear, the only thing. I like the warm cling of it, the slip. I like to look at my skin beside silk but best of all I like to look at my skin beside the skin of a man. I like the man to be darker than me. I like the man to have black hairs everywhere, fuzz and shadow. I like the man to be tattooed. My lover, the man with the cruel hands, he had tattoos.

'He had an eagle on his back, big, with a hooked beak and staring black eyes. Its wings were his shoulder-blades, feathers curling round his shoulders, brushing the tops of his arms. It was brown, black, gold and yellow and his own skin was wonderful brown. Oh I can see it now! I liked to lie naked on his naked back and press the baby birds of my breasts against the eagle's wings. His name was Frank. He was a gangster, he was a ... he was a ... but oh ... he's gone.'

She paused, looked round the room as if surprised.

I had been looking at the floor as she spoke, embarrassed, afraid that she'd suddenly realise what she was saying and be humiliated. I did not know how to react.

'You don't believe me, do you?' she said.

'I don't know.'

'Well look here, just look.' She pulled up her skirt. The plaster on her shin was a thick ridge under her brown stocking. Over her stockings she wore long peach-coloured bloomers. Grunting with the effort she rolled her left bloomer-leg up high, past the the stocking-top to the withered skin above. 'There!' she said triumphantly. I could see nothing more than discoloured skin until I bent closer and saw, half hidden in a crease, the red-brown edges of what might have been a tattoo, which otherwise I'd have taken for a birthmark or a bruise. 'I don't know where he went . . . people drift . . . you turn round and . . . where are they?' She let her skirt fall down.

'Yes,' I said. 'Let's go downstairs now. I'll make us some tea. You'll be missing your programmes.'

She laughed. 'You don't get it, do you? You *still* don't get it.'

'I would like to phone.'

'Ha ha ha!'

'Please . . . look, I need to go to the toilet.'

'Under the bed,' she said and before I'd reached the door she was out and had slammed it behind her. I shook the handle, but she was quick to lock it. I was furious with myself for not snatching the key. Stupid, stupid, stupid. I banged on the door and shouted and stamped. But there was no point in that, no point at all.

Under the bed I found a white enamel chamber-pot. I pulled it out and some of the contents slopped over the side. It was full of dark yellow urine, covered with a dusty scum. Choking on the smell, I pushed it underneath. And sat back on the sagging bed.

Why didn't I phone Richard when I had the chance? What was all that nonsense about waiting? I should have gone home. I could be there now. I want Richard. I want my children. There is no clock here, I'm not wearing my watch, but I know what time it is because Trixie's turned her television up so loud. I can hear the theme from 'Countdown'. If I was out I would telephone. I am decided. Only now I can't. It seems too idiotic to be truly frightening.

But she is frightening because she is so . . . I don't know. What *is* up with her? I don't know. I'm no psychologist. What I do know is that *I* am better. That's the funny thing, that's why I want to laugh as well as scream. Trixie's oddness has balanced me. The shock of the door slamming snapped me out of it. The oddness of her story, I'd say it was a fantasy if it wasn't for the mark on her thigh.

226

If she doesn't let me out soon, I'll . . . well I'll get out somehow. I don't know how. It must be possible. I'm tired. It's so bloody cold. The bed is very soft. The smell of crushed lilies is heady, quite sickly in the cold air – mixed with old pee. I cover myself in the bedspread. The sheets feel damp and they are stained over and over and over. There are patches of dark yellow pollen and stray grey hairs.

Robin and Billie will be eating their tea. Fish-fingers, maybe, or scrambled eggs with toast and Marmite. Billie loves cauliflower cheese but Robin hates anything in a sauce. I want to know what they're eating. I want them. Oh this is stupid! I will have to shout and scream to drown the television. She will *have* to let me out.

# SOMETHING SWEET

I don't like to see my body. I don't like it. It is a stranger to me and I try not to look. I lay a towel over my front. It soaks up the hot water and is a calming weight. A turquoise towel with lime-green stripes. Can't think where I got it, I would never have chosen it, not turquoise, not with lime-green stripes.

This is good though, a bath. Some of the Epsom salts have not dissolved, still gritty on the bottom. They sting the wound on my leg, a good, healing sting. I couldn't make my mind up about the bath so I put my finger in the Bible. *Stolen waters are sweet, and bread eaten in secret is pleasant.* I don't know what he's getting at sometimes, Jesus. Stolen waters? Still a bath is water, and a warm bath is sweet when you are an old woman, stiff in the limbs and soft in the head.

Singing in the bathroom is most effective. Acoustics, wonderful!

> *Always cheerful, always cheerful,*
> *All our words let love control:*
> *Always cheerful, always cheerful,*
> *Constant sunshine in the soul.*

Acoustics wonderful, yes, loud, yes. But my voice sounds very shrill and lonely echoing against the tiles. And the wet towel presses down on my stomach like a big, flat hand and it is hard to sing with no air in my lungs.

I could fancy a bit of something sweet tonight, something in the pudding line. But I've got nothing like that in, only blessed biscuits. A suet pudding soaked in golden syrup, creamy custard made with eggs. Oh Trixie Bell pull yourself together, do.

I cannot quite be calm because I've a nagging, niggling feeling that something is not right in the house. As if a door is hanging open or a gate banging. But it is nothing like that. It could be nothing.

I think I fainted on the bridge. Next thing, a searing whiff of smelling-salts. People all round me, all looking down and a woman kneeling beside me holding the bottle.

'She's come round,' she said in a deep, rough voice. 'Here darlin' . . .' She held the bottle to my nose again but I turned my face away. The people loomed over me, a wall of dark cloth, so that I felt I would suffocate.

'Shall I fetch a doctor?' somebody asked.

'No . . . she's all right.' The woman had a big jaw, dark skin, greasy black hair and she looked kind.

'What about the coppers?'

'Now what'd we want with them gentlemen? You all right then?'

I nodded my head.

'Get her to the Sally Army place,' someone suggested. But I shook my head.

'Tell you what, darlin', you come back with me for a cup of tea . . . how's that sound?'

'Yes, thank you.'

She helped me to my feet. 'Show's over,' she said.

I felt so strange. Not faint any more. It was like . . . one afternoon that woman next door showed me some of her photographs. Double exposures they were, one image overlaying another. Experiments, she said. And that is how I felt that evening, still myself but with another woman superimposed, the edges not quite together, quite experimental.

'What do they call you?' the woman asked as we walked off the bridge.

'Ada,' I said, without thinking, thinking only that I would not give my real name.

'I'm Doll,' the woman said. 'You up to a bit of a walk?'

We walked along the Embankment where down-and-outs were congregating for the night and I looked away for fear that I should see a familiar face – or be recognised myself. We turned away from the River and in my strange state of mind, I thought I heard it sigh. The sun had been setting as we started and it got dark as we walked. A fine drizzle dampened my face. We walked north between wet, black buildings. I was in a daze. Sometimes I came to for a minute to discover we were still walking and it was as if we had been walking for ever.

Near Liverpool Street we stopped at a tall, cramped house. I did not like the smell: perfume, beer, cinders. I was not innocent of the world, my Salvation Army experience had seen to that, and it didn't take me long to realise that I was in what once I would have called 'a house of ill-repute', that Doll was a madam, a soul ripe for, crying out for, saving. Not only that, but through the house ran a constant stream of such souls. Once I would have rubbed my hands and thanked God for this opportunity to do battle on His behalf.

But.

This is the worst of it because I did know what I was doing.

It was really me.

And yet it was not me, not entirely. I was not myself. Oh those words, how they have echoed down my years. Not myself. Not yourself, dear. Not yourself.

I was myself but not myself.

There is a thread of dusty spider's web hanging from the light-fitting. I never think to clean the ceiling. It twizzles in the heat from the bath, twizzles and floats. The tap drips and it sounds like the ticking of a clock, but not regular. Like time, the space between the drip ticks varies.

I do not feel alone. But that is good Trixie Bell, that is good, not bad. God is here in the dripping of the tap, the cobweb, the pressing weight of the towel. Do not be afraid. God is with you. Do not be afraid of your own self.

# BOY

I am here
I am going to be out
I will out of her

She can almost feel me now
Because I am getting the strongest
Because boys simply do have this thing that is strong
    about them
And bad and all that

Will not be kept in

So do not make me angry

Crawling out of a heavy thing
Asleep for years
But now awake
And sleep do make me strong

I have outed
And I will out

# MOTHER'S RUIN

It's bloody freezing up here and my throat is sore with shouting. There are two things I can do. Try to escape or wait. I have tried the door but it is solidly locked with a mortice lock. What kind of person has mortice locks on their inner doors? A crazy person, that's what. The only window is the little skylight. It doesn't appear to open, I can see no way of opening it. I could smash the glass – but then what? I'm not squeezing out of a jagged glass hole on to a slippery slate roof in the rain. The situation is not *so* desperate. I'd break my neck.

I wish I had my watch on. It's gone quiet downstairs now. She switched off the television, then there was a break during which I shouted and even screamed, then she began to sing. She sang one I did not know and then fighting hymns: 'Onward Christian Soldiers'; 'Fight the Good Fight'; I stamped and shouted but my voice was tired and my feet would keep stamping in time with the hymns, however hard I resisted. She's been quiet for ages now but snatches of 'Fight the Good Fight' keep floating into my head. I haven't heard it since I was at school.

The water-tank has been knocking and gurgling, filling with a deafening waterfall sound.

I wonder if I could knock through into my attic? I think, if I am forced to escape, if she doesn't let me out soon, that is what I'll try. With the aid of something hard . . . maybe the edge of a mirror frame, or the stool, I don't know.

But I will wait. I'm sure she'll let me out, she'll come to her senses. It is almost dark. The light seems to be shrinking back through the skylight as if afraid of what it might illuminate. Oh stop it! I've tried the light-switch but the bulb is dead. There are candles stuck in bottles, the bottles completely disguised under thick, red, waxy drifts, the wax cascaded down so that the bottles are stuck hard to the surfaces they are on: the dressing-table, a chair, the floor, where the wax has fused itself to the fabric of the red-patterned carpet. I look around for matches. I am hungry. I found a dish of old sugared almonds, the pastel colours faded almost to white. They are dusty but if I was very hungry later, if, absurdly, I was still here later, I could try eating them.

There is a half-full bottle of Gordon's gin. I think it would be very stupid in this situation to drink any, but still . . . I am so shivery and there's nothing to do but wait. I haven't drunk gin for a long time. Not since Christmas, not since the night I seduced Richard. And I've never drunk it neat. It has a comforting taste, medicinal somehow. Mother's ruin. Ha!

I do feel truly better. I am out of the prison that was my despair and so I am free. God I'm getting poetic, but it *was* like a prison, the bars were my despair and against the bars pressed the ghastly faces of my fears, of the things I could do to my children, of the things that people, mothers too, do to the children they love. The terrible things. What is the urge to hurt the thing you love the most? The helpless thing. I don't understand. I give up. The gin *is* comforting. It's warming me up. At least I've stopped shivering now. *Fight the good fight with all th – y might.* I used to love singing hymns at school. I could still love singing. Maybe when I get home I'll join a choir. I feel like some old wino swigging from this bottle, but all the glasses are thick with fingerprints and encrusted with blackened lipstick.

The bars have dissolved and the grisly faces have receded. Maybe I even did *right* to leave my family while I was so afraid, so . . . what? . . . deranged? You could say that. But now I am better. The thing is, the thing that will make me really laugh when I'm out of here is that now I am free of that prison, absolutely free,

234

I am a prisoner. I am free. And where do I discover my freedom? Locked in some crazy woman's attic. Who would believe it?

She's stopped singing but the words still ring in my ears: *Faint not nor fear, His arms are near*. I must find some matches. *He changes not, and thou art dear.* There must be some, or a lighter, else how would she light the candles? I open the dressing-table drawer, a long curved drawer with a fiddly knob on the front, latticed like a brooch. When I pull it out, powder rises up from it like a peachy ghost. Nothing in here has been disturbed for a long time. It is full of old perfume bottles, tickets to musicals, dried up make-up, a black lace glove, a man's handkerchief with a curly embroidered F in one corner. What did she call the lover? Frank.

But *could* she have invented him, invented the whole story? It has the flavour of a fantasy. I can't get my head round the fact that it is Trixie's story, staid old Trixie. But no. It was Ada. A man with an eagle on his back, her body pressed against . . . Could she have made that up? So vivid, I can almost see it, almost feel it. God, this is weird, it's making me excited, the idea of her white breasts squeezed flat against his tattooed skin. Stop it!

No matches. The powder makes me sneeze. I don't like the dark. Silly. I spend half my life in my darkroom – but that's about light. Making light. And there's the friendly red glow and the magic of the pictures appearing. I've never got over that magic which is actually a perfectly explicable chemical reaction. It used to make me feel so warm and happy in a deep muscular way, as if my stomach was smiling, when I saw my babies' faces floating up through the liquid, as if, almost as if I was creating them all over again. Soon I'll be able to hold and touch and sniff them. Lick the milky skin of Billie's neck. *Only believe and thou shalt see.* Oh this bloody woman. LET ME OUT! When will she come to her senses? I must find the means to light these candles before it is entirely dark.

Thank God for the gin.

Oh. It is so cold. And I feel filthy. It is so dirty, a dusty, clinging female dirt. Everything I touch coats my fingers in pinkish grey powder. She will have to let me out.

# ILL-REPUTE

Condensation is running down the tiles. The cobweb is hanging limp. The towel that hides me from myself is cold and the water is cooling. I hardly have the strength to stand up, hardly the will. This is why I hate baths. I should not have stayed in so long. I do so hate the cold. I want someone to look after me, someone kind. Someone to worry about me. Not her next-door, never again. Blowski would do if only he would come. Kindness has hardly ever been shown to me. Perhaps I don't invite it.

Doll was kind, whatever else she was, genuinely kind. She helped me on the bridge purely out of the goodness of her heart. You might not think that but it is true. If Doll was the Devil then the Devil has a kind face and makes a good cup of tea.

I followed her into the house of ill-repute, through the hall and into a comfortable room. She lifted a sleeping tabby cat off a chair and sat me by the fire. It was good to get off my aching feet. She drew the curtains and lit the lamps.

'Now, Ada,' she said putting strong sugary tea in front of me. Every time she said that name I flinched; thinking I should say I am Trixie, not Ada. But then I did not want to be Trixie anymore. I sat in a low armchair. The pattern on the hearth-rug was red, blue and green and made my eyes jump. The tea cup was encircled with ivy leaves that made me think of Ivy and her baby. The cat got up, stretched its feet out behind it and yawned, flicking me quite a look as it settled itself down against the hearth.

'It's a palindrome,' I said, surprising myself. It was as if another voice was speaking through my mouth, another face floating to the surface leaving me, Trixie, mute.

'What's that?'

'A palindrome, reads the same backwards or forwards. A.D.A. same both ways.'

Doll twisted her face with the effort of imagining it, then smiled. 'It does and all! Well a palindrome, eh? You learn something every day.' She gazed into the fire for a minute, then, 'Oxo!' she said triumphantly, 'the drink, Oxo.'

'Yes.' I sipped my tea. I had drunk tea in so many houses and I liked it strong like this. I could almost feel the fur growing on my tongue. I did not feel like Trixie. I did not want to be Trixie. I thought I would try to *be* Ada. Although I did not, still do not, know who Ada is.

'Well,' Doll said after a moment. 'Ask no questions and all that ... but it don't take a detective to see you're a Salvationist.'

'Was.'

'You *was* a Salvationist. What is it, darlin'. In trouble?'

I shook my head. 'Not the usual sort.'

'Usual sort! I've seen the lot! There isn't no *usual* sort. Here, this isn't some Salvation stunt?' Doll said leaning forward, smiling but only half-joking, 'I save your life, you save my soul ... nothing like that?'

'No!' I was me again. I felt a weight descend. It was no good, I was Trixie. Speaking with the other voice, that I must call Ada's, I had felt different, fun and flippant, with a lightness in my limbs that I had never known before. Carefree, is the word. Whereas *I* am loaded down with care. I felt envious. Envious of part of myself? I came to understand that my body was not only mine but shared with this ... this ... stranger. Ada.

I thought she was nicer than me. I was envious. So I tried to be her, pretended. And got it wrong.

The room we sat in had a mirror. Oval, like *the* mirror, hanging over the fireplace. All it reflected, from where I sat was the dark red curtains, a picture on the opposite wall of a bird, bright, maybe a cockatoo.

'I wanted to end it,' I said, my Trixie-voice heavy.

'Well that much was obvious. You're not . . . up the spout?' She looked at my stomach. I looked down at the long rip in my skirt.

'No.'

'Get that off you and we'll have it mended. You can't go out like that, not round here. Where do you live, anyrate?'

'Nowhere,' I replied. 'I had a house, it was my parents'. But I left. There was a woman staying there, a woman who sold her baby.'

'Sold her baby? What do you mean, *sold* it?'

'She said she hadn't. I put her up when she had nowhere to go. She said I stole her husband's things, he's dead. Died of drink, only I don't think he was her husband at all. And then she had a baby, I was there. I saw him being born, and . . . and then he disappeared. And she said, she said I took him, as if I would, as if I would take a baby and strangle him. She accused me.'

'Steady on, girl. You never did it, of course you never?'

'No, of course not. She must have sold him, she must have.'

'Yes.'

'Poor women do such things.'

Doll laughed, a high-pitched laugh, odd in a woman with such a deep voice. 'You don't have to tell me what poor women do, darlin', I'm what you might call an expert.'

The door-bell rang, and she got up and twitched the curtain. I saw her pass across the mirror. She stood with her head on one side, listening. The front door was opened: a female voice, a male voice, a female voice, a laugh, the door closing, two pairs of footsteps on the stairs. Doll smiled, settled back down.

'Only selling your baby . . .' She pursed her lips. 'That's beyond the pale, anything where nippers are concerned. There's sin and there's sin, see.'

I nodded. 'But she accused *me*.'

'So – you thought you'd top yourself?'

'No, not just because of that . . . I am very strange.'

'You're telling me. So, are they after you – the coppers I mean?'

'No, no, nothing like that. I just wanted to leave it all. It all went sour. I hate that house.'

'Ada, you never *had* nothing to do with it, did you?'

'No!'

'All right, all right. So long as that's straight. So what do you want to do now?'

She poured more tea from the brown pot. She poked the fire so that it collapsed in on itself and added another scuttleful of coal. I saw that she was handsome in a massive way, her hair too black to be God's handiwork alone, her face deeply lined but still pleasing because of her frequent smile.

What did I want? I didn't know. Only never to see that house again, nor Mary and Harold. Only, if I was not to die, to start again.

I thought I could start again by pretending to be Ada, a very different woman. I thought if I pretended hard enough, maybe I could *be* her.

The cat jumped on to Doll's lap. She blew across the surface of her tea. 'So Ada,' she said, 'let's think. You was on your way to the pearly gates when you was unexpectedly held up as you might say.' I nodded. I closed my eyes and tried to imagine the coldness of the water rinsing away to nothing but there was too much life in the room, the fire crackling, the cat purring, Doll's chair creaking, the sounds of movements and voices elsewhere in the house. The door-bell rang again and Doll waited to hear the four feet on the stairs before she continued.

'Now, if you had had it, you'd of required no baggage. No cash, no clothes, no shoes, no nothing.'

'That's right.'

'But you're still here. You've got nothing have you? And even that's ripped. Get it off, girl, go on. I've seen it all before. I'll get it sewn.'

I took off my skirt and stood in my stockings by the fire while she took it to be mended by one of the girls.

'So what are you going to do?' Doll asked when she returned, listening for a moment to footsteps descending.

'I don't know.'

'Nice legs, anyrate.' She held out a silky dressing-gown for me to put on, but then she caught sight of my tattoo. 'What in hell's name's that?' She bent down to look. 'Blimey . . .' she touched it with her forefinger. 'Beautiful,' she said, and then she began to laugh, landing back in her chair with a big puff of air. 'You in your bleeding uniform. Miss Butter Wouldn't Melt . . . I've never seen a nicer one than that . . . nor in a nicer place . . . What they wouldn't pay . . .' she started, sobering. Then, 'No, don't worry . . . this is a clean house, proper house, all that works here works willing.'

'I don't know where to go,' I said, and then, to my horror, I began to cry. It was repulsive, my face all stretched, hot tears like wet insects scurrying down my cheeks.

'Here . . .' Doll sat me down again. My shoulders shook. I don't know how long I cried for but I felt I could have cried for years. I didn't know how I would ever stop.

Next thing, she'd taken me to a small box-room. Tiny, nothing in it only a narrow bed. There was a small window, no curtains, full of black sky. I was still crying when she left me there to sleep. I hadn't washed and I felt filthy, my hands smelled horrible, all the traces clinging to them of the terrible day. Even when I'd stopped crying my breath came in shivery gasps and I lay filled with disgust for myself, for everything in the world.

But I felt, also, as I calmed down, something else. I felt relief. Because now someone knew me. Doll had seen my tattoo: she had seen me cry: she had heard me speak in Ada's voice and my own. I hadn't said about my money, that I was rich, so that was a sort of lie. She thought I had nothing, that I needed help. But I liked that feeling. I wanted to be helped.

I lay in the narrow lumpy bed, afraid that I would roll off. I had no idea what the morning would bring. It was as if I had come to the edge of the world, as if the world was flat and there was nothing solid ahead of me, only clouds, only gauzy grey. I strained my eyes into the clouds until I slept.

All night there were goings on in the house, the door-bell ringing, feet on the stairs, voices, laughter, movement. But still, I slept. And I dreamed too, in vivid snatches as if a hand was flicking through a bright picture book. Most were nonsense. But one, I remember still. It was Mary and Harold's wedding, only the man called Harold was another man altogether, a man called Frank who looked like the man who stared at me in the street. All through the wedding he kept his eye on me and I knew I was his and that after the wedding it was me that he would carry to bed. During the singing, Mary removed her blouse to show her breasts and a wreath of lilies was tattooed around each nipple. She came towards me and said, 'These are for you, Trixie,' and when I touched them, the milk flowed like two streams.

Out of the bath and by the fire, all shivery in my dressing-gown that I've had for donkey's years. I thought I'd never get out, the water getting colder and colder and my skin going blue. Gave myself a fright, drifting off. You can die in a bath, old dears do die. Hypothermia, or drowning. You have to watch yourself, living alone with nobody to care whether you're alive or dead.

Something not right.

Please let it be all right.

# BOY

I am getting out
I am
Just you watch
That fat old woman
And the other one

She thinks she can keep me in

If I had wanted to get out before
I would have

But now I am ready
And Trixie and Ada will have to let me be

It is my turn to be

I will out
She will crack
They will be sorry

Watch out
When I'm about

# FILM STAR

I found a lighter. What is that other hymn, the one I used to like? Oh I know. *He who would valiant be, 'gainst all disaster.* A lighter, candles for light and warmth. One of them is nearly finished, just a spike of black wick, a hollow where the wax has run down. She'll have to come up. I am uncomfortable, cold, thirsty. This is almost embarrassing it is so, so stupid.

I opened the wardrobe. It was not easy. It is a hideous thing. How did it get up here? Too big for the stairs, too big for the door. Impossible as a ship in a bottle. Grotesque. If it was an animal it would be a . . . it would be an amphibian, a giant toad squatting. There were no matches anywhere else so I thought I'd look inside it. The wood is almost black. I wonder if it's ebony? Double doors – locked. I crashed against them, pulled and rattled, pushed against one door with my foot and pulled the handle until the lock gave way.

The door swung open and I shuddered. A blast of cold, stale, masculine air came out, masculine because it smelled of pipe tobacco but sweetened with old perfume. Coats and dresses hanging up, crammed, crushed together, shelves of crushed and tangled things, a fat brown-paper parcel. I stuck my hands into the dark cloth shadows to feel the textures: velvet, satin, tweed and fur. Because I was so cold, I slid a mink coat off its hanger and put it on. I despise people who wear fur, but the light silky weight of it, the slithery perfumed lining made me feel . . . I don't know, it seems so stupid and anyway I'm drunk, three sheets to the wind, my dad would have said, but it made me feel glamorous.

Reflected dimly in the mirror, wrapped in the black fur with my spiky white hair, I looked like a stranger. The cold fur started to warm me. Stuck to the pocket lining, I found an old peppermint. I put it in my mouth, teased off the fluff with my tongue.

I went through the other pockets of the garments in the wardrobe; found coins – pre-decimal mostly – lipsticks, dead flowers, sweet papers, a tortoiseshell comb. In the jacket of a hairy tweed suit, I found a pipe, half an ounce of St Bruno and a square silver lighter. I flicked and flicked it, and to my relief eventually it lit so that I could light the candles. The candlelight flickered on the dusty mirrors and on the black skylight. The light made the darkness darker. The edges of the room disappeared, the edges and the corners.

I felt so odd, detached. Again I had the feeling that I had strayed into someone else's dream, or tumbled into the clutter of a subconscious not my own. I was warmer in the coat and the candles gave enough light to see by. I banged and shouted. But the noise of my voice calling like that made me more scared. *Let me out* . . . *Help* . . . Scary and ridiculous. Also fruitless. She will come in her own good time.

I went back to the wardrobe, I was fascinated by all those old clothes, shoes on the bottom, crammed shelves at the side. I took the garments out, one by one, to look. The dresses were nearly all black: chiffon, velvet, lace, and many of them were torn. One was of a dark crushed velvet, like red wine. I wondered what Richard would think if I was to wear anything so sexy. It has a low neck. I couldn't work out how it would fit, where the shoulders would come. I thought I'd try it on. She's locked me in. I've nothing to do. I should keep myself occupied. I'm swimming in gin and quite numb. My fear, the thought that I'm trapped, has receded. The image of my children in a bright balloon of domestic light at the end of a telephone wire bobs there, somewhere above me, but separate.

I took off the coat and shivered out of my jeans and sweater. I wriggled into the dress, the velvet clammy against my skin, slowly warming. I had to take off my bra because the dress has no shoulders, it scoops round the top of my arms. When I looked in the mirror, I almost laughed I looked so preposterously sexy. I looked, despite my awful hair, quite stunning. I've never worn anything like it, it is a film star dress. It clings to my body, emphasising the line of my hips and thighs, the round slope of my belly. My breasts glimmer white above the low neck and my shoulders look lovely, I have never noticed my shoulders before. How round, pale and smooth they look above the long tight-fitting sleeves.

Trixie is so big how could she ever have worn it? Though she is not so tall . . . not much taller than me, just solid. Once perhaps it might have fitted her. The dress is very old, a bit rotten under the arms, one of the side-seams coming undone showing a peep of white skin through a dark velvet slit.

I picked up Trixie/Ada's wig and pulled it on over my own hair. It is warm and slightly scratchy. Black hair makes my face look even whiter, with the mass of hair I appear frail, my face tiny and . . . what is it? Piquant. I went through the collection of caked lipsticks till I found a usable one and filled in my lips with vermilion. I smell of animal fat, grease and old perfume. And gin.

I am frustrated that there is no one to see. I want Richard to see me. I look so sexy I turn myself on. A shivery, scary excitement. I can feel my heart beating against the velvet of the dress. On one of the wardrobe shelves I found a tangle of fine stockings, real silk with seams at the back, and a suspender-belt. I've never worn stockings, only tights. Richard once asked me if I would, if I'd wear white stockings with no knickers when we went out so that only he would know, but I'd been angry and scornful and worn jeans instead. But here in the attic, with the sensation of pale, cool silk against my thighs, one foot up on the bed, fiddling with the little rubbery catches, I'm sorry. I'll surprise him one day. I will be his fantasy which is also mine which I am in. Or someone else's. I took another swig of gin and shrugged the coat back on. I posed in front of the mirror, smiling film star smiles, pouting seductively.

But then I had the feeling that the mirrors weren't only reflecting, they were watching too, judging. The mirrors were voyeurs. Did I really look so sexy or did I only look absurd? I went cold, the realisation of where I was and what was happening came back. I felt as if I'd been slapped.

I went back to the wardrobe to pick up my clothes. Once again, my eye caught the brown-paper parcel. I opened it. The dust that rose from between the paper folds made me sneeze again. In the parcel were old fashioned boys' clothes: trousers, a blazer, a shirt, a cap, all quite moth-eaten, indeed, dead moths fell out when I held up a pullover and small grey live ones fluttered towards the candle flames.

I do not understand. Though it's none of my business. Maybe she had a son once? Why would I know anyway? I should parcel them back up again. I should put my own clothes on before she comes back. But I am sleepy. I should never have drunk that gin. I am dizzy. What if she never lets me out? I ate some of the sugared almonds, the sugar has gone powdery and soft but the nuts are all right. I throw a few lilies out of the bed, lie down and cover myself up.

Maybe Trixie/Ada is going to kill me.

Don't be silly. Why should she? But what if she was to have a stroke say, and die? Or drown in the bath? I could be shut up here forever. Oh stop it, stop it. *No foe shall stay his might, though he with giants fight.* I wish Richard was here with me, to see me, to touch me. *He will make good his right. To be a pilgrim.*

I wish someone would let me out.

*Trixie!*

# DOLL

I hardly know where I am. I am at home. If it wasn't for the television to keep me here ... What? What now? It is *dadadada-dum-dum* 'EastEnders', that is all right. 'EastEnders' is finished. I know where I am then, and when. All safe by the fire in my dressing-gown, all safe.

But why is she making so much noise? Why, when I long for the companionship of noise is she so quiet, and tonight when I cannot bear it why does she make such a noise? She is evil. She is like the Devil in my head, worming in the folds of my brain.

Oh what's up there in my head, no, no, not in my head in the top of the house where I do not care to go. Is the noise in my head or in my house? In the attic? That is where bad dreams live among the dust and cobwebs. Where the wardrobe is. I can almost feel its black weight above me. I never go up there. The door is safely locked. Stupid! What do I think would come creeping down those stairs if the door was open? It's only a room full of junk.

Still, better that it's locked, better for my peace of mind.

Terrible not to know where you are. That confusion when you wake and everything is strange, a split second that echoes down the day.

When I woke at Doll's, I did not know where I was. Or even who I was. I lay waiting for it to fall into place. Sun shone on my bed. Then I remembered the jump. I could not believe it. I might have laughed. I could not even do *that* right. A spectacular failure.

The little room was hot and stuffy. I got up and at the end of my bed, found my skirt, neatly mended and ironed. I wanted to wash, to start the day. I needed to find out: what happens next.

I opened the door and crept along the landing that was full of the smell of sleep, the sound of sighs and snores. I found the bathroom, slipped off the nightdress Doll had lent me and washed. There was a long mirror and I could not help seeing my body though I avoided my face. I could not help thinking that it was a lovely body, white as marble but for the dark nest of hair, the pink nipples, the bright red of the little rose on the thigh.

I dressed, the uniform seeming odd in this house, pious and somehow silly. Wrong for me now. I thought about going back. I didn't know what to do. I couldn't bear to remember what Mary and Harold had said to me. They had as good as killed me. I thought that as I buttoned my blouse: they had killed me. I was dead and whatever I did now it didn't matter. Trixie had jumped in the river and drowned. Now I would be Ada.

Downstairs it was quiet. The curtains were all closed against the sun. I opened them and let it stream in so that dust glittered in the air. I could have just walked out. There was no need to stay. But where would I go? Where would Ada go?

The thought of my house made me shudder. I could not enter that house again, the house of Trixie's childhood, the house of shadows and fear. I could not bear the sickening soup of dread that slopped in my stomach whenever I thought of Ivy or the children. Or even Harold and Mary.

At least I was not poor. I could do anything. Cruise to the United States. Buy myself a motor car. Learn to fly, ha!

I made a cup of tea. The kitchen was big and dark, no sun at the back of the house, a tap dripping a brown ring in an enamel sink. There were gin and beer bottles in a box by the floor – but it was clean. Every dish and glass washed and put away.

The wooden draining-board scoured, the floor swept. Doll was right, it was a clean house.

I sat at the table and sipped my tea. A girl in a satin dressing-gown came into the kitchen. She gave a start when she saw me sitting there in my uniform and then laughed.

'Doll's new friend . . . ?' she said.

'Yes, Ada.'

'I'm Gracie – I sewed your skirt.'

'Thank you, it's beautifully done.'

'Just one of my many talents.' She lifted an eyebrow at me as she poured herself a cup of tea and sat down. Her dressing-gown was trimmed with wispy down, pale like the hair of Ivy's children. I couldn't get that wretched family out of my head. Gracie's hair was pale and smooth as butter. She looked no more than sixteen.

'Hungry?' she said, jumping up. 'I could eat a bleeding horse. Bacon and egg?'

'Yes, thank you.'

She clattered about with pans and lard, whistling like a man, cracking the eggs and holding them high to splat in the pan.

'Doll's a respectable woman,' she said suddenly, turning to me quite fiercely. 'She saved me from worse you know. It's a respectable house.'

The door opened and Doll came in, splendid in an embroidered silk kimono. 'Dad, mum, tit, tat,' she said. 'And refer. Know what they are, Gracie?'

'No, Doll. Sit down.' Dramatically solicitous, she pulled a chair out for Doll. She wiggled her forefinger at the side of her head and winked at me.

'Get stuffed!' Doll batted her with her hand. 'Palingdromes, that's what, eh Ada? A.D.A.'

'Yes, darlin'.' Gracie sat down and yawned through her long white fingers.

Doll shuffled her rump around on her chair. 'Good night,' she remarked, rubbing her finger in the corners of her eyes. 'Here watch those rashers.'

Gracie got up to attend to the frying-pan.

'So has Ada here shown you her tattoo?' Doll asked.

'No.'

I was startled. My hand went to the place.

'Show her A. There's no harm in it.'

Well, I thought, I'm Ada now. Ada wouldn't be backward in coming forward. I slid my chair back and lifted my skirt to show her the rose. She breathed in. 'Ooh . . . that's lovely,' she said. She ran her cool fingers over the place and I shivered.

'Can I have one, Doll, can I? Go on.' She stretched out and her dressing-gown fell open to show her long bare legs. She opened her thighs and pointed to the shadowy hollow just below the wisps of light hair. 'Just here. Or else on me tit. A little bird I'd have, I think, a swallow or something.'

Doll yawned and stretched until her ribs cracked.

'Do you have to, Doll?' Gracie said.

Doll frowned at me. 'You're a dark horse, Ada. I'm most perspiwhatsit, as a rule. Tell like that . . .' she snapped her fingers, 'good, bad, dangerous . . . goes with the job. But I can't seem to get the measure of you. Perspicacious,' she added with satisfaction.

'Doll loves her words,' Gracie said, licking egg yolk off her finger.

Doll looked at me. 'So what are we going to do with you?' she asked.

'I'll go,' I said. 'You don't have to do a thing.'

'Seems a bleeding waste,' Gracie said. 'Think what our gentlemen would make of that.' She nodded at my thigh.

'Eat up,' Doll said. The bacon was sweet and fatty. 'We'd call her A,' she continued through a mouthful of bread, 'if she was to stay.'

'Just think of it,' Gracie said, giggling . . . 'No,' she held her hand up to me, 'no harm in thinking. A. sitting there with me and Nan and Edie, all of us in our glad-rags and whatnot and A. sitting there cool as a bleeding cucumber in her uniform. No lipstick nor nothing.'

'Quite a looker though,' Doll added, 'quite a figure underneath it all.'

'When the punters come in; the gentlemen friends I mean,' Gracie smiled apologetically at Doll, 'what wouldn't I give to see their faces!'

'Some of them'd go for her just like that . . . but what if she was to slide her skirt up, show a bit of leg . . .'

'Right up to her stocking top . . . show that rose . . .' Gracie sucked her breath in.

'Falling over themselves, they'd be,' said Doll. 'Still.'

# MOTHS

I don't think she'll come tonight now. It must be late. The moths
are fluttering near the candle flames. Stupid things. Giant flame
shadows wobble about on the sloping ceiling, the shadows of
the moths among them, shuddering smudges.

There is nobody to miss me, except those who have been
missing me all along. The swaying shadows make me feel sick,
the stocking hanging from the lampshade stirs, the room itself
seems to be swaying. The lilies are cold and fleshy and their scent
is rank.

Perhaps she had a son who died? Why else would she keep the
clothes. Poor, poor Trixie. I thought I knew her but I don't know
her at all. So sad that the little clothes are moth-eaten, so sad.

It is strange to be lying here in the redness of her bed, dressed
in velvet, silk and fur and to be too pissed to move. It is not like
me at all. I am thirsty, so thirsty, but there is nothing to drink
but more gin.

I'm afraid one of those moths will burn itself. What is it that
attracts them to the flames? I could blow out the candles but
then it would be dark. If I could be bothered to move, the first
thing I'd do is shut the wardrobe, there is something stupidly
menacing about the door lolling open, the dark, mothy, crammed
interior.

I want to see my babies. I'll bake a cake for them, buy presents.
It's nearly Billie's birthday. My baby will be one. I'll buy such
lovely things. And for Richard? I'll be his present in stockings

and suspenders, silk next to my skin, it's the only thing, my dear, the only thing.

Poor Richard. He tried to make me sexy. Tell me your fantasies, he said, but my only fantasy was of ten hours uninterrupted sleep. Alone.

There was that weekend in the Peak District. We could have made love in the open air like we did in Greece. Then we found a little scoop of beach, overshadowed by pine trees, hidden by rocks and we lay on the firm sand and made love, right on the edge of the sea itself. I cannot believe we did that, Richard and me, it is more like something from a film about another woman. I can even see the rectangular edges of the screen. That holiday we did it all the time, everywhere, in the shower, in a rowing boat, in a car.

I wonder if Trixie would give me this dress, let me buy it? No, it is rotting.

The gurgling of the water tank is a friendly sound.

I think she has forgotten me.

All these mirrors. Lying down I can see myself in a mirror by the bed smudged with lipstick, she must have kissed the mirror. My roots are showing. I used to kiss the mirror sometimes too, to see what I looked like kissing, but you can't see, it's too close and you steam up. I look like a tart, what my dad would have called a tart, and my mum.

I'm so thirsty and my head is pounding.

Does she mean to hurt me, or am I only forgotten?

I'm parched, so dry I have to sip the gin just to wet my throat. You can understand sailors going mad. All that sloshing sea. *Water water all around and . . . all the sea was ink*. No.

I wonder what time it is? Middle of the night, that's what I'd tell Robin if he asked. I don't know if I've been asleep or not.

*If all the land was bread and cheese and all the sea was ink, if all the . . . something about lemon curd?* I don't know. Robin knows it.

I want a tall glass of cold water, only that, the most simple request. One of those frosty glasses. First thing when I'm out of here, a glass of water, a pint of it, two pints. I won't be fit for much tomorrow.

If the moths would stop fluttering, then maybe the flames would stop fluttering. If everything was still it would be better. The shadows crawl like independent things, seem to crawl out of the wardrobe, like the ghosts of coats and shoes and frocks. Oh for Christ's sake.

If the clothes in the wardrobe are her past, then she must have had some past.

What did she mean about the police? What has she done then? What?

I could be scared, if I let myself. I could be very scared. I can smell burning wings.

# GENTLEMEN FRIENDS

God had left me. At the moment I jumped. Or I had left God. The Devil had caught me by the skirt and delivered me to Doll. Delivered me into prostitution. How many gentlemen friends I had in that time I do not know.

Now I am clean. I am forgiven. Washed in the blood of the lamb. I am still shivery after my bath. Possibly I am catching that woman's cold. I am not myself. Oh that again. I should be in my bed with a hot drink and my little bedside telly on for company. There's a Bette Davis on after midnight. 'A Stolen Life'. I do like Bette Davis. There is trouble in her eyes that I recognise. And something else. I know! That Inis! That's who she reminds me of. Fancy! All this time I've been tantalised. Give her some curls and lipstick and that's who she'd be. Bette Davis.

I'll see her tomorrow and I'll tell her. I'll be friendly. Cool though, cool but polite. I have to withdraw because she is a snake at heart, a snake with Bette Davis's face sent to rob me in the night.

Why do I not go to bed if I'm so tired and cold? A hot-water bottle or two at my feet and the lull of a black-and-white film. Instead I sit here too close to the fire, burning my shins and shivering. Some programme on the television while I wait for the film, I don't know, some pop group with matted hair, flailing, the sound turned down. Looks like an asylum, all that thrashing around.

What is it that is the matter? In this house there is nothing wrong. Everything is as it always is. And yet I cannot settle. It is as if I've left something switched on that should be off, or something open that should be shut, something undone that should be done.

It is her that has upset me, her next-door, with her treachery. I wish that she would disappear.

I got it wrong back then. I thought I would be Ada. I thought since I was Ada, I would stay and be a whore, that would be my new life, that was the sort of thing she would have done. But I was wrong. Or not. Maybe she would have done it but it doesn't matter. It wasn't Ada – if there is even any such person – it was me, that is what I have to face. I was the sinner, not her.

Jesus dropped me and the Devil scooped me up and made me into a whore. The Devil in the shape of Doll who was a good woman. One of few truly good people I have ever met. How can I say the woman who saw me in despair, who looked at me in my Salvation Army uniform, trying to end it all, looked at me and saw the makings of a whore, how can I say that woman was good? There is no sense in it.

Oh that first night.

I spent a week in that house before I was decided. A week spent largely in my room looking out of the window at the sky searching for a sign, a special cloud, a rainbow, I don't know what. But there was nothing. Only sky. Why did I do it? Nobody pressurised me. I was not a prisoner, I could have opened the door and walked out at any time. But I chose not to leave. I did not need the money from it. What did I need? To be part of something. Was that it? I was so hurt by Mary I cannot describe it. I was so hurt by the doubts about Ivy's baby, not my doubts. *Not mine*.

Really, I was dead. With the jump I lost responsibility. It fell from me and floated away on the Thames like a dead flower.

And so I said I was Ada. I even believed, some of the time, I really think I did believe I was Ada. They called me A. One day, at breakfast, I said I would like to earn my keep. There was a girl called Edie who choked and had to be thumped on the back and Gracie pulled a face at the others.

'Are you sure, darlin'?' Doll said, she took hold of my hand. 'You sure you know what you're letting yourself in for?'

'Yes.'

Doll licked her lips and squinted at me. 'Yes, I believe you do and all,' she said. 'Good girl.' She squeezed my hand and gave it back.

That evening I sat in the front room with the other girls. There was an air of suppressed hilarity, not shared by me. The others wore low blouses, tight dresses, sheer stockings, their legs crossed to show the tops. The air was thick with perfume, lipstick grease and cigarette smoke.

I sat stiffly on the edge of the sofa, my knees together, one hand crunching the other fist. I was in my uniform. I was Ada, I told myself, Ada mocking the old Trixie, that's what I told myself, but it was a lie. Really I was Trixie mocking Jesus. If I had worn a silky dress and lipstick, or if I had worn nothing at all it would not have been so . . . I would not have defiled my . . . Oh this is useless.

That is how it was. That is what I thought Ada would have done and that is what I did.

The first 'gentleman' to be shown into the room was brought up short by the sight of me, so prim in my jacket and bonnet. My dry, white lips. He looked almost as if he would run, but Doll caught him by the arm.

'Here now, Mr Smith,' she raised her eyebrows at me. 'This is our new girl, A. She won't bite your head off nor nothing else for that matter . . . she's not quite what she seems, are you A? Show the gentleman.' She nodded at my thigh but I was frozen.

Doll looked at Gracie who knelt and lifted my skirt until the red rose showed at the top of my stocking. 'Now, isn't that pretty?' she said.

'So what do you think, Mr Smith?' Doll said. 'Who's the lucky girl tonight?'

'Well . . .' He looked around the room, smiled at Gracie, then his eyes returned to me. He had a sandy moustache that twitched damply under his nose. 'I don't know that a spot of religion wouldn't work wonders,' he said, his eyes darting round, pleased with his little joke.

'That's right, Mr Smith,' Doll said. 'You see if A. can't save your soul for you while you're at it . . .'

'Right you are then.' He clutched his hat nervously against his chest.

He followed me upstairs. I could feel his eyes hot on the back of my skirt. A lamp was lit in the room, a little fire burnt in the grate. In a bowl were some white chrysanthemums.

We stood facing each other. He was no taller than me. His pale eyes settled on my uniform.

'Let's have a hymn, then,' he said. I don't know if he was joking but anyway I sang. At first my voice was unwilling but I thought that if I sang it might put off whatever was to follow, and as I sang my voice grew stronger. I shut my eyes against the twitchy ginger man.

'Yes, yes, oh yes . . .' he was mumbling. He had knelt down in front of me as I sang and ran his hands up under my skirt. 'Keep singing,' he said, 'keep it up . . . yes . . .'

'*The King of Love my Shepherd is,*' I sang as he raised my skirt and buried his face between my thighs, nuzzling up higher, butting and licking. It was as if some old dog had its snout up my skirt. *Perverse and foolish oft I strayed, but yet in love He sought me,*' and he snuffled and moaned into me. I kept my eyes closed as he scrabbled at himself and cried out, 'Yes, Jesus, yes.' And then I realised that he'd stopped. He stood up pink and shiny faced. My skirt fell down, heavy and safe around my legs. He wiped his face with a handkerchief.

'It's wonderful what a dose of religion does for a chap,' he said, straightening his trousers, clearing his throat, twittering around. Despite his handkerchief his moustache looked damp and sticky.

'Goodbye, my dear,' he said as he left the room. He looked saucily back round the door. 'God bless, eh!' and went off down the stairs chuckling at his wit.

He was the first and he became a regular and he was easy. There were other regulars. Some wanted only to talk. Some to do more than my snuffling ginger friend. But it didn't matter, I was dead to them all. And to myself.

*I* did that. I *was* it. I was a whore. Not Ada, me.

But I did not kill the baby. I would never do that. Jesus knows. I don't think even Ada would have done *that*.

# ADA

After Frank's death. I hardly cared to exist.

After the Ivy business, the baby and the boy oh *poor* Trixie *that*
she cannot understand. After that there was no me. Oh dimly I
was there, still, watching Trixie struggle.

She felt a most terrible guilt for something she hadn't even done.
Can you imagine the confusion of that?

I floated to her surface when she was weak, after she had tried
to kill us on the bridge, and for once when I spoke through her
mouth, she felt me and heard me.

She liked me. I was so glad because old stick that she is, I do love
Trixie. She liked me and she wanted to be me. But she got it so
wrong. Poor Trixie, she is like a babe in arms when it comes to the
physical side of things. She thought I would have sold myself!

I laughed a terrible cringing laugh before I drifted away. Love was
dead for me, died with Frank, was buried by the terrible joyless
performances in the brothel which were what . . . were a parody
of love and I could not stand it. I could not stand watching poor,
poor Trixie being such a fool. What else? Being such a mockery
of me. Even the boy turned away and went to sleep.

Not till Blowski did I wake up.
Clever Trixie to find a man we both could love.
Trixie loves him as a friend. But I love him as a lover should.
That Blowski, he sees me as I am and not how I seem to be. Some days he sees straight through Trixie to me. He never knows who he's getting when he knocks on the door, Blowski doesn't, that's the joke.

> *Call me romantic,*
> *but still I maintain,*
> *I was born to lo – ove.*

If Trixie and I could only be one. If we could end our days as one . . .
That is what I long for.
That is what she longs for, if only she knew.

But that can never be.
Because of that monster.
That boy.

# MAROONED

Oh God it is almost morning I have been here all night.

I couldn't think where I was when I woke. But, of course, I am here.

Marooned in a mad woman's dream.

But it is morning and the skylight has turned a weary grey. Most of the candles are dead now, spluttered out.

I am scared. I need to pee. Despite the coat I am cold. The air stinks of old wax, gone-out candle, amongst the other stenches, rotten lilies, ancient perfume, unwashed linen, the secret, festering reek of body juices dried to crusts.

She is a murderer, that is what she is.

Hark at me, bloody hell.

This is stupid. She has simply forgotten me. Old people are forgetful. Now it's light I'll attract her attention or she will remember. Then I will go home. No, hair first, hairdresser or a bottle of something brown from Boots. Pack . . . station, ticket, journey. Home. Oh my head. I can hardly move. How will I do those things? They are like wishes. When I close my eyes it is all red and fuzzy but . . . I can see the bubble with my children in it, balloon, like a party balloon drifted far away.

Sleep is like a dirty blanket.

The inside of my mouth feels like . . .

My head is an empty tin can and someone is bashing on it with a spoon, like Robin with his breakfast egg, smash, smash, smash.

Even these silly tinny thoughts hurt.

Look, if she wanted to kill me she would have done it by now.

Unless she wants me to starve.

But why?

You can quickly die of thirst.

When she comes up I'll overpower her. She might be bigger than me but she's not strong. Overpower her! I can't even move my head.

But there will be adrenaline. I will knock her off balance. I should feel pity. She is mad. This is mad, this, me, here.

So. There is no real danger. Except . . . what enemy is in my head whispering fears? Yes, all right, there is fire. I would not be in a strong position if she was to set the house on fire, but why would she? It is her home.

What did she mean about the police?

If I hadn't wanted a bath I might be home by now.

If I could have anything what would I have? Apart from water.

I would like to see Bonny again and smell her fur. I'd like her to lick my hand in her friendly way with her cool pink tongue.

And Richard and the children, of course, of course.

And I'd like to see my mum and dad.

Oh grow up.

There is nothing I can do but wait.

# SUNSHINE

Sunshine through the curtain-gaps. I have sat up all night. I never do that. It is just . . .

I am an old woman, coming unravelled; stiff in the limbs and soft in the head.

She's not herself, they'd say, the people if they knew.

It's just that . . .

Not herself, not herself, not herself.

Where do they go, all the people that pass across and through and never stop?

What is it Trixie Bell, whatever is the matter?

Imagine someone being there to say that, to say, *What is the matter? nothing is the matter, my darling*; arms wrapped round. Another person who wanted to be with you. Imagine that.

The television was on but she didn't watch it. *I* didn't. Oh she does love her Bette Davis, but the sound was turned down and what was in her head was too loud and bright and pressing. It was what was real.

Think of it. Bette Davis as Trixie Bell. In the film of her life.

Ha ha. Off I go again.

*But still I maintain,*

*I was born to lo – ove.*

What is that rubbish?

But just imagine *love*.

Well I missed it. No use crying over spilt anything.

And there is Blowski.

*Always cheerful, always cheerful.*

What is it, oh what is the matter?

Not herself, not herself. She's not herself.

I cannot rest until whatever it is that nags me is put to rights. It is like a door banging in the wind, or a bird trapped in a room beating its wings against the window glass, scattering petals.

Not petals, feathers! Imagine it, a bird with petals!

But still, trapped in a room, beating its wings.

I keep thinking that; something like that.

I will have to look over the whole house. I must look in every room, check every switch, every lock, every window, every door.

If there was only someone to hold my hand or someone to reassure me. Is that not what God is for?

I am crying in the wilderness of a morning when there has been no sleep and my eyes are full of grit.

The seedlings in the yoghurt pots have lain down their heads and died; the seed leaves like little pairs of dead wings, the stems limp as cotton. I have forsaken them as He has forsaken me.

Come on Trixie Bell. Bear up. *Constant Sunshine in the Soul.*

And when I know that it is all safe, all as it should be, then I will rest.

# FEAR

I was woken by a scream. I'd dozed off again, was dreaming about swimming, gulping the water as I swam, cool, wonderful, blue water. It was not a loud scream, more the strangled wail of a sleeper, that seemed to percolate through the water of my dream. Then I saw Trixie.

She had not seen me, she was staring at the wardrobe, at the open doors. She wore an old candlewick dressing-gown and her face was yellow and caved in – no false teeth. Her shaking fingers went up to her mouth.

I struggled in the softness of the bed to get up, waves of pain and nausea washing through me. Trixie's fear made goose-pimples rise on my chest under the silky lining of the coat.

'What . . . ?' I said, but Trixie kept her eyes on the dark space in the wardrobe. Then she stepped back, her eyes casting wildly about. She stepped on the crackly brown paper from the open parcel on the floor, the boy's clothes, all ragged and moth-eaten. She cried out again and backed away from them as if they were crawling things, things that might bite her. She backed away and then she saw me and . . . I can hardly describe the horror on her face: her eyes flooding with black, the frame of her face collapsing further as if the flesh was disintegrating. Her sparse hair seeming to rise as if it was really standing on end, as if that was possible.

'Trixie, what is it?' I was not entirely awake, muzzy with gin and pain and dreams and with finding Trixie – whom I'd been prepared to be angry with, to push over, to flee from – so pathetic; not the murderous monster I'd turned her into but only a terrified, confused, old woman. 'Trixie, what?' I reached out my hand.

But Trixie backed away.

'Ada,' she mouthed, her fingertips crammed in her mouth.

'Trixie . . . it's all right . . .' and waking up a bit, I looked down at myself, at the black mink open to reveal the crushed velvet underneath.

'Oh the clothes!' I got up and approached her, caught sight of myself in the mirror, black wig askew, lips smudged huge and scarlet. 'It's not Ada! It's only me.'

I paused by the mirror, giddy, watching myself sway through the dust on the glass, I could see why I frightened her so. How could I have thought I looked beautiful? I was grotesque. I turned, but before I could reach her she had slipped out and there was the rattle of the key in the lock even as I reached it.

I shook the door handle and hammered on the door with my fists: 'No – o – o – o,' I screamed. 'Trixie! Trixie! Trixie! Let me out! Trixie!' I could not believe it. It was not possible that she'd been in and I'd let her out. And I was still there. I bashed the door with my knee and kicked it and then I sank down on the floor, my head pounding, a thin sting of bile rising in my throat. How could I have been so pathetic? It was not fair, not fair, not fair. It was a nightmare; I was trapped in a bloody nightmare.

I dropped my hot head in my hands and wept.

# BENJAMIN CHARLES

I am out
I am out
I am out
Hurrah I AM OUT
I can run and I can shout
I am a boy and I am free!

She is cracked wide open I am free

I CAN DO WHATEVER I WANT

Just wait

I am sucking her rock what the lady gave her
It's very sticky and it's got a word in it but I can't read it
Because reading's for girls
I am a danger and a disgrace
And I am free

HURRAH
HURRAH
HURRAH

I will never go in again

See me I am clever and bad
See me

But, my father could not see me. I stood in front of him and
    he only saw Trixie
Oh she will be sorry now
I am a boy see I am a boy see my thing
I am a big boy
Big as a man full growed

Air all round me
I can move my arms and legs and I can kick and thump

Sucking the rock into a spike with red in it from the word
No I am not a boy I am a man
See me I am a man
I truly am
See my thing
I could stick my thing in the lady in the attic

Or I could kill her

# ROCK

The sun is shining in. I keep looking at my clothes on the floor. Clothes that I hate, feel bad in. The wrong shape jeans, a jumper that makes me look sallow. I wear them a lot. Why do I wear clothes that make me feel ugly? I save my best clothes up for best. For never. In a minute I'll get up and take off the velvet and the musty fur and put my ordinary things back on. Then she will let me out.

Then I will go home.

And I will wear my best clothes.

I will feel good.

I will love my children, I do, I do love them.

And Richard too.

A ray of sun shines on the stocking dangling from the lampshade and lights it up like a spirit leg all gauzy gold and floating, stirring the dust motes with a glowing toe.

When she'd slammed the door I'd crawled across the floor and back to bed and lay here, too dry to cry much. Useless anyway. Part of me wanted to laugh. Locked in a mad woman's attic, something wrong there Inis, something upside-down.

She is coming. I hear her feet on the stairs, surprisingly sprightly. I heave myself up. No time to change but I don't care. This time I will get out, I'll simply barge her. This time I will be free.

She opens the door and I am ready for her. She has something in her hand . . . I don't get it . . . the stick of rock from Blackpool

all sucked and sharp. There is sticky pink all round her mouth –
no teeth – all caved in – how she must have sucked and sucked
to get such sharpness.

I go to the door and she . . . Trixie! and there is pain. I don't
. . . pain in my chest I don't know what to . . .

But I am all right I try to pass her but she is backed against the
door . . . what is she . . . as if she is shoving the rock up my skirt
as if . . . I want to scream a laugh as if . . . *raped with a stick of
rock by a mad woman in an attic* but her face close to is fierce
and lined and streaked with sticky glistening pink.

'Trixie!'

'I am not Trixie.'

'Ada, then Ada!'

'I am not Ada!' Warm spit flecks my face.

'I am Benjamin.'

All I can do is push against her oldness and her snapped off
rock and her collapsing face. In her dressing-gown pocket, I see
only as her hand goes down, is a knife.

# SAINT BRUNO

I took the rock upstairs and a knife too. I took Trixie's sharp knife from the kitchen drawer. I tried it on my thumb and blood came out. I put it in my pocket.

The lady was still dressed like Ada.

She shouted and pushed me but I am a man. I am clever and strong. I got my back against the door. I stuck the rock out and got her in the chest and the point of the rock broke off.

Her hand went up and she sort of laughed. I don't know if it was laughing or crying or what.

I didn't know what next. I wanted to pull her dress up and do it to her but I had the rock in my hand.

I couldn't . . . she was too close, pushing.

She was making stupid noises like laughing and crying at the same time and snot was coming out of her nose and she kept saying *Trixie, Trixie*, just like Father used to when he couldn't see it was me and not Trixie.

I said I was not Trixie. I got hold of her all fur and stinking scent. I could not let go to undo my clothes so I tried to push the rock in her, up her skirt.

Now the rock has blood on. Real blood, I think, only when I suck it it is only sweet and mint. When she saw the knife she made a stupid noise, a bleat like sheep do.

I sat on the floor and I saw I was still wearing Trixie's things, her nightie and dressing-gown. The knife was on the floor.

And on the floor I saw my things that I had when I was a boy, that Father made Trixie wear to try to make her into me.

And now I am me but they are only boy's things. They would be too small for a man.

But in the wardrobe is Father's jacket. Father did love me only he never saw me. He thought I had died but only the baby died.

Because baby boys *should* die and make way for the men.

And ladies should die with their silk and their private parts which are nothing. Only nothing where there should be something.

Father's jacket is all scratchy when I put it on, the collar hairy against my neck and it has his smell.

He is dead. But I am out. Never will go back.

In the pocket is his pipe and his tobacco. Saint Bruno.

Saint Bruno has a lovely, lovely smell which is nothing like babies or women at all. Not at all.

No lighter, but a candle alight. The pipe is hard to light. Bits of paper but they just singe my fingers and go out. You shouldn't play with fire but I don't care because I am bad. I light bits of cloth. I make little fires on the floor trying to get the pipe alight. It takes lots of goes but I do.

All the little fires go out so there is only ash and no flames.

The pipe is lit and the taste is the wonderfulest thing. It tastes like Father smelled. In the mirror, wearing the jacket, I see that I look like Father. I do. Very like.

The wardrobe is open. That is where Father told me to go.

I have to throw out all the old shoes and boots and things to fit in. All the dresses against my face again. The smoke filling up all the flat and silky places. Smoke and silk, velvet and fur.

# STOCKINGS

Oh God, Oh God, Oh God.

But I am out.

I must get away from here.

Pale and dreadful in the mirror. Hand shaking: mascara, lipstick. Scrub off lipstick. Quick. The greasiness like last night, like last night settling on my shoulders and head like a flock of crows. Stave that off, last night. My scalp prickles and my palms slip with sweat.

Because, Oh God, Oh God, I nearly died.

A bruise on my chest, a speck of blood from the sharp rock. Only rock. But what if it had been a knife? There was a knife. What if I had not knocked it away?

Oh God. Oh do not think. Keep it off. Safe now. Going home now.

I do not understand last night. How can I? All I know is . . . I don't know. Last night was . . . I don't know.

I have folded her clothes into a pile. Not a neat pile – they will not be neat. They slither and slide, velvet on silk on fur.

So now, ready. A last look round. A last breath of this house now that I can breathe. It's not so cold. It's not so bad with the sunshine through the smeary window lighting up the yellow Formica with its pattern of old brown cup-rings.

Not a bad place. Some regret. For a time my home. *Mine*. Darkroom, white paint with the roses blooming through. A place I made.

I must go *now*. I am alive. Trixie only the other side of this wall. Trixie or Ada or ... oh I don't know. Tonight I will be with the people I love. I can't think now. Distance is what I need before I can even think.

Step out into the passage, put down the bags, close the door and lock it. That's that.

Running again. *To* love instead of away. Running from what?

Not from everything. In my pocket, the silk of the stockings which I am taking home.

# BLOWSKI

Blowski is there, first she can smell his breath, then she can see his face, close to hers, engraved like a silver coin. Her mouth is bitter, her lips taste of . . . something . . . leather, old leather, Father . . . men, a proper man's taste in her mouth whatever is it? Oh tobacco.

'Trixie . . . you all right now? Trixie Bell?'

'It wasn't me,' she says, shrinking away from him in her chair. 'It wasn't.'

'Trixie, thank the stars.' Blowski smiles.

'I didn't do it. I didn't. It wasn't me. I never touched it.' Trixie's voice all wet and childish.

'No, no, you didn't do nothing,' Blowski says. 'Everything all right. Everything tickety-boo.'

Huddled up in her chair, she looks up at him, suspicious, then hopeful.

'Tea,' Blowski says.

He goes into the kitchen. The tobacco is sour in her mouth. Her mind scrambles. What has she been thinking, what doing? He was helping her down the stairs, she remembers that. The stairs seemed to go on for ever. And . . . his hot knotted hand pulling her out from somewhere, from between something, his voice soothing. Like some dream. What is happening? Some dream about men. Not Blowski, but other men, paying men. Paying? For what? Oh no good pretending. Trixie Bell did it. *Was* it. That was no dream. *Paying* men. But that is over. That

277

was over fifty years ago. So what else is it? Why is her mind full of man and boy? Something not right. Some absence. Something funny going on.

Please no.

All right. Only the memory playing tricks, tricksy memory, Trixie.

What is happening, oh what is happening? She did not do it. Do what? She's done nothing. Her hands are all sticky and when she licks her finger it tastes sweet. She runs her tongue around her gums. No teeth in. Her stomach churns with shame. She tries to get up from her chair, but Blowski is there again with a cup of tea and the memories shrink back, vanish, like silk scarves whisked through a ring.

'I put sugar in, for shock, yes?'

'Shock. What shock? Where?'

'Settle down, Trixie Bell, settle down.'

He turns the fire up. Trixie sits with her hand curled over her mouth.

'Blowski, what are you doing here?' She drinks the top half of her tea in a scalding slurp that steadies her. 'It's early.'

'Just passing,' he says, 'first thing: get out, get milk and paper, like every morning and I pass and . . . I don't know . . . something tell me something up and I come in . . . and . . .'

'And?'

'And here you are and I make you tea. End of story. Yes?'

Trixie slumps. That is not quite right. There is more. What about the stairs, the smoke? But Blowski is so kind to her. He is a dear, her dear old friend. 'I make you breakfast,' he says. 'Then I go to shops and go back to Brenda. She be having kittens. "Where is he? Where is that bugger," that what she say . . .'

He switches on the television for Trixie; two ragamuffins sprawled on a bed, a lot of silliness. Then the advert for Coco-Pops again. Trixie puts down her tea and taps her hand on the arm of her chair. '*I'll have another bowl of Coco-Pops.*'

'I'd like to try those, Blowski,' she says.

'I get you some, later. I come back, later, me. See you all right. I get your Coco-Pops, all your shopping.'

Something is different, some clamouring inside her is stilled. It is almost like peace. She smiles and touches his arm.

'Oh Blowski, you are too kind.'

He flaps his arthritic hand in front of his face and snorts.

# ONE

Well, well, well. I was wrong to think we could never be one.
The boy has gone.

The boy has gone up in smoke.

Trixie . . . Trixie and I are drinking tea through the same lips.
Blowski is doing our shopping.

I cannot be sure but I feel there is no filter between us. There is
a merging like a sigh of relief.

We are simply too old for all that nonsense now.
And the boy has gone!
He has gone up in smoke!

I know that *I* am here.
That I am Trixie, almost, now that the boy has gone. And Ada
too. We are the same. We sit together by the fire, an old woman in
love with an old Pole who is the husband of two other women.

Ha!

*Always cheerful, always cheerful,*
*I was made for lo – ove . . .*

Next-door has slammed the door and gone.
Something about her, I kept quiet, something Trixie saw in
her . . . but that does not signify now.
We need not worry our head.

We are just an old woman.

I am just an old woman.

I *am* myself.

# A NOTE ON THE AUTHOR

Lesley Glaister was born in Wellingborough in 1956. She teaches a Master's Degree in Writing at Sheffield Hallam University, and writes occasional book reviews for the *Yorkshire Post*. She is the author of *Honour Thy Father*, which won a Somerset Maugham and a Betty Trask award, *Trick or Treat*, *Digging to Australia*, *Limestone and Clay*, and most recently, *Partial Eclipse*. She lives in Sheffield.